boss, but rarely complains. Happily married with children, her personal life is relatively calm in comparison to her professional life.

CINDY THOMAS

An up-and-coming journalist who's always looking for the next big story. She'll go the extra mile, risking life and limb to get her scoop. Sometimes she prefers to grill her friends over cocktails for a juicy secret, but, luckily for them, she's totally trustworthy (most of the time...). She somehow found the time to publish a book between solving cases, writing articles for the *San Francisco Chronicle* and keeping together her relationship with Lindsay's partner, Rich Conklin.

> **"When your job is murder, you need friends you can count on"**

YUKI CASTELLANO

One of the best lawyers in the city, she's desperate to make her mark. Ambitious, intelligent and passionate, she'll fight for what's right, always defending the underdog even if it means standing in the way of those she loves. Often this includes her husband – who is also Lindsay's boss – Lt. Jackson Brady.

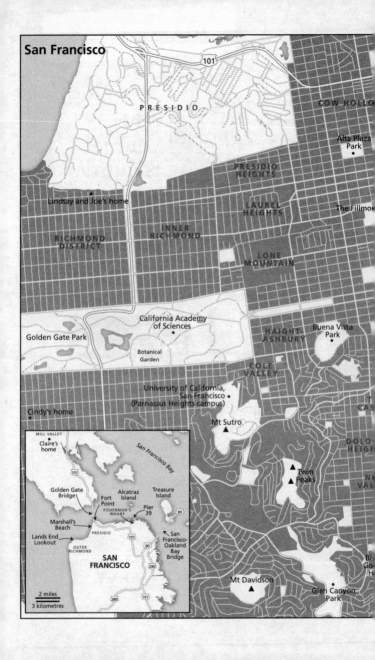

San Francisco

101

PRESIDIO

COW HOLLO

Alta Plaza
Park

PRESIDIO
HEIGHTS

Lindsay and Joe's home

LAUREL
HEIGHTS

The Fillmo

RICHMOND
DISTRICT

INNER
RICHMOND

LONE
MOUNTAIN

California Academy
of Sciences

HAIGHT
ASHBURY

Buena Vista
Park

Golden Gate Park

Botanical
Garden

COLE
VALLEY

Cindy's home

University of California,
San Francisco
(Parnassus Heights campus)

T
CA

Mt Sutro

DOLO
HEIG

MILL VALLEY

Claire's
home

San Francisco Bay

Twin
Peaks

N
VAL

Golden Gate
Bridge

Alcatraz
Island

Treasure
Island

Fort
Point

FISHERMAN'S
WHARF

Pier
39

80

Marshall's
Beach

PRESIDIO

101

San
Francisco-
Oakland Bay
Bridge

Lands End
Lookout

80

Bi
Go
H

OUTER
RICHMOND

SAN
FRANCISCO

Mt Davidson

Glen Canyon
Park

2 miles

3 kilometres

280

101

19th
CHRISTMAS

JAMES PATTERSON is one of the best-known and biggest-selling writers of all time. His books have sold in excess of 385 million copies worldwide. He is the author of some of the most popular series of the past two decades – the Alex Cross, Women's Murder Club, Detective Michael Bennett and Private novels – and he has written many other number one bestsellers including romance novels and stand-alone thrillers.

James is passionate about encouraging children to read. Inspired by his own son who was a reluctant reader, he also writes a range of books for young readers including the Middle School, Treasure Hunters, Dog Diaries and Max Einstein series. James has donated millions in grants to independent bookshops and has been the most borrowed author in UK libraries for the past thirteen years in a row. He lives in Florida with his family.

MAXINE PAETRO has collaborated with James Patterson on the bestselling Women's Murder Club, Private and Confessions series. She lives with her husband in New York State.

Meet The Women's Murder Club

EXCLUSIVE PROFILES by Our Crime Desk

LINDSAY BOXER

A homicide detective in the San Francisco Police Department, juggling the worst murder cases with the challenges of being a first-time mother. Her loving husband Joe, daughter Julie and loyal border-collie Martha give her a reason to protect the city. She didn't have the easiest start to life, with an absent father and an ill mother, but she didn't shy away from a difficult and demanding career. With the help of her friends, Lindsay makes it her mission to solve the toughest cases.

CLAIRE WASHBURN

Chief Medical Examiner for San Francisco and one of Lindsay's oldest friends. Wise, confident and viciously funny, she can be relied on to help whatever the problem. She virtually runs the Office of the Coroner for her overbearing, credit-stealing

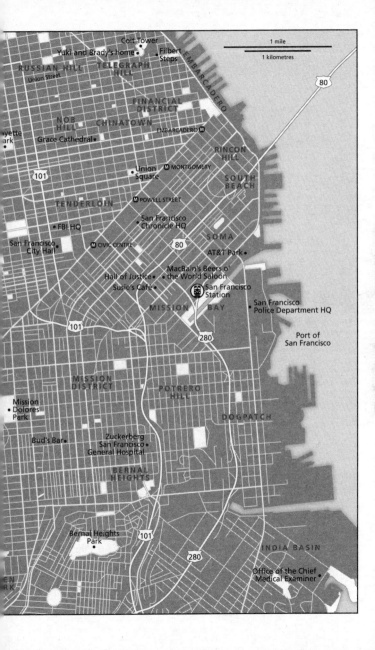

A list of titles by James Patterson appears
at the back of this book

19th CHRISTMAS

JAMES PATTERSON

& MAXINE PAETRO

arrow books

1 3 5 7 9 10 8 6 4 2

Arrow Books
20 Vauxhall Bridge Road
London SW1V 2SA

Arrow Books is part of the Penguin Random House group of companies
whose addresses can be found at global.penguinrandomhouse.com

Penguin
Random House
UK

First published in Great Britain by Century in 2019
Paperback edition published in Great Britain by Arrow Books in 2020

www.penguin.co.uk

A CIP catalogue record for this book is available from the British Library

Printed and bound in Great Britain by Clays Ltd, Elcograf S.p.A.

MIX
Paper from
responsible sources
FSC® C018179

Penguin Random House is committed to a
sustainable future for our business, our readers
and our planet. This book is made from Forest
Stewardship Council® certified paper.

AUTHORS' NOTE

Part of the joy of writing a long-running series is the opportunity to watch the characters develop lives of their own. Just like all of us, the Women's Murder Club (and those they care about) have a present—and a past. In *18th Abduction*, the first scenes and the very last scenes take place in the present day, but the main story takes place five years earlier, before Julie Molinari was born. We referenced this time line shortly after the Prologue, but probably didn't make it clear enough. We heard from some readers asking after Julie. Thank you for caring about this character so very deeply. Read on for more about Julie, and all your other favorites.

PROLOGUE

DECEMBER 20

IT WAS FOUR nights before Christmas Eve, and the city of San Francisco had decked the halls, houses, and grand public edifices in a sparkling, merry Christmas display.

My husband, Joe, our three-and-a-half-year-old daughter, Julie, our aging border collie, Martha, and I had piled into the family car for a tour of the lights.

Julie was wearing a red leotard with a tutu and a blinking tiara. The antlers she had assigned to Martha had been rejected by our doggy, so Joe wore them to keep the peace and Julie approved. I was wearing the sweater my baby fashion coach had picked out of a catalog—Santa and his sleigh sailing over a cheesy grinning moon. It was so tacky it was hilarious.

Joe said to me, "Lindsay, give me a C."

I did, perfectly pitched.

As we headed down Jackson Street, we sang "Jingle Bells," and then Martha joined in—definitely off-key.

3

Dear Joe knew the way to guide our sleigh, and we headed toward Cow Hollow, parked, and walked along Union Street to see the Fantasy of Lights. The Victorian buildings, both shops and homes, were twinkling red, green, and white. Joe carried Julie on his shoulders, and I laughed out loud when she parted his antlers to get a better view of the window displays.

Julie clapped her hands at the sight of the snowmen guarding the entrance to Santaland, and I was elated. This was one of the wonderful things about motherhood, watching Julie make Christmas memories.

"Where to next?" Joe asked Julie. "The fishing boats will be all lit up from the Holiday Lights Boat Parade."

"Chocolate factory!" she shouted from her top-of-Daddy seat.

And we were off to Ghirardelli Square, near Fisherman's Wharf, to see the fifty-foot-tall tree decorated with giant chocolate bars, Julie's idea of the prettiest Christmas tree in the whole wide world.

Yuki Castellano was in the kitchen, and there was not a holiday decoration in sight. She stirred the guacamole and then set a tray of brownies in the oven while her husband, Jackson Brady, mixed up a pitcher of margaritas.

"Ah love to see you giggly," he teased in his Southern accent.

Yuki giggled just hearing that. From her Japanese mother and her Italian-born American-soldier daddy, she had inherited a ticklish funny bone, no tolerance for alcohol, and a decided weakness for tequila.

4

"You just want to take advantage of me," she told her husband.

"I do. My first night off in I don't know how long, and I think we should trash the bedroom."

Yuki felt the same way. She'd just finished prosecuting a case from hell, and Brady had been working overtime as a homicide lieutenant and doubling as the acting police chief. They'd barely had time for sleep, let alone each other—and it was almost Christmas.

She said, "No phones, okay? Not a single phone call. And that means both of us, agreed?"

"Say the word and I'll fill up the sink and drown those dang things in it."

She said, "The word," laughed again, and popped open a bag of chips.

"Plate alla that, will you? I'll grab the liquor."

They headed for the bedroom with drinks, chips, and dip. They'd chosen to screen an action classic that some considered the greatest Christmas story ever told. Yuki had never seen *Die Hard* and was wondering now if she'd ever get to see it. Odds were she and Brady were going to be naked before the opening credits rolled.

"Don't start without me," she said. "I'll be right there."

She went back to the kitchen and turned off the oven. Brownies could wait.

Cindy Thomas and her live-in boyfriend, Rich Conklin, stood on the tree-lined path that divided Civic Center Plaza. The attractions of the seasonal Winter Park were in full swing.

Up ahead, centered on the path, City Hall was alight in wide, horizontal red and green bands; the brilliant Christmas tree in front of the impressive old granite building pointed up to the magnificent dome.

Rich squeezed Cindy's hand and she looked up at his dear face.

She said, "Are you going to forgive me?"

"For us not going out to see my family?"

"I wish I could, Richie. Your pops always makes me feel like a movie star. But I've got that interview tomorrow."

"And a deadline," he said. "You think I don't know the drill by now?"

"You. Are. The best."

"Don't I know it," he said. He grinned at her and she stood up on her toes to kiss him. He pulled her in and made a corny thing of it, dipping her for effect, making her laugh between the dramatic rows of trees. People cut around them, taking pictures of the view.

Cindy said, "Hang on."

She ran up ahead to the couple who had just taken a photo of City Hall.

"Sorry," she said to the surprised couple. "I wonder if you might have caught me and my man in your pictures?"

The woman said, "Let's see." She flicked through the photos on her phone and squealed, "Hey. Lookee here."

She showed the phone to Cindy, who beamed and said, "Can you send it to me, please?"

"My pleasure," the woman said. She took Cindy's email address and said, "There you go. Merry Christmas."

Impulsively, Cindy threw her arms around the stranger, who hugged her back.

"Merry Christmas to you, too. Both of you," Cindy said, and she ran back to her sweetheart.

"Rich, look." She showed him the photo on her phone.

"Instant Christmas card. Beautiful. I'll send it to my family. And now let's go home, Cindy. Home."

Claire Washburn had slung her carry-on bag over one shoulder and her computer case over the other and was forging ahead toward the gate. She and her husband, Edmund, were at SFO, which was decorated for the season with over three million LED bulbs—not that Claire took any notice. She turned to look for her husband and saw him far behind, gazing out at the light show.

She called, "Edmund, give me one of those bags."

"I've got them, Claire. Just slow down a little so I can keep up."

"Sorry," she said, walking back to him. "Why is it you can never find a luggage trolley when you want one?"

He made a face. "You want me to state the obvious?"

The airport was always busy, and it was even busier today, with mobs of people flying out to spend the holidays with relatives in far-flung places.

It was a working holiday for Claire. As San Francisco's chief medical examiner, she had been asked by National University in San Diego to teach an extra-credit course for students in the master's program in forensic medicine.

She was glad to do it.

The quick course would be held during Christmas break

and was the perfect amount of time for a case study of a crime Claire had worked years ago. The body of a young boy had been discovered in a suitcase chained to a concrete block in a lake miles from home. Claire's work on that case had helped the police solve the crime.

Along with giving her a nice paycheck, the City of San Diego was putting Claire and Edmund up at the Fairmont Grand Del Mar, a resort-style hotel with a gym and a gorgeous pool. It promised to be a great respite from the somewhat harsher NoCal winter.

Edmund had resisted going with Claire on this trip. He had made plans with friends from the San Diego Symphony to lay down a track for a CD they were working on. But Claire knew the real reason he didn't want to come: Edmund was becoming more introverted by the year, and he just wanted to stay home.

Claire had told him, "Edmund, it's a chance for us to be together with a heated pool and room service. Your mom is dying to babysit her youngest grandchild over Christmas, and Rosie *wants* to be babied. Tell me I'm wrong."

He couldn't honestly do that.

Edmund knew how much Claire loved talking to students, encouraging them and sharing her experience on the Thad Caine case. It would be a needed lift to her spirits, and if Claire wanted his company, he couldn't say no.

Edmund saw a lone luggage trolley by the newsstand and he grabbed it.

He called to Claire, "I got wheels. We are definitely not going to miss our flight."

PART ONE

DECEMBER 21

CHAPTER 1

JULIAN LAMBERT WAS an ex-con in his midthirties, sweet-faced, with thinning, light-colored hair. He was wearing black jeans and a down jacket as red as a Santa Claus suit.

As he sat on a bench in Union Square waiting for his phone call, he took in the view of the Christmas tree at the center of the plaza. The tree was really something, an eighty-three-foot-tall cone of green lights with a star on top. It was ringed by pots of pointy red flowers and surrounded by a red-painted picket fence.

That tree was *secure*. It wasn't going anywhere. But he would be, and soon.

It was lunchtime, and all around him consumers hurried out of stores weighed down with shopping bags, evidence of money pissed away in an orgy of spending. Julian wondered idly how these dummies were going to pay for their commercially fabricated gifting sprees. Take out a loan on the old credit card and worry about it next month or not worry about debt at all. Julian's phone vibrated, almost catching him by surprise.

He fished it out of his pocket, connected, and said his name, and Mr. Loman, the boss, said, "Hello, Julian. Are we alone?"

"Completely, Mr. Loman." Julian knew that he was meant only to listen, and that was fine with him. He felt both excited and soothed as Loman explained just enough of the plan to allow Julian to salivate at the possibilities.

A heist.

A huge one.

"The plan has many moving parts," Loman said, "but if it goes off as designed, by this time next year, you, Julian, will be living the life you've only dreamed of." Julian dreamed of the Caribbean, or Ipanema, or Saint-Tropez. He was picturing a life of blue skies and sunshine with a side of leggy young things in string bikinis when Loman asked if he had any questions.

"I'm good to go, boss."

"Then get moving. No slipups."

"You can bank on me," said Julian, and he was glad that Loman barked back, "Twenty-two fake dive, slot right long, on one."

Julian cracked up. He had played ball in college, which was a very long time ago, but he still had moves. He clicked off the call, sized up the vehicular and foot traffic, and chose his route.

It was go time.

CHAPTER 2

JULIAN SAW HIS run as a punt return.

He charged into an elderly man in a shearling coat, sending the man sprawling. He snatched up the old guy's shopping bag, said, "Thanks very much, you knucklehead."

What counted was that he had the ball.

With the bag tucked under his arm, Julian streaked across Geary, dodging and weaving through the crowd, heading toward the intersection at Stockton. He sprinted across the street and charged along the broad, windowed side of Neiman Marcus where a Christmas tree laden with lights and ornaments rose forty feet into the rotunda. Revolving glass doors split a crowd of shoppers into long lines of colorful dots going inside or filing out onto the sidewalk accompanied by Christmas music: "I played my drum for him, pa-rum-pum-pum-pum." It was all so crazy.

Julian was still running.

He yelled, "Coming through! No brakes!" He wove

13

around the merry shoppers, sideswiped the UPS man loading his truck, and, with knees and elbows pumping, bag secured under his arm, dashed up the Geary Street straightaway and veered left.

Another crowd of shoppers loaded with shopping bags spilled out of Valentino. Julian shot his left hand out to stiff-arm a young dude, who fell against a woman in a fake-fur coat. Bags and packages clattered to the sidewalk. Julian high-stepped around and over the obstacles, easy-breezy, then broke into a sprint again and turned left on Grant Avenue.

Julian chortled when the oncoming pedestrians scattered as he headed toward them; he gave the finger to a wiry guy who yelled at him. He ran on, knocking slowpokes out of his way and shouting, "Merry flippin' Christmas, one and all." God, this was fun. He couldn't see the goalposts, but he knew that he was scoring, big-time.

Julian's long strides ate up the pavement, and despite the blood pounding in his ears, he listened for sirens. He still had the ball, but the clock was ticking. He glanced over his shoulder and saw, finally, two people who looked like cops running up behind him.

He was winded, but he didn't stop. *Show me what you've got, suckers.* He put on another surge of speed as he headed toward Dragon's Gate and the Chinatown district. He slowed only when a lady cop's authoritative voice shouted, "Freeze or I'll shoot!"

He thought, *In this crowd? I don't think so.* And he kept running.

CHAPTER 3

MY PARTNER, INSPECTOR Richard Conklin, was running out of time, and he needed my help.

He said desperately, "Would be nice if she'd tell you what she wants."

"Where would the fun be in that?" I said, grinning. "You figuring it out is kind of the point."

"I guess. Make our own history."

"Sure. That's an idea. Romantic, Rich."

We had slipped out of the Hall of Justice to do some lunchtime Christmas shopping in San Francisco's Union Square because of its concentration of upscale shops. Richie wanted to get something special for Cindy. He wanted his gift to make her speechless, but when he asked her for a hint about what she wanted, she'd offered practical ideas. A multiport device charger. New cross-trainers. A gel-foam seat for her car. He grinned, thinking about her.

Rich had wanted to marry Cindy from pretty much the moment he met her. And she loved him fiercely. But. There's always a *but*, right?

Rich was from a big family, and while he was still in his thirties, he'd always wanted kids. Lots of them. Cindy was an only child with a hot career—one that took her to murder scenes in bad places in the dead of night. And Rich wasn't the only crime fighter in the relationship; Cindy had solved more than one homicide, had even shot at and been shot by a crafty female serial killer who'd become the subject of Cindy's bestselling true-crime book.

All this to say, Cindy was in no hurry to start a family.

It was a conflict of priorities that in the past had broken up my two great friends, and it was tremendous that they were back together now. But as far as I knew, the conflict remained unresolved.

Rich pointed out an emerald pendant around the neck of a mannequin in the window of a high-end jewelry shop. "Do you like that?"

Just as I said, "Beautiful, Rich. And very Christmasy," I heard a scream behind us.

I whipped around to see a man in a red down jacket running hard, bowling down shoppers. He closed in and then passed us, yelling, "Coming through! No brakes!" He collided with a group of people walking out of Neiman's. They scattered and he just kept going.

An elderly man in a shearling coat was hobbling down the street in pursuit, blood streaming out of his nose. He cried, "Stop, thief! Someone stop him!"

Rich and I are homicide cops, and this was no murder.

But we were there. We took off after the man in the red down jacket who was running with all the power and determination of a pro tailback.

I yelled, "Freeze or I'll shoot!" But the runner kept going.

CHAPTER 4

I DIDN'T TRUST myself to run full out. My doctor had recently benched me for two months because I was anemic. So I slowed to a walk and yelled to my partner, "You go! I'll call it in."

I got on my phone and summed up the situation for dispatch in a few words: There had been a robbery, a grab-and-dash. Conklin was pursuing the suspect on foot, running east on Geary Street between Stockton and Grant Avenue.

"Suspect is wearing a red jacket, dark pants. We need backup and an ambulance," I said and gave my location.

I trotted back to the elderly man with the bloody nose who was panting and leaning against a building.

He said, "Are you the police?"

"Yes. I'm Sergeant Boxer. Tell me what happened," I said.

He said, "I was minding my own business when that guy

in the puffy red coat knocked me down and stole my shopping bag. How could he do that to a senior citizen?"

"What's your name, sir?"

"Maury King."

"Mr. King, an ambulance will be here in a minute."

He shook his head. "No, no. I'm okay."

"We won't let him get away. My partner is in pursuit. Stay right here," I said. "I'll be back with your shopping bag."

The man in the red jacket had cleared a wide path for Rich, as screaming shoppers had thrown themselves against parked cars and buildings. I took off again, jogging in their wake.

I could see that Rich was keeping up with the runner but not gaining on him. I was following behind them on the wide, shadowed corridor of Grant Avenue, close enough to see someone pop out of a doorway and step right in front of the runner.

The runner stumbled and almost fell. I saw him push off the pavement with his free hand. He regained his footing but he had lost his momentum.

I yelled again, "Freeze or I'll shoot."

Just then, Rich fully extended himself, lunged—and tackled the runner. They both went down.

Breathless and dizzy, I caught up in time to hold my gun on the runner as Rich pulled the man to his feet and shouted, "Lace your fingers behind your neck." Rich kicked the runner's legs apart and patted him down.

"He's not packing," Rich told me.

"Good."

I unhooked my cuffs and, with shaking hands, linked

the runner's wrists behind his back. A cruiser pulled up to the curb.

I asked the runner for his name as I closed the cuffs.

"Julian Lambert. Still smokin' after all these years," he said, sounding far too pleased with himself.

I arrested Lambert for battery, theft, disorderly conduct, and resisting arrest. Conklin read him his rights and stuffed him into the back seat of the cruiser. After my partner slapped the flank of the departing vehicle, I said to him, "Did you notice? That jerk actually looked glad to see us."

CHAPTER 5

THAT DAY YUKI was in sentencing court, standing before the bar.

Across the aisle, defense counsel Allison Junker stood with her client Sandra McDowell. McDowell was a fifty-three-year-old woman who had lost control of her car and plowed into a gang of kids exiting a sports bar on Fillmore Street.

There had been no fatalities, thankfully, but three of the boys she'd hit had been hospitalized with an assortment of injuries to heads and limbs and one had been in a coma since the incident, which had happened weeks before. McDowell had admitted to driving while intoxicated and making an illegal left turn. She had pleaded guilty, been remanded to the court without bail, and been in jail since her arraignment. Yuki expected the sentencing hearing to be swift, smooth, and punishing.

Judge Judie Schlager was on the bench, presiding over

a full courtroom. It wasn't yet the end of the day, and she'd sentenced over two hundred people since nine a.m. She looked unfazed, even chipper. A small pin reading "#1 Nana" sparkled on her collar.

The judge said, "Ms. Castellano. Talk to me."

Yuki looked up at Judge Schlager and said, "Your Honor, Mrs. McDowell was indisputably drunk when she took an illegal left turn and plowed into pedestrians crossing with the light. She injured four young college students, one of whom, a rising football star, is still comatose. First officer on the scene gave Mrs. McDowell a Breathalyzer test. Her blood alcohol was 0.15. In his words, she was severely impaired."

The judge flipped through papers in front of her and asked, "She called the police of her own accord?"

"Yes, Your Honor," said the defendant's counsel, Ms. Junker.

"And she pleaded guilty?"

"Yes, Your Honor."

Yuki said, "Your Honor, this is not Mrs. McDowell's first DUI. We're asking for a sentence of three to five years, time commensurate with the pain and suffering of her victims. It's too soon to tell, but some of their injuries may be permanent."

The defendant was now weeping noisily into her hands.

Judge Judie Schlager addressed the defendant. "Mrs. McDowell, it says here that you're a pharmacist, married, two children in college. And this prior DUI was a one-car accident?"

"Yes, Your Honor. I hit a tree. Came out of nowhere."

The judge said, "Don't you just hate those jaywalking trees?"

"Your Honor," said Ms. Junker, "Mrs. McDowell is a good citizen. Her entire family is dependent on her income, including her husband, who has MS and is confined to a wheelchair. She has accepted responsibility for this accident from the time it happened and is unbelievably sorry. She intends to join AA upon her release. We urge the court to show leniency."

Judge Schlager wrinkled her brow and looked toward the back of the courtroom at a scuffle that had gotten out of control. She banged her gavel and demanded silence in the court even as Sandra McDowell continued to cry.

Yuki would be happy with a three-year sentence. It would get McDowell off the street, and during that time, she hoped that those college boys could recover from their injuries, get PT, and return to the lives they'd had planned before McDowell ran into them with her Buick.

Judge Schlager said, "Mrs. McDowell, before I impose a sentence, do you have anything to say?"

Mrs. McDowell dabbed at her face with a tissue and blew her nose. When she had regained her composure, she said, "Your Honor, I'm more sorry than I can say. I'm only grateful that I didn't kill anyone, but what I did was inexcusable. Whatever sentence you think fair is acceptable to me."

Judge Schlager said, "Mrs. McDowell, I'm revoking your driver license and giving you a year of probation, including eight months of community service, twenty hours a week. Do not drive. If one year from now your probation officer reports to me that you've attended AA and completed your community service and automotive abstinence, this court will be done with you.

"I'm releasing you today for time served. Next time there will be no leniency, do you understand me?"

"Yes, Your Honor. Thank you very much."

"Thank my Christmas spirit. That's all. Next?"

Allison Junker smirked over her client's shoulder, and Yuki gave her a *Drop dead* look before leaving the courtroom feeling like she'd been punched in the face by Santa Claus.

CHAPTER 6

CONKLIN AND I faced each other across our abutting desks in the Homicide squad room. The exasperation on his face mirrored my own.

The Robbery Division was overworked in the first degree. Likewise, Booking was packed to the walls. Conklin and I had caught this case, literally, and now we owned it. Julian Lambert was in cuffs, swiveling distractedly in the side chair while we wrote him up for larceny, assault and battery, and, for good measure, resisting arrest.

Lambert handed over his driver license and answered our questions, telling us his full name and address and that he worked in the stockroom at Macy's. Just before I accessed our database to see if the guy Conklin and I had tagged as the Grant Avenue Dasher had a record, he made an announcement.

"I'm on probation," he said.

"For what?" I asked.

"Shoplifting, from Best Buy. I did four months and was let out on good behavior, long as I don't screw up this year. My parole officer is a hard-ass. If you don't violate me, I can help you out," he said.

I asked, "How can you help us out, exactly?"

"I've got some information to trade for a get-out-of-jail-free pass."

I seriously doubted Lambert's claim, but what the hell. Let him try. I ran his name and found the arrest from three years ago as well as his release for time served and his current ongoing probation.

Conklin had read him his Miranda rights. He knew he could have an attorney present but apparently didn't want one. We were free to hear what he had to say and use it against him—if there was anything worth using.

We walked Lambert out of the bullpen and down the corridor to Interview 2, entered the small interrogation room, and took seats around the scarred metal table.

Conklin said, "Okay, then. You see that mirror?"

"Two-way. This isn't my first time in the box."

Conklin grinned. "You probably think there's someone back there listening in, watching your body language, right?"

"Yep." Lambert waved at the glass and said, "*Joyeux* fucking *Noël*, everyone."

"Well," said my partner, "you just waved at nobody. We're short-staffed this week. So lay your cards on the table and there's a good chance we can move you along with a minimum of red tape. You could be out on bail by New Year's."

"Okay, but I'm supposed to go to Florida, to my mom's place in Vero Beach, the day after Christmas."

I jumped in.

"Mr. Lambert, your victim is going to have something to say about your traveling across state lines. You threw an old man to the ground, broke his nose, and took about twenty-eight hundred dollars in Prada belts and Hermès ties. Sorry to tell you this, but that's grand larceny. And your victim is not feeling well disposed toward you. Last thing he said to us was 'Toss him in a dark cell and leave him there for good.'"

"I thought there was food in that bag. I swear," Julian Lambert said to the camera in the ceiling. "But he'll get his property back, right?"

Conklin said, "Yes. But you hurt him and traumatized him. You want us to help you, let's hear what you've got. Make it good. And quick. And truthful."

CHAPTER 7

LAMBERT GAVE A long, reluctant sigh, clasped his cuffed hands in front of him on the table, and said, "This is going to blow your minds."

He paused for effect, and when he got no reaction, he said, "I heard that something *big* is going down in a couple of days. I promise this is worth more to you than this little bust for stealing what I thought was a fruitcake and then bowling with pedestrians."

Conklin said, "Get serious, Lambert. You scared a lot of people, and Mr. King is looking to press charges. What's this 'big' something? Be specific."

"There's going to be a heist on Christmas Day," said Lambert.

"A heist?" Conklin said. "An armed robbery?"

"Yeah. Maybe the biggest one in the history of this town."

I thought, *Yeah, sure.*

But movies with big heists flashed through my mind. *Heat, Ocean's Eleven* through *Thirteen, Diamonds Are Forever,* and *Goldfinger.* And my favorite, the Pink Panther movies. My sister and I still found them hilarious and watched one whenever we spent time together.

I said to the dasher, "So you're talking about a bank robbery? Underground tunnels, things like that?"

"I overheard this conversation in a bar, so I don't have all the pieces."

"How about *some* pieces?" I said. "Do you have *some*?"

Crickets.

I turned to Conklin and said, "Mr. Lambert is just making stuff up. It's been a long day already, and I've had enough. Time to send him up to his cell and move on."

Lambert said to Conklin, "A little patience, please, Officer. I'm *getting* to it. It's dangerous for me to talk to you, understand?"

Conklin shrugged, stood up, pushed his chair in, and said, "Sergeant Boxer is the boss. She says we're done, we're done."

"Okay. Listen," said Lambert. "I've got the crew chief's name. Loman. You'll have something on him in your database."

I asked, "Like the off-price clothing chain? L-o-e-h-m-a-n-n?"

"No idea. I've never seen his name in writing."

"Mr. Loman's first name?"

"Mister. Look, he just calls himself Mr. Loman. That's all I know."

"Wait here. I'll be right back," I said.

I went to my desk, said hey to a couple of colleagues, then brought my computer to life.

I ran the names Loehmann, Lowman, and Loman through all available databases. Too many hits came up, dozens in San Francisco. I'd need more information about who we were looking for to do anything with this tip, and the first name "Mister" wasn't cutting it. My fingers were warmed up, so I ran Julian Lambert's name again. As he'd said, he'd served short time and was currently on probation for shoplifting. But now that he'd claimed knowledge of a huge heist, I punched his name into the FBI database. I found zip, zero, nada. And Lambert had no known associates named Loman on record.

Our runner looked to be a liar, a nobody, and an utter waste of time.

CHAPTER 8

I RETURNED TO Interview 2 with two guards from our jail on the seventh floor.

I said, "Stand up, Mr. Lambert. Your escorts will take you to your cell. You should consider using your phone call to get a lawyer."

"Wait. Wait a minute, will you?"

"I don't have time for bull, Mr. Lambert. Tell your story to the judge."

Lambert asked, "What? You found nothing on Loman?"

"I found a lot of names like that with many different spellings, dozens in Northern California, dozens in town. Without a first name and a location, your hot tip isn't worth jack."

"I have more information," he said.

Our petty-thief runner was sounding desperate and no longer looked as happy to see me as he was when we arrested him.

Conklin said, "I've worked with Sergeant Boxer for a

31

long time, Mr. Lambert. I know when she's ready to lock up for the night."

"Okay, I hear you," he said. "Just—I need to tell you about this heist. Alone."

I asked the guards to step outside, but I didn't sit down.

"Speak," I said to Lambert.

"I know one of the crew. I've got his name and address and I know that he's the kind of guy who is always heavily armed."

I sat down.

"His name is Chris Dietz. I know there will be a lot of people by that name. But that's his real name."

"What does he have to do with this heist?"

"He's a hitter. Psycho variety. Loman hired him for this job. I met Dietz here, in the seventh-floor jail, about three years ago. It was memorable."

I said, "I'll pull Dietz's sheet, but save me some time. What was he in for?"

"He was charged with holding up an armored car. Witness disappeared and the charges didn't stick."

"Okay, Mr. Lambert. Let's have his address."

After Lambert gave me the name of a cheap hotel located squarely in the pit of hell, I stood up, opened the door, and asked the guards to come in again.

"Please take Mr. Lambert up to seven."

"Hey, I cooperated," Lambert protested.

"If your information pans out, I'll speak to the DA. The DA will speak to Mr. King. Your lawyer will tell you to be remorseful when you're in front of the judge. Make it real."

When Lambert was gone, Conklin and I walked back to

our desks in the squad room. Shifts were changing. Day turning to night.

I did a search for Christopher Dietz. I found him.

I said to Rich, "There's an arrest warrant out for Christopher Alan Dietz, whose last known address was Seattle. He was charged with armed robbery. Someone put up two hundred thousand for bail and he skipped. He's got priors for shootings that didn't stand up due to lack of evidence. We should get the Feds into this."

Conklin picked up the phone, punched in a number, and said, "Cin. I'm working tonight. I know. I know. I'll try not to wake you up."

Cappy McNeil stopped by our desks. Cappy was a friend, a fellow cop who'd been working homicide longer than me, which made him an old-timer.

"I overheard the name Chris Dietz," he said. "I know of him. A CI of mine just mentioned that Dietz could be planning some kind of job. Big one."

"No kidding."

I thanked Cappy for the tip, which gave some validity to Julian Lambert's story and turned my thoughts about the interview with him upside down. And then I saw how this was going to go.

Conklin and I would brief Brady. He would call the SF branch of the FBI and our most senior SWAT commander, Reg Covington. Then we were all going to pay a call on Mr. Dietz, a bad guy with a gun said to be living in the Anthony Hotel.

I tried to imagine Dietz coming peacefully with us to the Hall.

I couldn't see it.

CHAPTER 9

THE ANTHONY HOTEL was in the middle of a grubby block in SoMa, flanked by two buildings—on the left, a low-rent office building with a tax-preparation business on the ground floor; on the right, a liquor store with a sputtering neon sign and a massage parlor on the top two stories.

I'd been to this nightmarish six-story "hotel" before, once to investigate a suspicious death by hanging and once to disarm a drug-addled father who had threatened to take out his family of six. It was amazing that we'd gotten all of those kids out alive.

I knew the Anthony's nearly bare lobby by heart, the scabby front desk, two broken-down armchairs, a bank of vending machines, and the pervasive smell of urine. Above the ground floor were five stories of rent-by-the-month rooms where drug addicts could indulge their habits in private and with all the amenities, like sinks and toilets and beds.

The hallways were pocked with bullet holes and in some places had been bloodied by heads being bashed against the walls. Inside the rooms, sinks had been pulled out and pipes in the ceiling had exploded, and I didn't want to think about what passed for bathrooms.

To call the Anthony Hotel a dump was to flatter it. But Christopher Dietz, the professional hit man Julian Lambert had named, had taken a room here among the psychos, drug addicts, and many poor families with small children.

At eight that night Conklin and I, wearing Kevlar over our SFPD Windbreakers and armed with semiautos and two warrants, entered the lobby. With us were two FBI agents, Reginald Covington, the head of our SWAT team, and three of his men, all in full tactical gear. Four other SWAT commandos were outside, watching the front and rear entrances and standing by for whatever might come.

Was this overkill for one bail-jumping presumed hit man?

Only if he put up his hands and let us bring him in.

Covington asked the frightened desk troll which room Dietz occupied.

"He's in 6R. Top floor, rear of the building."

Covington said to the clerk, "Be cool and get out." He didn't have to be told twice.

The elevator wasn't working, so the eight of us thundered up the stairs. A woman on three dropped her laundry basket and locked herself behind her door. Good idea. Little kids playing in the stairwell yelled for their mothers—and then they just stood there and stared.

We swept them out of our way, ordered them to go home

and close the door. One child left his pile of small wheeled toys in our path, and a girl of about eighteen months just sat on the landing and bawled until her father grabbed her up and carried her away.

My pulse was pounding from both exertion and dread. Kids could get hurt. We all could.

When we reached the top floor, we paused to scope out the hallway. It was dim, silent, and empty. Room 6R was at the far end of the execrable corridor, which was lined with five doors on each side.

Covington and his men stood on either side of Dietz's doorway.

As I was lead investigator on this case, my job was to knock, announce, then step away. When the door opened, SWAT would toss in a flashbang grenade and pull the door closed. A moment later they would open the door again and immobilize Dietz, who would be sprawled out on the floor, temporarily deaf and blind and wishing he were dead.

I knocked, called out, "Mr. Dietz? SFPD," and stepped to the side of the door. I listened for the sound of footsteps.

Instead I heard metallic clicks coming from behind us, down the hall and at the front of the building. It sounded like locks being thrown open.

Was a neighbor coming out to see what was happening?

Or was a child coming out to play?

I turned toward the sound and a heavy weight fell on me, covering me and dropping me to the floor. I heard shocking reports of gunfire and the reverberation of hundreds of rounds hitting the walls. The sixth floor of the Anthony Hotel had become a war zone.

CHAPTER 10

A MOMENT LATER, the deafening fusillade of gunfire at close range just stopped cold.

There was an echoing silence, then I heard the clattering of boots on tile and men cursing: "Shit." "Jake. Speak to me." "God damn it to hell."

I said to Conklin, "Rich. Let me up. Please."

He scrambled off me, got to his feet, and peered down into my face. "You okay, Boxer?"

"I think so. Yes. How about you?"

"I'm good," he said.

"You're great. A human shield," I said to my partner, who might have saved my life.

"Pure reflex. Let's get you up."

He reached down and I grabbed his hand. He pulled me to my feet.

My ears were ringing and I was on adrenaline overload as I stared along the narrow hallway. Most of the ceiling lights had been shot out. Five feet away, an FBI agent with what looked like a fatal head wound sat propped against a wall. The other agent had taken a bullet to his shoulder. Blood spurted as he tried to coax his partner back to life.

I called for backup and an ambulance, stat. I wasn't sure how the shit had hit the fan, but I gathered what I could from the chaotic scene and tried to piece together what had just happened. I'd been standing to the side of room 6R, waiting for SWAT to kick in the door, when the hallway had exploded in gunfire—the first shots coming from *behind* us—and Conklin had thrown himself on top of me.

We'd been told by the desk clerk that Chris Dietz, the professional hitter, was in 6R, rear. But apparently he'd been in 6F, *front.*

Had Dietz been so paranoid that he'd kept two rooms? Had he heard us running up the stairs and taken defensive action by busting into someone else's space? Or—the simplest explanation—had the terrified desk clerk given us the wrong room number?

The door to 6F had nearly been shot off its hinges. The dead man inside, cut down by our return, and more intense, gunfire, blocked the threshold. Even in the dim light I could see his blood pooling on the tiles. Me, Conklin, Commander Covington, and two of his people went to 6F and the body.

A SWAT officer kicked the dead man's gun aside, and he and Conklin rolled him. I pulled a wallet from his back pocket. His driver license told me he was Christopher Dietz, Caucasian male, no corrected vision. Height, five ten; eyes, hazel; born in 1985. An address in Boise. If there had been a place for occupation, I suppose it would have said *freelance hitter.*

I was glad he was dead but very, very sorry I wouldn't get a chance to interrogate him.

Covington shouted through 6F's open doorway for any people inside to show themselves, put their hands above their heads. When no one answered, he and his team stormed the small room, clearing it to the corners.

Conklin and I stepped around the dead man and peered into 6F, which was lit by the sporadic flashing of red neon coming from the liquor store next door.

Covington hit the light switch and the room lit up.

I saw a coffee table made of two milk crates and a plank, and a bare mattress in the corner. A rag of a shirt hung in the open closet. There were empty beer and liquor bottles everywhere, and the smell of excrement permeated the air.

We touched nothing, corrupted nothing, just looked for something that would reveal what Chris Dietz had been doing before he decided to commit suicide-by-cop in grand style.

If a clue was there, I didn't see it.

I heard sirens screaming up Sixth Street, ambulances and cruisers. Conklin and I backed out of the doorway and returned to the rear of the building, and I told the wounded FBI agent to hang on, EMTs were on the way.

Covington rammed in the door to 6R, rushed in, and, a moment later, pronounced it clear.

Paramedics jogged up the stairs with a stretcher. Uni-formed cops followed. Conklin told them to cordon off the rooms at both ends of the hall and start checking for wounded residents behind the other doors.

I called Brady, briefed him, and gave him the bad news: "Our best and only lead to the Christmas Day heist has expired."

CHAPTER 11

YUKI AND BRADY were at home that evening, dressing for a pre-Christmas dinner with DA Len Parisi and a handful of coworkers. They had promised each other that they would pick out a tree together. There was still time.

Yuki fastened the clasp of her jet necklace, and it curled neatly above the rounded neckline of her little black dress. She brushed her hair and then sat on the edge of the bed, watching Brady get ready.

He said, "I'm looking forward to getting out, talking to people. Wonderin' if I still have any charm left after all these years."

"You've still got it, sweetie. Charm to spare."

In Yuki's opinion, he underplayed his appeal and it was a pleasure to see him dressing for a night out. She liked his pink shirt, a sweet complement to his buffed body and white-blond hair. He held up three ties for her review, and she selected one with a pattern of jumping dolphins.

"This place is going to be jammed," said Brady as he knotted his tie in front of the mirror.

The restaurant they were going to was the new hip successor to LuLu's, also specializing in local seafood, suckling pig, and gourmet pizza cooked in wood-fired brick ovens. Yuki thought about her first dinner at LuLu's with Len Parisi.

Yuki and her new boss had been discussing a case in which a ferry passenger had pulled a gun and unloaded on the other passengers, killing six innocent people. The Brinkley case was Yuki's first prosecution of a mass murderer, and it was personal: the killer had shot her friend Claire Washburn and her teenage son, both of whom, thank God, had survived.

She and Len had been deep in conversation over wine and pizza when he suddenly clutched his chest and toppled backward onto the restaurant floor.

To this day, Len credited her with saving his life. She had only made a phone call, but he insisted that it was because of her clearheaded actions—waving off the fellow diner who had volunteered to drive him to the hospital, calling 911, staying with him, riding with him in the ambulance—that he was alive today.

In Yuki's opinion, Len didn't owe her a thing. It was the other way around. She'd learned so much from him, and she liked him, too.

It had been at least a year since she and Brady had had a social evening with Len and friends, and she was thinking ahead to what she knew would be a memorable event.

Brady was lacing up his shoes when his phone vibrated. Yuki had tried instituting a no-phone-after-eight-p.m. rule, but it hadn't lasted for even a day. She got calls. He got calls. Drowning "those dang things" in the sink was a fun idea but definitely impractical.

Brady grabbed his phone off the dresser, and Yuki listened to his end of the conversation.

He said, "Tell me everything, Boxer. But y'all are okay? I need the name of the FBI agent. Okay. Got it. You need to get all of those tenants off the sixth floor and into the lobby. I agree. Wait for the ME. I'll call the mayor. Absolutely. Twenty minutes, traffic permitting."

Yuki knew what was coming next. She sighed.

He ended the call, speed-dialed the mayor, and left an urgent message.

"I'm sorry," he said to Yuki. "Our investigation just turned into a shootout with two fatalities. I've got people on the scene, more on the way, and a lotta displaced tenants needing a place to bunk."

Yuki was disappointed, but she didn't say so. Dinner was dinner. This was life and death. Brady had been talking with Lindsay, and that meant that her friend had been in danger. Yuki tuned back in to what her husband was saying.

"I have to go. Yuki, tell Red Dog I'm sorry."

"He'll understand," she said. "Be safe. I love you."

CHAPTER 12

AFTER LIVING THROUGH the terrifying shoot-out at the Anthony, I was weak-kneed, shaky, and ready for sleep, a shower, hugs, and dinner, not necessarily in that order.

I took the elevator to our apartment and had stabbed my key at the front-door lock several times when the door opened. Joe said, "Hey, just wondering what happened...oh, man, look at you, Blondie."

"That good, huh?"

I got my hug. I held on to Joe, thinking once again that my love for my job could cost me everything. Any day. Any time.

I told Joe that I loved him, my voice cracking in the middle. He said, "Hey, hey, you're home now. Take a look at what Sugarpuss and I have been up to."

Sugarpuss, a.k.a. Julie Anne Molinari, screamed, "Mommeee," and ran into the foyer. Joe grabbed her up so I could get out of my jacket and lock my weapon in the antique gun safe high above Julie's curly-haired head.

Martha woofed and waddled in and got her paws up on my knees. We all headed into the big living-eating-relaxing room with its tan leather furniture and big TV.

And there, standing between two tall windows looking out onto Lake Street, was a beautiful Christmas tree, winkin' and blinkin', intensely decorated on the branches that Julie could reach. The star for the pinnacle was sitting on the windowsill, and a pile of wrapped presents filled the seat of Joe's big daddy chair.

"Oh, my God," I said. "You two did all of this?"

"*I* did, Mommy!" said Julie.

I didn't know I still had an ear-to-ear grin left in me. I picked Julie up and she gave me a tour of the tree: the snowflakes and icicles, the globes with little scenes inside, and the now-traditional silver star from my sister, Catherine, engraved with *First Christmas* on one side and *Julie* on the other.

After the tour and Joe's promise to place the star on the top of the tree in the morning, we put our little girl to bed. We doused the light, blew some kisses, and closed the door. As we tiptoed back to the living room, Joe said, "If I were you…"

"Hmmmm?"

"If I were you, I'd have a bowl of mushroom beef barley soup. Then a shower. Then ice cream."

"We have that soup?"

I must have been staring at him with stray-dog eyes,

because Joe laughed long and hard. "You think I would offer soup and not have any?"

"You made it from scratch?" I said.

"Mrs. Rose did that."

Mrs. Rose, Julie's part-time nanny, was an amazing cook.

"I'm reheating it," said Joe. "That counts."

"It certainly does."

He sat me down and turned a flame up under the soup. When I was tucking into a bowl with a spoon in one hand and half of a buttered baguette in the other, I told my husband about my day.

I started with Christmas shopping for Cindy, then the chase along Grant Avenue, the capture of Julian Lambert, and our Q and A with him back at the Hall.

"He asked for a deal," I told my husband. "A walk-in exchange for info on an upcoming 'heist of the decade.' He said the mastermind was called Low-man."

"Humph."

"Or Loman."

"Like Willy Loman? Lead character in *Death of a Salesman*?"

"Hmm. Maybe. Julian didn't know how to spell it. What he did know was that a professional hitter by the name of Chris Dietz was one of the crew. Dietz was renting in the Anthony Hotel."

"I get a rash just thinking about that place," Joe said.

I nodded and said, "Tell me about it. We cornered Dietz, we thought, but then he pulled a switcheroo. Decided to have SWAT mow him down."

Joe asked questions. I told him what I could, and we continued talking as I took a hot shower. When I was dry and dressed in pj's, sure enough, there was a bowl of chocolate chocolate chip ice cream waiting for me. Joe, Martha, and I went over to the tree, and I watched Joe write out gift labels, most of them from Santa. He shook a small, flat box. "From Aunt Cat," he said. "Bet it's Julie's annual Christmas star."

Would I see the next one? I was thinking again about the Job versus Life. Everyone I knew, certainly my closest friends, was trying to balance this conflict every day.

Joe read me. "You're thinking about the shootout?"

"I was feeling bad that I missed the J-Bug hanging balls on the tree."

"There will be other Christmas trees," he said.

"I know." I said it again for emphasis and maybe for luck. "I know."

But what I was thinking was *God willing*.

PART TWO

DECEMBER 22

CHAPTER 13

CINDY THOMAS WAS in her office at the *Chronicle*, laptop open and coffee cooling as she dug into the assignment that had just arrived in her inbox.

The paper's publisher and editor in chief, Henry Tyler, had asked her to do a piece for the Living section about how undocumented immigrants in San Francisco celebrated the Christmas holidays. Undocumented immigrants were tangential to her usual crime beat, but Cindy was charged up by the story idea. For once she wouldn't be reporting on bombings or mass murderers or parents who'd locked their babies in hot cars.

Cindy created a new folder and shut out the sounds around her—the coffee-cart lady's bell, her coworkers laughing and chatting as they passed her office, and the traffic noise coming from the street below.

She would begin her research with the Christmas

traditions of people from Mexico and Central America, focusing on a central question: Was it possible to keep cultural tradition alive when you were living under a shadow? Sometimes that shadow was decades long.

Cindy began reading about Las Posadas—"the Inns" —a nine-day Mexican Christmas tradition celebrating Mary and Joseph's journey to find a safe place to stay while awaiting the birth of their child. How had she never heard of this festival? It sounded so joyful. It started every year on December 16 with a costume parade down a main street, after which friends, families, and neighbors would take turns acting as "innkeepers," one home hosting a posada each night through December 24. As tradition had it, once the crowd had gathered inside a home, there were prayers and a Bible reading before the good times rolled. Cindy found photos of the piñatas, the hot drinks and yummy food, and the take-home bags of candies for the celebrants.

Today was the twenty-second. Cindy figured that in some places in San Francisco, Las Posadas was in full swing, but it would be ending soon. She had to work fast if she was going to center her story on that. Research alone did not a story make.

Five days a week Cindy published a crime blog that was open to her readership for comments. She clicked on her crime-blog page and wondered how to ask for assistance from Latino immigrants without it looking like an ICE-inspired sting.

She wrote, "If you're from South or Central America or Mexico and would like to share your Christmas tradition with our readers, please write to me. Your real name is not required."

Within the hour she was looking through dozens of responses to her query, and one of them was tantalizing.

But it had nothing to do with Las Posadas. At all.

CHAPTER 14

THE RESPONSE THAT grabbed Cindy's attention was from Maria, who wrote, "My husband is in jail for a murder he didn't do. We are undocumented and he has been in jail for two years, no trial. I am lost. Please help."

Cindy replied, "Thank you for your message, Maria. Can we meet?"

Maria wrote back in minutes. "Can you come to my apartment? I have to work at noon."

Less than an hour later Cindy was driving through the Mission, a neighborhood heavily populated by Spanish-speaking immigrants from Latin America.

She checked off the landmarks Ms. Maria Varela had given her—the tattoo parlor on one corner, a *mercado* on the opposite one, vividly colored signage and murals on the sides of the three-story wood-frame building on Osage Street where Maria lived.

Cindy parked in front of a coin-op laundry, walked

a block west to Osage, and buzzed the button marked VARELA. A return buzz unlocked the street-level door. With some trepidation, Cindy entered and climbed two flights of stairs.

Maria was waiting for her outside the apartment door.

"I *love* you for coming," she said. "Thank you very much."

Cindy thought Maria looked to be in her forties, average height and weight, hair pulled into a bun. She wore a loose-fitting flowered top over tights and flat shoes, pink lipstick, and a smile at odds with the sadness in her brown eyes.

The small apartment was tidy with a nice sectional facing the TV, a print of the Crucifixion over the faux fireplace, and Christmas lights strung along the wall above the windows. A small Christmas tree stood on the kitchen table, and there were framed family photos—everywhere.

Cindy declined an offer of coffee, took a seat on the sofa, and began to interview Ms. Varela, noticing that her English was excellent.

"Tell me about your husband," Cindy said.

Maria lifted a photo from the lamp table and showed it to Cindy. It was a picture of herself and her husband, Eduardo Varela, taken some years before. Maria's hair hung loose to below her shoulders, Eduardo wore a white linen shirt, and the two had their arms around each other, radiating love and hope.

Maria said, "We got married in Guadalajara when we were eighteen. Three little ones came the first five years. Then the farm where we worked burned down. We couldn't get work. We had a cousin here. We tried to get visas for ourselves and our children so we could come to America. The papers never came."

Maria told a harrowing story of the type that had become almost commonplace in the pages of the *Chronicle* and all over the country. She and Eduardo had paid a "coyote" everything they had, and he had arranged for them to be driven in a packed truck to the border and then smuggled over. In the process, they had been separated from their oldest child.

"But God answered our prayers. We found Roberto in a shelter four months later. He was six."

The cousin got Eduardo a job in the tomato fields, and Maria did laundry. They scraped by.

"We were illegal. We couldn't apply for green cards.

"Roberto, Elena, and Geraldo are now in high school. I work at the Trident Hotel. Cleaning. Eduardo had two, sometimes three, jobs to support us all—and then the nightmare happened."

Maria seemed stuck in the memory of that nightmare until Cindy encouraged her to go on.

Maria looked grief-stricken. She told Cindy, "A boy was shot on the street. Some other boys said Eduardo did it. They knew him—knew his name and said that to the police. Ms. Thomas, Eduardo was in his car, sleeping. He doesn't want to wake us up when he leaves for his night shift. He heard the shots but he had nothing, *nothing*, to do with the shooting. That night he was arrested for murder at his job, and he is being held for trial two years now."

"Two *years*? Can they do that?"

Maria nodded sadly. She told Cindy that her husband

had prior arrests before the shooting. "He was stopped for speeding. And he had a fake driver license. He needed to work, drive from the auto-body store he cleaned during the day to the gas station where he did the overnight shift," she said. "But he never hurt anyone in the world. He is the best husband and father. Sweet. Gentle. He has never shot any gun."

"Maria, do you have a lawyer?"

"We did. He got all our money, and Eduardo is still in jail. Now I'm afraid if I fight, *I'll* be deported, and then there is no one to protect our children."

"I'd love to see more pictures of your family," Cindy said. Maria brought an album over and sat next to Cindy.

"The pictures are not so good but very valuable to us."

She turned the pages slowly, saying who was who in photos of events, birthdays, and gatherings. There was even a picture taken at a parade along Osage Street of the family dressed as peasants and angels in the Christmas pageantry of Las Posadas.

"But we won't be celebrating Las Posadas this year."

"What can I do to help?" Cindy asked.

"When I saw what you wrote, I felt that God was saying that you are a lifeline. I have no place else to turn."

"No promises," Cindy said, reaching over to take Maria's hands. "But I'll talk to a friend who might be able to help."

CHAPTER 15

CINDY DROVE BACK to the *Chronicle*, thinking about what she could do before she called Yuki and begged her to get involved. There were so many people like Maria, hopeless, living in fear. And there had to be many others who would feel this family's pain. People who could easily think, *There but for the grace of God go I.*

As she drove, Cindy thought of Maria Varela's sadness and desperation. In her mind she composed a pitch to Henry Tyler about Maria's family and their tragic situation.

If Tyler approved, Cindy thought she could write a story about this family that would get attention. It might melt some bureaucrat's heart or attract a legal pit bull who could take a bite out of the system. Suddenly she was feeling a lot of pressure to write an impassioned story about the Varelas as well as her assigned feature about Las Posadas in time for both pieces to appear in the Christmas edition.

She just needed to stay focused and keep her fingers on the keys. Research first.

Back at the *Chronicle*, Cindy found the coffee wagon, brought a cup of cocoa and a muffin, took both back to her desk, and began looking up resources about immigration law, which she knew to be complex and sometimes arbitrary. She pulled several articles from LexisNexis and read for hours. In regard to law enforcement, she learned that ICE could bring an unauthorized migrant to immigration court, where he or she would most likely be deported and barred from reentering the United States for ten years or more. Depending on the offense, the individual might also be prosecuted under the laws in his or her home country.

In Eduardo's case, the officers had chosen to hold him on criminal charges. He'd been indicted by a grand jury and then left in jail in San Francisco pending trial—whenever that would be. Cindy now knew that long-term pretrial detention happened with regularity. Courts had backlogs, and detention ensured court appearances and preserved public safety. But the real reason many stayed in jail was that most undocumented immigrants couldn't afford bail.

Maria had told Cindy that Eduardo was sleeping in his car when he heard the shots. She said that the witnesses had lied—he didn't own and had never fired a gun. Maybe when they'd seen Eduardo, they had decided on the spot to pin the shooting on him.

Cindy thought about the possible outcomes of a trial. Could those witness statements be refuted? Or was it more likely that two years after that murder, in a transient neighborhood with an immigrant population, no one would testify in Eduardo's defense? And if the case went to trial and Eduardo was found guilty of murder despite the sketchy evidence, he would go to prison, probably for life.

With her new understanding of Eduardo's situation and what he was up against, Cindy decided it was time to pitch Tyler the story and then, if he approved it, go see Yuki Castellano and try to get her on board.

CHAPTER 16

YUKI WAS BEHIND her tidy desk in her office when Cindy came to the door. She said to Cindy, "Come on in. Have a seat. Put your feet up. What's going on?"

Yuki was usually the fast talker of the group, but Cindy could put some speed on when she was worked up. The two friends went over to the small sofa, where Cindy filled Yuki in on her meeting with Maria and the research she had done.

Her proposed article about Eduardo Varela wasn't an investigative report. It was an opinion piece, a human-interest story. She hadn't interviewed cops or the ME or gone over crime scene photos.

She had pitched Eduardo's story to Henry Tyler, the publisher and editor in chief, saying that she *believed*, based on talks with his family, that this undocumented immigrant had been wrongfully charged and jailed without trial for two years.

Cindy had told Tyler that she was convinced that an injustice had been done, and she and Tyler had discussed the Varela family's backstory.

After ten intense minutes Tyler had said, "Go for it." And he was holding space for her on the front page of the Christmas edition.

Now she had to write it—and fast. Could Yuki help Eduardo?

Yuki said, "Are you asking me to lean on an ADA and get this man out of jail? Today?"

"Can you?"

"Hell no."

Cindy laughed. "I thought you could do anything."

"Not exactly," said Yuki. "I can do *nothing* to defend this man. I'm a prosecutor, remember? But I have some questions for you."

"Shoot," said Cindy.

Yuki asked for the names of the victim, the arresting officers, and the witnesses against Eduardo. Cindy referred to her notes.

"The victim was Gordon Perez, twenty years old, body found on Bartlett Street two blocks from Eduardo and Maria's apartment. Here's a transcript of the arresting officers' statements," Cindy said as she emailed the police report to Yuki from her phone.

"Let me see," said Yuki. She went to her laptop, read the report, then looked up and said, "The police didn't find the gun."

"That's good or bad?"

"If they'd found a gun that belonged to Eduardo, there's

your slam-dunk conviction. If they'd found the murder weapon and it was registered to someone else but Eduardo's prints were on it, ditto. Slam dunk. If they'd found the gun but there were no prints, that would have worked in Eduardo's favor. Without a gun, it's much harder to prove that he's the shooter. Did Eduardo know the victim?"

"Yes. They were acquainted."

"How did they get along?"

"From what Maria told me, they just lived on the same street. That was all."

Yuki said, "Okay. Assuming Eduardo Varela had no motive to shoot Gordon Perez, the case against him is based on witness statements. Varela has a crappy alibi. As it says here, he was sleeping in his car, heard shots, got out, and saw some boys run off."

"He didn't call the police," said Cindy. "He just drove to his second job."

"Hmm. Or, as the state will put it, he shot the guy, got rid of his gun, then drove to his second job."

Yuki had worked for a nonprofit lawyers' organization. Cindy knew she had defended a couple of undocumented immigrants while assisting the head of the Defense League, who was now a friend.

Yuki said, "I'm thinking about that big case that gets talked about a lot. Jorge Alvarez was deported five times and got back into San Francisco, where he fatally stabbed a man in a hotel lobby. It was an unfortunate criminal career path," Yuki said, "but it made a big impression on the public consciousness, and it hardened the courts against illegal immigrants."

63

"What happened to Alvarez?" Cindy asked.

"He's awaiting trial. He could be your guy's cell mate, for all we know. But there's another guy I just read about, an immigrant convicted of murder, Jaime Ochoa. Ochoa got a break—after twenty years."

"Twenty?"

"The one and only witness retracted her statement. She maintained that she had told the cops she wasn't sure at the time, but the state ran with the witness testimony and got a conviction. After twenty years, the witness was willing to swear she'd ID'd the wrong man."

"Holy crap. Twenty years of life, wasted."

"Ochoa walked out a free man. He wasn't deported, and he thanked the court and went home to his family," Yuki said. "He was undocumented, but he had no prior record.

"Varela, on the other hand, is not only here illegally, he's a repeat offender with a murder indictment."

"So there's no hope at all?"

"I'll make a call to Zac Jordan, the lawyer I worked for at the Defense League. He's good, Cin. He's smart as can be. Still, I wouldn't bank on Eduardo Varela walking on this one. He has the right to a fair trial. But unless he has a brilliant lawyer and the state is too overwhelmed to pay attention, odds are he's going to prison for the rest of his life."

"Please call your friend, Yuki," Cindy said. "I believe in miracles."

CHAPTER 17

THE DAY AFTER the shootout at the Anthony Hotel, the bullpen was standing room only, packed wall to wall with investigators from our station and representatives from Northern and Central as well.

Brady had called an emergency meeting. Two FBI agents had been hit; one had died, and the other had been moments from bleeding out. The tension in the room was expressed with tight body language and nervous chatter.

I watched Brady leave his office at the back of the bullpen and edge through the crowd. When he got to the front, he grabbed a chair, stepped up onto it, batted away a garland of tinsel tacked to the ceiling, then ripped it down.

He said, "Good morning, everyone."

The chatter immediately shut down, and our lieutenant and acting chief got right to it.

He said, "We've been tipped off that there is going to be

a big, likely heavily armed robbery in the next few days. We'd like to head that off.

"Here's what we know."

Talking over the fresh round of murmurs, Brady detailed the chase and capture of petty thief Julian Lambert, the info he'd given us on a hitter hired to work the upcoming robbery, and the tip that the hitter was staying at the Anthony Hotel.

"That hitter," said Brady, "is now laid out at the morgue. Everyone here heard what happened last night?"

A murmur of "Yes, sir"s rumbled through the room. The story of the one-man ambush and Dietz's utter obliteration on the sixth floor had traveled fast, first over the police and fire department channels, then by word of mouth, then via the internet, and finally as a "Sources tell us" piece on the broadcast news.

Conklin and I exchanged looks, both of us still shell-shocked, hoping for answers. After this, we planned to go back to the Anthony and meet with CSI director Charlie Clapper. He and his team had been processing the scene all night, and I was dying to find out what he had learned from Chris Dietz's rented room. Julian Lambert was still in our custody, and Brady would interrogate him again. If Lambert was holding anything back, I was pretty sure he'd give it up to Brady.

Brady said, "Here's what we know about this robbery scheme. Supposedly, a man named Loman is behind it, and supposedly, it's going down on Christmas Day."

He paused and everyone waited.

"That's all I've got," said Brady. "No idea what the

target is, what part of town it'll be in, who else is involved. Heck, Loman might have decided to pull the plug on this operation, given all the publicity on last night's action.

"But let's say he's still going forward. If you hear something, say something."

Feet shifted. A voice called out, "Over here, boss."

"Bentley," Brady said. "Whatcha got?"

Sergeant Roger Bentley was from the Robbery Division. I didn't know much about him, but I knew he was well positioned to hear rumors about a heist.

Bentley said, "I've heard the name Loman. People are afraid of him, like he's a drug lord or a capo. But nothing more than that. I've asked, and what comes back is 'I don't want to talk about him.'"

Another hand went up and Brady called on Anderson from the Criminal Investigations Unit upstairs.

Anderson said, "Rumor has it that Loman was behind that casino heist in Vegas. The one at the Black Diamond. Netted nine million. Almost got out clean, but three of his crew—the guys transporting the take—were killed when their getaway car was T-boned by a gas truck on the way out of town."

We had all heard about that heist gone wrong—a TV movie had been based on it. As I remembered it, the gas-truck explosion was shown in slow motion and it had been a mesmerizing special effect. But I hadn't known that the man behind the heist that went way wrong was named Loman.

"Let's have some ideas on possible targets," Brady said.

Hands went up around the room; people suggested

banks, museums, jewelry stores. Opportunities for potentially big hauls, like the nine million taken from the Black Diamond Casino.

When the brainstorming was over, Brady asked those present to work their informants and uniforms in their divisions and forward all possible leads to him.

"Crime's not going to take a holiday while we go after Loman. I'm calling people back from time off so we're covered. One of those people is Chief Warren Jacobi, who has volunteered to step out of retirement and work out of this unit with Boxer and Conklin."

Jacobi came through the doorway to a big round of applause from about sixty cops who knew that, even after retiring under a cloud, he was a helluva cop.

I was very glad to see my old partner, my old boss, my close friend. Conklin and I grinned at each other.

The gang was all here.

CHAPTER 18

I WAS STILL on adrenaline overload from last night's shootout at the Anthony Hotel, and now Brady's full-house staff meeting had tweaked me to a turn.

The clock on this mysterious big heist was running out and we needed answers—fast. Conklin parked our squad car in front of the Anthony Hotel behind three cruisers and the CSI van. I was glad to see that van. If anyone could read tea leaves in the dregs of this cesspool, it was Charlie Clapper and his team.

I zipped my Windbreaker over my vest and yanked up the chain holding my badge so that it hung outside my jacket. I got out of the car and took in the sights. Morning on Sixth Street looked like a flashback to the Great Depression. Clouds blocked the sun. Trash blew up the pavement and collected in the gutters. Pedestrians drifted purposelessly, and the thin traffic slowed when drivers saw the CSI van.

Uniformed officers leaned against their cruisers, protecting the perimeter. Others had door duty, barring the press and checking IDs of hotel residents. An old man vomited in the alley next to the liquor store.

My partner said, "Ready?"

"You bet. Can't wait."

We crossed the buckled sidewalk to the hotel entrance, entered the stinking lobby, and identified ourselves to the desk clerk, who was twenty years older than the clerk working the night shift. He had been informed, no doubt. He said, "Don't mess up the place, okay?"

Conklin said, "Got it," and we took the stairs, an obstacle course of discarded crack vials, condoms, Thunderbird empties. We exited through the fire door onto the sixth floor.

All but two of the doorways were taped off; tenants had been relocated and their rooms cleared. I noticed now that a couple of those doors had wreaths circling the peepholes. Another was hung with a stocking, the name *Mia* stitched on the cuff. Meager hopes for a merry Christmas, dashed.

At the front of the long hallway, room 6F looked as I had seen it last night, the bullet-perforated door left hanging by one hinge after Dietz had sprung his surprise attack on a team of trained SWAT commandos armed with military-grade automatic weapons. The bloody outline of Dietz's body was like an unwelcome mat in front of the door. Why would he pick a fight he so obviously would not win?

At the far end of the hallway, the door to 6R was wide open. I called out to Charlie Clapper and he stepped out to meet us. Clapper was director of Crime Scene Investigation, a former LVPD homicide cop with deep knowledge and no attitude. He always looked as though he'd dressed for a business meeting, and despite the booties over his shoes and the blue latex gloves he was wearing, today was no exception. His blazer and tie were snappy, and his graying hair was immaculately cut and combed.

"Welcome to the morning after," he said.

"Always a pleasure to see you, Charles," I said.

Clapper told us to view the scene from the doorway. "For anything you want to see close up," he said, "I'll be your eyes."

The room was lit by a couple of halogen lights and was small enough that we could see everything in it from the threshold. Three CSIs, gloved up, wearing booties, and armed with cameras and evidence bags, stepped gingerly around the periphery of the room.

Done correctly, processing a crime scene is a slow, methodical procedure of documentation and analysis because of the underlying need to keep the scene intact. If there were clues to Loman's plans, they could be here.

I looked around and saw an open can of beer on top of the old-fashioned TV set, a plate of half-eaten spareribs on the kitchen table. The closet door was open, revealing two men's coats and assorted pieces of casual clothing. A coffee table in front of a sagging sofa was laden with what looked to be expensive cameras and technical equipment I couldn't identify.

"So what do we have?" I asked Clapper.

"Looks like he was living here alone," said Clapper. "And

he was working on something not exactly kosher. Those are the tools of his trade: cameras, sophisticated listening devices. No expense was spared. Oddly, there's no laptop in either of his rooms, but we got his phone.

"Unrelated, there was a stash of porn over there," he said, pointing in the general direction of the sofa. "And in the bathroom. And under the bed."

"Regular porn or something special?"

"Straight-up busty women. Two semiautos plus ammo were in the closet. I sent the guns and the phone to the lab. Before I did that, I mailed this from his phone to mine. You may find it interesting."

Conklin and I stood beside Clapper as he swiped through the crime scene photos. He stopped on one and angled the screen so we could see it: a map of Golden Gate Park. He enlarged it. The de Young Museum, located inside the park, had been circled in red.

Hot damn.

Finally. We had a clue.

CHAPTER 19

CONKLIN AND I were heading down the fire stairs to the Anthony's lobby when a curvy young woman stepped out of the shadows on the fourth-floor landing.

She said, "Hey. Inspectors. I got something to tell you about Savage. I mean Chris."

She looked to be around twenty years old and was wearing frayed black tights and a tight red top with sequins at the neckline. Her haircut was choppy and there were studs in her face, hoops in her ears. The tattoo on one arm read BITE ME. One of her hands was inked with a baby's face under a banner reading ANGEL.

I asked her name.

"I go by Dancy."

"And Savage is?"

"Your boy. Chris Dietz," she told us.

Muffled shouts, Christmas carols, and door slams

resonated through the stairwell, as if it were acoustically designed to pull sound upward through the thin walls of adjoining apartments.

I asked her, "How well did you know Chris Dietz?"

"I lived next door to him for two months. Since he moved in," she said. "When I got jacked outta my room, I found an empty one downstairs. When can I go back to my place?"

I said, "When the crime scene guys are done. Probably take another day."

"What about all the holes in my door?"

I shrugged an apology and said, "That'll be up to hotel management and Nationwide. You have something for us?"

She scowled. "I need a hundred dollars. Savage was my rent money."

Conklin said, "A hundred? That's a little much, isn't it?"

"It's cheap for what I've got for you," she said. "He used to talk to me when we were done. He told me his plans."

I didn't want to take a witness statement in a fire stairwell if I could help it. If Dancy had something, I wanted her in an interrogation room on camera.

We had a map of Golden Gate Park with a circle around the museum that had come from Dietz's phone. It was a good start. Maybe we had the where. But I wanted more. Much more. Times, dates, names, all the details needed to flesh out this sketchy story. If Dancy had answers, truthful ones, a hundred bucks *was* cheap.

I said, "I have to get the boss to sign for that. Let's take a ride to the station."

She scoffed and trotted down toward the lobby.

I shouted after her, "Dancy. We'll get the money."

She spun around. "You want to lock me up."

"No," I said. "I want to talk to you in private—"

"Listen, and make sure you hear me," she said. "I'm not going to no damned police station with you."

A door opened on the floor below us. Children's voices rang out and their footsteps clattered in the stairwell.

I sighed. Our potential informant was dancing away.

"Come back," I said. "I'll give you what I've got on me."

The young prostitute walked up to the landing and stuck out her palm.

Conklin dug his wallet out of his back pocket and I searched my jacket for spare change.

I handed him my little wad.

Conklin counted his bills and said, "I've got sixty. All together, we've got seventy-five dollars and thirty-five cents."

Dancy looked at it and snorted. "Keep the change," she said. She plucked the bills from Conklin's hand and stuffed them inside the bodice of her red spangled blouse.

She said, "Dietz told me that he was going to hit the mayor."

"Caputo?" I said stupidly.

"He's the mayor, right?"

"Why was Dietz going to kill the mayor?"

"He didn't say why. Savage always wants to be a big man. There was supposed to be a huge paycheck in the hit. He said he knew where the mayor was and when. He was just waiting for the call and it would be a go."

"Waiting for the call from whom?" Conklin asked.

Dancy looked at him like he was an idiot.

"You don't know anything, do you?" she said. "Loman. Savage was working for Mr. Loman."

CHAPTER **20**

CONKLIN AND I sat across from Brady in his small, glass-walled office at the back of the bullpen.

Our lieutenant had a few to-do lists in front of him, yellow pads marked with a red grease pencil. A flurry of Post-it notes covered his lamp and walls. Every light on his phone console blinked red.

The stress of several punishing months of double duty showed in Brady's face and posture. I wondered how much longer he could take it, how long before either a new chief was hired to replace Jacobi or Brady took the bump up to the bigger job. He had the chops to be chief, but the position was 100 percent administration and politics.

I didn't think he would like it.

Brady punched a button on his phone console and said, "Brenda, can you clear these calls before the phone shorts out?"

To us he said, "Y'all have to make this quick."

Conklin and I told him about our morning with Clapper at the Anthony and dangled the two shiny objects: Dancy's tip about a contract on the mayor and the circled museum on the hit man's phone.

Brady leaned back in his chair and stared out at the traffic on the freeway.

When he turned back, he said, "We're swimming in tips, none substantiated. Loman's crew is going to hit one of two banks, a jewelry store, or all of the above.

"Now we add in a target on the mayor. Why the mayor? Is this political? Is it terrorism?"

Conklin said, "Dancy told us that Dietz was given a contract. That's all we've got."

Brady said, "I'll get to the mayor. He's too willing to put himself in front of microphones. Cameras. He should cancel any public appearances. I can beef up his security detail."

He stood up, shouted out across the bullpen, "Brenda, please get Wroble on the line."

Ike Wroble was captain of the Homeland Security Unit, now reporting to Brady in his role as temporary police chief.

Brady sat down, drummed his fingers on the legal pad.

"About a robbery at the de Young," said Brady. "It's a rich target. If Lambert, your shopping-bag thief, is right that there's going to be a heist, that sounds more like the way to go than taking out the mayor. There's a fortune in artwork at the de Young.

"Either way, we've got three days to get ahead of this. I

don't have to tell you, we have limited resources and not one goddamn reliable fact."

We kicked it around for ten more precious minutes. Conklin argued that we should lean on Dancy. "She says Dietz confided in her. She's skittish, but motivated by cash."

"Okay," said Brady. "Grab up a partner from the bullpen or get a couple of unis and pick her up. If she's uncooperative, hold her as a material witness. And, Conklin, you interview her alone. Do your magic. Boxer, we've still got Lambert upstairs?"

"Yes, his arraignment is tomorrow."

"Good. You and Jacobi squeeze him *hard*. What else does he know about Dietz, about Loman, and does he know anything about any possible hits on, say, local politicians? And get ahold of security at the de Young. Tell them what we've got."

Brady's phone lines were blinking like a flock of rabid bats, and Brenda was at his door.

Conklin and I got out of his way and went to work.

CHAPTER 21

CONKLIN FOUND A pickup partner in Robbery, and they left the Hall to bring Ms. Dancy in.

Jacobi swooped in, took Conklin's vacant chair, and plugged in his laptop.

I said, "Must suck to get dragged back into this mess."

"Not at all, Boxer. It's *retirement* that sucks."

Job one for us was the de Young Museum in Golden Gate Park. We were both familiar with the spacious modern showplace that held a permanent collection of great American art as well as priceless jewelry and special exhibits. With the opening of the annual holiday artisan fair and special viewing hours, foot traffic would be up.

"You call museum security," I said.

"And you hit the keys."

I grinned at him. It felt great to be partnered again with my old pal. We had always been able to read each other's minds and finish each other's sentences. We hadn't lost the knack.

I booted up my computer. If the de Young was the target, I could envision gunfire spraying throughout the galleries. I could imagine a bloodbath.

Jacobi said, "Guy named James Karp was head of security last I checked. I used to know him."

As Jacobi dialed out, I hit the keys, asking our software for museum robberies. Pages of them unfurled on my screen.

I clicked on the first link and read about an audacious museum heist in Boston. In this case, a couple of armed cops arrived after the museum had closed for the day and told a security guard that they'd received a call reporting a disturbance. Breaking the rules, the guard let the supposed cops in, and they promptly handcuffed him, threatened another guard, and made off with thirteen high-value paintings worth five hundred million dollars. There'd been no shooting. No mayhem. Just a well-planned and -executed robbery.

The return on investment was, frankly, unbelievable. The fake cops were never ID'd or caught, and the property was never recovered.

A similar job had taken place in a Swiss museum. Two bad guys in ski masks had forced their way in, bound the security guards with duct tape, and gone out the back with four paintings by the all-star masters' club: Cézanne, Degas, Monet, and van Gogh.

As with the Boston heist, there'd been good planning, a huge haul disproportionate to the number of men in the crew, and, surprisingly, no bloodshed.

Jacobi sighed loudly and said into the phone, "Yes, I can continue to hold."

I saw the beauty of these robberies that required very few people and had such enormous payouts. I went on to read about more sophisticated, over-the-top B-movie-type heists involving explosives and tunnels that had taken years to dig. A robbery of a Swedish museum had one team to lift the masterworks while another detonated cars in other parts of the city, closing off roadways so that police couldn't fully respond.

I thought about that. Code 3, adrenalized cops swarming in from all points with lights, sirens, the works, and slamming into gridlock—everywhere. Damn. *Frustrating* wasn't a strong enough word for that.

Jacobi had the receiver to his ear and was twisting the cord around his fingers, but he was still on hold, so I gave him the highlights of my research.

I said, "From what I can tell, you don't have to come through the skylight on a rope with suction cups and a glass cutter or crawl under laser beams. You want to rob a museum, go at night. No civilians, small security detail. Threaten and terrify the guards, bind them with duct tape, get the keys and codes, lift the loot that is hanging in plain sight, and get the hell out.

"I wonder if that's Loman's plan. Do the hit not on Christmas Day, as we've been led to believe, but after museum hours on Christmas *Eve*. Not many security guards working then."

Jacobi said, "I like your thinking," and turned his attention back to the phone. "James Karp? It's Warren Jacobi.

Yeah, I know, long time. Listen, Karp, I'm helping out at Southern Station on a tip we got that the de Young is going to be burglarized."

"Put him on speaker," I said.

Jacobi hit the button and introduced the security head, adding, "Boxer, Karp and I were patrolling a beat when you were in high school."

I laughed politely and said, "That can't be right." I cut to the chase, telling Karp about our unconfirmed lead pointing to a possible well-armed hit on the museum on Christmas Eve or Christmas Day.

Our call was interrupted when Officer Bubbleen Waters texted me from the seventh-floor jail. *Sgt. I got your prisoner in a box. Lambert, Julian.*

Jacobi told Karp he'd call him back and signed off.

We went upstairs to the jail. I was ready and eager to talk to Julian Lambert. I had news for him about his friend Dietz.

And we weren't leaving Lambert until he had actionable news for us.

CHAPTER 22

JULIAN LAMBERT WORE a day-old beard and the same odd expression I'd noticed when Conklin and I arrested him yesterday. He took a chair at the table in the jail's small meeting room, seeming wan and pale, as if lockup was having a bad effect on his morale.

"Sergeant Boxer, right?"

"How're you doing, Julian?"

I saw that I was going to be the good cop; Jacobi's age and interrogation style made him a natural heavy. I introduced him as Chief Jacobi, and we all sat at the table, which was twice the size of a luncheon tray.

Would Lambert talk? Our deal with him was paying out tomorrow. He'd given us Dietz, and in exchange, when he went to arraignment court, the ADA bringing the assault and theft charges would drop them and he would be released.

Julian had made good on his side of the deal. We had no leverage.

I said, "We found Chris Dietz at the Anthony."

"Like I said. I hope you didn't mention my name."

"We found him, Julian, but we didn't talk to him. He pulled his weapon and fired on us. He was killed in the return fire."

"Oh, no. You *killed* him?" The jolly expression was gone.

Jacobi jumped in, all business.

"Mr. Lambert, we need some help. We're getting miscellaneous tips about what Loman's crew is up to."

Lambert said, "I can't believe you killed Dietz. This is *my* fault. He's dead because of *me*—because of what *I* told *you*."

I took temporary leave of my good-cop role. "He's dead because he fired on police. He knew he was going to die."

Jacobi refused to be sidetracked. He said to Lambert, "The calls we're getting say Loman's going to hit a bank, a museum, or some other high-value target—"

"Wow. Well, I'm not surprised. Loman has a rep for thinking big."

Jacobi said, "I've got some questions for you, Lambert, and here's your incentive. Tell us what we want to know, or we're going to hold you as a material witness until you give us what we need to close this deal down."

"No. Wait. I'm supposed to be released tomorrow."

Jacobi said, "How do we find Loman?"

"I have no idea. He could live in outer space for all I know."

"I know this," said Jacobi. "You're keeping back information."

"Jezusss. I told the sergeant. I heard that Chris had a

job working for Loman. I didn't speak with Loman or with Chris. I guess it's too late now."

Lambert seemed genuinely broken up. Jacobi didn't care.

I gave Jacobi a look and he pushed his chair back from the table. I said, "Julian, listen to me. More people could die. You want that on you?"

Lambert said, "I've told you *everything* I know. Supposed to be a *big heist* on Christmas. Loman is the boss. I've never met him, thank God. Who do you think I am, CIA?"

"Who's your informant? Who told you that Dietz had a job with Loman and that there was going to be a heist?" I asked. "Give me a name, Julian."

"I can't say. *I can't say.* It wouldn't do you any good if I did. I got it from a nobody who happened to overhear a phone call."

"Your story is changing, Julian. You overheard it? Or someone else overheard it? What's the truth?"

"It's getting to where your guess is as good as mine. I'm not sleeping. I'm not eating. I can't even think anymore."

Either Lambert was digging in or he really was empty.

I stood up from the table, walked to the door, hit it with the flat of my hand, and called, "Guard."

Jacobi said to Lambert, "Be smart. Speak now, or we'll hold you as a material witness. We don't mind keeping you while we file additional charges. Obstruction of justice comes to mind."

Lambert appeared startled. He said, "Look, I can't verify this."

The door opened and two guards came into the room.

"Hang on a minute," Jacobi said to the guards. Then, to Lambert, "We're listening."

"What I heard was they were going to hit the mint."

"The San Francisco Mint? Who told you that?" I asked.

He shook his head—no, no, no.

"Give me a name."

"Marcus, okay? That's all I know about him. Calls himself Marcus, no known address. He's harmless, so try not to kill him, all right?"

"What else?" I said. "Anything about a hit on a museum? Any targeted political figures?"

"No," said Lambert. "Marcus said the mint."

I didn't think an army could get into the mint. The gray stone structure located on Hermann Street in the Lower Haight was completely closed to the public. Currency was no longer produced there, but the mint did strike commemoratives, special coins, and sets—it was a highly fortified fort full of gold and silver bars.

"Don't use my name," Lambert pleaded. "Keep my name out of this."

Jacobi and I left Lambert with the guards and took the elevator down to the squad room.

I said to Jacobi, "Could this be true? The mint is impenetrable. Guns and ski masks won't cut it. What's your bullshit detector tell you?"

Jacobi said, "That it's time to call the Secret Service."

PART THREE

DECEMBER 23

CHAPTER 23

JULIAN LAMBERT LEFT the jail in the Hall of Justice on Bryant Street with his backpack over his shoulder and wearing the red down jacket and dirty clothes he'd had on when he was arrested.

He'd felt like a vagrant in court, but the cops had made good on their promise. The ADA had said, "We're withdrawing the charges, Your Honor."

He was freed into a blustery morning. He walked northwest into a high, damp wind, trying to shake off the feeling of cuffs and bars, the omnipresent glare of fluorescent lights and psychopathic guards, the echoing shouts of prisoners.

He'd spent only two nights in a cell, but it felt like a year. And now the rest of his life was ahead of him.

With the wind blowing his hair around, Lambert adjusted his backpack and headed toward Victoria Manalo Draves Park, thinking of the job to come. He was sure that it would be a well-oiled process, and just as with a spy cell, he wouldn't know the others on the team and they wouldn't know him.

When the job was done, Loman would give him a passport, a new name and address, and a flush bank account in a city with a coastline. That was the deal. He was thinking he just might have some work done. Lose the bags under his eyes, shave down the nose. There was nothing he would miss about San Francisco, USA.

He had just crossed Columbia Square when a car horn honked behind him. He turned and watched as the blue Ford sedan pulled alongside him and slowed to a stop.

The car had one occupant, the driver, who buzzed down the passenger-side window and called out to him. "Lambert, right?"

Lambert walked over to the car and peered in. "And you are?"

"Dick Russell. Loman's man."

Lambert said, "I thought Loman was coming."

"He wants to have lunch with you," said Russell. "Get in." Lambert got into the passenger seat and closed the door, and the car took off.

Loman's man looked nothing like a criminal. He wore old-man clothes, a cap with a button-snap brim, a khaki Windbreaker, and perforated leather driving gloves. His face was unlined and ink-free, and he was carrying a spare tire around his waist. To Lambert's eyes, Russell looked like an accountant.

"Lunch, huh?" Lambert said. "Mind driving by my crib so I can change? I'd rather not smell this bad, you know?"

Russell said, "We don't have time, and besides, it's not necessary. Loman is very impressed. Tell me how you got yourself arrested, if you don't mind."

Lambert relaxed. A light rain pattered on the windshield, and the wiper blades smoothed it away. He was thrilled to be able to tell the story to someone, and Dick Russell was a very eager audience.

Lambert began, "It was Mr. Loman's inspiration."

Then he gave Russell the play-by-play, how he'd planned his moves as he ran, knocking down the old man and grabbing the bag, feinting, dodging, slowing so the cop could lunge and catch him.

Russell cracked up at the punch lines, then asked him what happened once the cops had him in the box.

Lambert told him about giving up Dietz as instructed. "The cops just told me about Dietz getting killed. Did you know?"

Russell nodded, slowed for the light on Howard Street. "I heard. Did *you* know he had cancer?"

"No. I didn't know him very well."

"It was sad. Terminal. In his brain. Dietz didn't want to die in a cell with his mind turning to mush, so he decided to go out in a blaze of glory."

"No shit."

Russell continued, explaining that Dietz's cut of the take was going to his daughter in Newark. "We're funneling the money into her bank account."

"Nice," said Lambert. "The cops bit on the map of the park Dietz left on his phone—I take it that was part of the plan?"

"Absolutely," said Russell. "So, Julian, where did you leave things with the cops?"

Lambert told Loman's man the whole story of the second interrogation—the threats, the pressure, how the two major-league cops finally dragged "the truth" out of him.

Lambert said, "I told them I heard Loman's crew was going to hit the mint."

"You're kidding," Russell said, turning to grin at Lambert. "That's brilliant. Protecting the mint will drain their resources. What made you think of that?"

Lambert was laughing now, enjoying the ride and the company. He said, "I always wanted to hit the mint. Must be pallets of gold bars and vaults full of coins in there. I'm a pretty good safecracker. But wait—that isn't the target, is it?" he asked. "I didn't accidentally give it away?"

Russell said, "Not at all. Make sure to tell Loman all about this; he's going to love it. He'll be meeting us in about five minutes. He's never late."

CHAPTER 24

THERE WAS A lull in the conversation between Lambert and Russell as Russell negotiated the traffic in the rain, looking at his watch every few minutes. Lambert didn't want to interrupt Russell's thoughts, so he tuned in to his own.

He thought again about Dietz. He didn't know much about the guy, but he'd gleaned that Dietz was a sports fisherman, owned a boat called the *Mai Tai* he talked about a lot, and had a seventeen-year-old daughter named Debbie. When he'd known Dietz, he hadn't yet been diagnosed with cancer. Shit. He'd been only about forty.

Lambert tried to picture what the cops had told him about Dietz firing on armed SWAT like he wanted to die. They didn't know that Dietz and Loman had planned this "blaze of glory" in exchange for a payout to Dietz's daughter. Generous of Loman to spring for it. But then, Dietz had come through for Loman even in death.

Lambert appreciated Loman's game plan, throwing down fake clues like spike strips in the path of the police, distracting them from the real plan and, at the same time, scaring the citizens with random chaotic events. It took tremendous skill and confidence to do that.

Lambert's own strength was that he was a complete athlete, almost a player-coach. The coach had foresight; he could diagram plays and knew when to call them. The player saw the whole field, *anticipated* events and knew what to do in the moment. His movements were quick and instinctive. He executed.

Lambert had used these skills in football and in life, and they had never failed him.

For this job, he would work with Loman's playbook and carefully script out his plays. He had a nose for the goal line—in this case, the money. And he'd know how to make it to the end zone.

Right now Lambert was seeing himself at a nice restaurant at a table with a view, having a three-course lunch, Loman telling him what he expected from him in the upcoming heist of the century.

Russell made a turn onto the Great Highway, followed the signs toward Lands End. There was a good restaurant out there, the Cliff House, where on a clear day you could see 180 degrees of ocean beyond the rocky bluff.

"What we're going to do," Russell said, "is stop at the Lands End Lookout off El Camino del Mar. Loman is going to meet us there, and you'll go in his car with him. I'll drive around for a little while, make sure I wasn't followed, and then I'll meet you at the restaurant. There's our turnoff."

Russell turned left and drove toward a paved parking area flanked by trees and, ahead, the USS *San Francisco* Memorial. On the left was a breathtaking view of the Pacific, to the right, the Golden Gate Bridge.

"I need a little help," Russell said. He angled the car and backed it up so that the rear was against the parking barrier and the front was pointed toward the road. Lambert noticed that the weather had kept the tourists inside. The parking lot, usually busy, was empty.

"Sure, Dick. What do you need?" Lambert asked.

And now he noticed that Russell seemed edgy.

"Everything okay?" Lambert asked.

"I've got a ton of weapons in the trunk. They're in duffel bags, so no worries. We'll transfer them to Loman's car, but let's get them out now."

Russell pulled up on the trunk release and got out. Lambert climbed out of the passenger seat and, walking straight into the wind, reached the back of the car before the older man. He pulled up on the latch. The trunk lid sprang up.

The cargo space was carpeted in black. Lambert saw a duffel bag, but it was flat; it didn't seem like it held "a ton of weapons." He leaned in and patted it.

The bag was empty. Was he missing the obvious, or had Russell exaggerated?

Lambert was straightening up to ask when he felt a jolt of fear.

It was animal instinct, a realization that he'd read this game all wrong.

CHAPTER 25

THE MAN WHO had said that his name was Dick Russell fired a round into the back of Lambert's neck.

Lambert was dead when Russell pushed him into the open trunk. The gunman didn't look it, but he was strong enough to easily fold Lambert's body into the rear compartment without getting any blood on himself.

He frisked the dead man for his wallet, took it from his back pocket, closed the trunk, then went through Lambert's backpack, still in the front seat. Finding no other ID, he left the backpack and locked up the car. By now it would have been reported stolen, but it would be days before a car left here would be called in or even noticed.

Standing at the rear of the Ford, the man in the old-geezer clothes tossed the car keys, the wallet, and the unregistered gun over the cliff, one after the other, and watched each one bounce down over the sharp rocks and land.

Then he made a call with his burner phone.

"Dick, where are you?…Good. I'm leaving the parking area now. I hope you brought my clothes. All right. See you soon."

The phone followed the wallet, gun, and keys over the edge almost two hundred feet down to the rocks above the crashing waves. After double-checking that no one was around the parking area, Loman started walking along the verge of El Camino del Mar.

Only a few minutes had passed before a horn blew behind him and his black Escalade stopped. Russell reached across the front seat and opened the door for him.

Loman got in.

"Man, I'm wet. And hungry," Loman said to his number two.

"Clothes are in the back seat and I've got reservations," Russell said. "Table with a hazy view."

"How's it going from your end?" Loman asked.

"Like clockwork," said Russell.

"That's what I like to hear," said Loman.

He grinned at Russell, who grinned back and stepped on the gas.

CHAPTER 26

CINDY WAS ALREADY hard at work in her home office at dawn, polishing the article about Christmas in San Francisco's barrios.

Her interviews with undocumented immigrants had left her feeling sad. There was nothing uplifting about people celebrating Christmas in the darkness, wondering if a slipup or a traffic stop could turn into a deportation. Was it even possible to keep cultural tradition alive when living in shadows that could stretch for decades?

She attached a photo to her file, an image of a Christmas tree with a handmade papier-mâché manger underneath. She titled the piece "Feliz Navidad" and sent it to publisher and editor in chief Henry Tyler.

Cindy drained her third mug of coffee and texted Yuki. *Are we still on?*

Yuki responded, *I'll be at the office at eight. C u soon.*

Cindy closed her laptop and dressed, then nudged Richie and told him she was his requested wake-up call.

He kissed her, tried to roll her into bed.

"Can't. Rain check. Love you." She kissed his ear and fled.

She drove through the misty morning toward the Hall of Justice along streets lined with lights and houses adorned with twinkling Christmas characters. They didn't lift her mood at all, wired as she was about her meeting with Yuki.

Twenty minutes after leaving home, Cindy tossed her keys to Brad, the parking attendant in the All-Day lot on Bryant. She shouted to him over her shoulder, "I'll be back in an hour."

She raced for the crosswalk, but as she reached the corner, she heard Brad calling her.

"Ciiiiiiiindyyyy. You dropped this."

He held up her scarf. She trotted back, said, "Damn. Thanks, Brad," and headed off again. Even after turning her ankle, she still made the green light.

She jogged up the granite steps, cleared security, crossed the lobby, and got into the elevator, her mind still fixed on Eduardo Varela and his lovable wife, Maria. After Tyler had green-lighted the jailed-undocumented-immigrant story, Cindy had spent enough time with Maria that she was totally convinced of Eduardo's innocence.

But believing in someone's innocence didn't make a publishable story, and it wouldn't spring him from jail, either.

Yuki had offered to help even though, as a prosecutor, she couldn't work the case herself. Yet in a couple of hours, Yuki would be visiting Eduardo in the jail where he had been detained for the past two years.

Cindy couldn't go with her, but Yuki would not be alone. She was bringing her old boss Zac Jordan, who worked at the not-for-profit Defense League. Zac was a do-gooding superstar with a Harvard law degree. He would decide if he wanted to take Eduardo's case and defend him at trial.

Cindy jerked her thoughts back to the present, exited the elevator, and opened the door to the DA's suite. Although the office was officially closed for the holiday, the reception area was lit by a gooseneck lamp at the front desk and the blue-and-gold twinkling of the tree in the corner.

She was about to phone Yuki when a man in a mail-room shirt entered reception through the side door and held it open for her to come through.

Cindy headed along the main corridor and knocked on the frame of Yuki's open door. Her friend looked up and said, "Come in, come in, Girl Reporter. Sit yourself down. We have to work pretty fast. Want coffee?"

Cindy said, "No, thanks." She was maximally caffeinated already.

Yuki said, "You brought the papers?"

Cindy opened her bag and put the folder in front of Yuki. Yuki flipped through the arrest record, police report, court transcript, and two witness statements, then transferred the folder to her own handbag.

Cindy asked, "What have you got for me?"

Yuki said, "There's no central database for this, Cin. So I can't get ahold of actual comprehensive data. The best I can do is give you the overview from thirty thousand feet."

"That's fine, Yuki. Right now I know less than zilch."

CHAPTER 27

CINDY SAT ACROSS from Yuki, her arms folded on the desk, looking at her friend with her trademark intensity.

Yuki said, "You sure I can't get you some coffee?"

"Only if you want to see me levitate," Cindy said.

Yuki said, "Okay, then, Cindy, here are the basics. If you're an undocumented immigrant—that is, living here without citizenship, green card, or visa—and you commit a crime of any kind, ICE can detain you."

Cindy nodded. She knew.

Yuki went on. "Once you're in custody, ICE decides whether or not to initiate removal proceedings. If you're charged with a felony, ICE can deport you, or local or federal law enforcement can process you through the system. You know the drill: arraignment, then a bond, if you can get one, or else you stay in jail pending trial."

Cindy said, "Eduardo has been charged with murder and has been detained pending trial for *two years*."

"I hate to hear that," Yuki said. "That really stinks."

"Doesn't it, though," Cindy said, clearly in full crusade mode. "And worse, according to his wife, the case against Eduardo is *entirely* based on false statements. He was framed."

"As you know, that's why there are criminal defense attorneys."

Cindy said, "Apparently, Eduardo had a lawyer at one point, but not anymore."

"What happened?"

"The Varelas don't know. They can't reach the guy. He doesn't return their calls. They think he just took their money and ran."

Yuki sighed. "That's crazy."

"Agreed," said Cindy. "I don't get the feeling that this has never happened before. I'm sure this isn't the first time an immigrant has paid a lawyer and then been blown off. Can you give me an idea how many undocumented immigrants are overcharged or poorly defended?"

Yuki said, "Hey, do I look like your research assistant?"

Cindy laughed. "Sorry. I'm on a tight deadline."

Yuki said, "If this helps, you're onto something. Even US citizens get improperly detained, and some are intimidated into waiving their rights or confessing when not guilty. Immigrants with no criminal record have been bused over the border and abandoned in wide-open spaces with no papers, no money."

Cindy nodded. "I read that, last year, eighty people who

were detained in California died of injuries or untreated illnesses. And in the US, four hundred thousand people pass through detention every year."

"See, you don't even need a research assistant," Yuki said. "But your primary interest right now is Eduardo Varela."

"True."

"And why are you so convinced he's innocent?" Yuki asked her friend.

"I believe his wife. There's that—and my solid-gold, award-winning gut instinct."

Yuki laughed. "Don't go public with your gut-instinct opinion until Zac and I meet him, okay? Not all undocumented immigrants who are arrested are innocent."

"I know, but Eduardo only has a traffic violation and a fake ID on his record. He's not a criminal."

"Did you hear me say I was going to help?"

"Yes. Yuki, you are the best of the best."

Cindy got up, hugged her friend, and said, "I wish I could go with you."

There was a knock on the door frame, and they looked over to see a tall man standing there. Yuki said, "Zac, come in and meet Cindy. Cindy, Zac Jordan of the Defense League. From time to time, Zac's been known to save the day."

"Great," Cindy said. "Nice to meet you, Zac. I think today is a day worth saving. It's almost Christmas, after all."

CHAPTER 28

YUKI GOT INTO Zac's old baby-blue BMW, and they took off toward County Jail #5 in San Bruno. She hadn't seen him in a year, and she was struck by how much he'd changed. He had a pierced ear and a bunch of string bracelets, and he'd swapped his cords and camel hair for denim. His longish hair needed a cut.

He saw her looking at his attire and smiled. "My day off," he said.

"You look younger," she said, meaning it.

The drive was a great opportunity for Yuki to catch up with her old friend. She told Zac about her most recent case. "I believed the victim, but he lied to me from the moment we met."

Zac commiserated and shared with her what he called his "extremely rotten year." Not only had Zac lost more cases than he had won, but his wife had filed for a separation. Then Mike Stoddard, the mega rich donor who kept the Defense League's lights on, had died at the age of fifty-two.

"It was sudden," Zac said. "Mike was such a good friend to us. I'll miss him, and not just for the money. He kept me fighting the good fight."

"But surely he provided for the Defense League in his will?"

"Nope. He just…never expected to have a massive coronary."

A few moments of silence ensued. Then Yuki said, "Zac? You okay? Will you be able to keep the Defense League going?"

"I'm fine. Really. Enough about me, Yuki-san. Tell me more about Eduardo Varela."

Yuki was glad to get into it. According to Cindy, she explained, Eduardo was a hardworking undocumented immigrant with a family who had been arrested for going ten miles over the speed limit and driving with a fake license. Then he claimed that he'd been falsely charged with murder.

"Eduardo's friends and family would all testify that he's innocent," she said, "and now he's got the indomitable Cindy Thomas of the *San Francisco Chronicle* on his side. If you take the case, his odds of acquittal zoom from 'no frickin' way' to 'maybe a shot.'"

"Nice of you to say so," Zac said. "We'll have to see."

Of course, Zac was right to reserve judgment. He was a good-as-gold person, a terrific lawyer and a busy one, but she had taken a chance asking him to look into this sad and likely hopeless case a couple of days before Christmas. Her pitch to Zac was based only on Cindy's enthusiasm and gut instinct. Of course, in Yuki's humble opinion, Cindy was right about 90 percent of the time. She was an investigative reporter. Her instinct was always supported by research.

Maria Varela had given Cindy a fat packet of letters from Eduardo along with gigabytes of family photos. Cindy had met their kids, individually and privately. She had also paid a call on Eduardo's employer at the Stop 'n' Shop gas station and convenience store where he had worked for years.

This was a small sample, but according to Cindy, they were all on Team Eduardo and of the same mind. Eduardo could *never* have shot anyone.

Cindy was sold. And despite Yuki's lawyerly reservations, she was on the Varela train and looking to get Zac on it, too.

A half hour after leaving the Hall, Zac and Yuki cleared the security systems at San Bruno and were brought to a small interview room. They had just taken seats when the door opened again and two jail guards escorted an unchained forty-eight-year-old Mexican in an orange jumpsuit and flip-flops into the room.

Judging from his blackened eyes, swollen nose, and stitches above his right eyebrow, Yuki surmised he'd recently taken a beating.

Yuki introduced herself and Zac and explained who they were and why they had come.

"You're a Christmas gift from my wife," Varela said, shaking his head, "I swear to God." Then, to Zac, "But if you're going to be my lawyer—I have no money."

Zac said, "I'll decide if I'm taking your case after we talk, Mr. Varela."

"Eduardo. Please."

"Eduardo," said Zac. "We've got only fifteen minutes. Tell me about the murder."

CHAPTER 29

"I DIDN'T KILL that guy. I didn't kill anyone," Varela told Yuki and attorney Zac Jordan.

He looked anguished, defeated. Two years in a maximum-security jail would have that effect on anyone. Double that if he was innocent.

"Do you know who *did* kill him?" Yuki asked.

"It was one of the three damned gangsters who put it on me," said Varela. "Their names are in my file. Pablo Esteban, Miguel Perez, Antonio Vasquez. Gangsters on our street. They told the cops it was me."

Zac asked him to start at the beginning. Eduardo nodded and collected himself.

He said, "I had three jobs. On the weekdays I kept the auto-body repair shop clean, then at night, I worked at the Stop 'n' Shop gas station and convenience store. I did house painting on the weekend. This happened on a Wednesday night."

Zac nodded. *Go ahead.*

Varela said that he had left his day job at the auto-repair shop and gone home to wash up. He had dinner with his wife and kids. Then he walked to his car, reclined the seat back, and took a nap before to driving to his night job.

"I heard a bang," said Varela. "I was still in my dreams. Did someone hit a car with a pipe? But then another bang. Then two more."

He was breathing heavily now.

"I think, *What's happening?* I sit up and look out. A man is lying in the street up near the corner. I get out to see, and three thugs I know from the neighborhood see me—and run very fast up the street. Like the devil was chasing them."

Varela looked panicky as he said, "I go over to the man lying in the street. It's dark. He is facedown in his blood. The back of his head—*gone.* I see his brains." He tapped the back of his head to indicate where the man had been shot. "I think maybe I should call for help, but he's *dead.* I don't want to talk to the police. Maybe they take me in. I have a family. I can't go to jail. So I go to work."

He lowered his head and shook it: *No, no, no.*

"Police come to the Stop 'n' Shop and arrest me. They tell me the three gangsters—"

"They used that word, *gangsters?*" Zac asked.

"They say men called the police and gave my name as the killer. The policemen drive me to the station. They take my fingerprints and my picture and fill out forms and ask me, 'Where is the gun?' I tell them, 'I don't have a gun. I never have a gun.'

"They ask me the same questions all night. They tell me that the dead man is my neighbor. First time I knew."

"Did they tell you you had a right to have a lawyer?" Zac asked.

"I don't know. I think so."

"Did you waive your rights?"

"I don't know. I answer all the questions they ask. They tell me the dead man is Gordon Perez. I *do* know him. He lives across the street. We had arguments about where we park our cars. It was never anything. Some shouting. But no fights, understand? So I tell them that. After all night of this, they put me in a cell."

Zac said, "Eduardo, this is important. You didn't have a gun? You've never had a gun? No one is going to show up with a gun that your fingerprints are on?"

"No, no. Never."

"Were you given a gunshot residue test?"

"I don't know. The whole night was like a bad dream. I was very afraid of the cops. I see too many people deported. That's all I can think. They will drop me off in the desert."

Varela put his head down on the table and started to cry.

Guards came into the room.

Zac said, "I need another minute."

One of the guards, a young woman, said, "One minute."

Zac said, "Eduardo. Who is your lawyer?"

Eduardo stopped crying. "Peter Bard. He took my money. He didn't get me bail. He didn't say he quit, so I wait to hear from him. I need a public defender maybe, but they haven't said anything about that."

"Okay. Okay," Zac said. "If you want, I'll be your lawyer. No charge."

Eduardo started crying again. Zac patted his hands and gave him his business card.

Yuki said, "I'll call Maria for you, Eduardo. I'll tell her you have a lawyer now. A good one."

CHAPTER 30

'TWAS THE DAY before Christmas Eve, and I was not in my house.

At the desk across from mine, Conklin muttered to himself as our internet connection winked off-on-off and then went down completely. Curses flew up from surrounding desks. A wastebasket was kicked. Brady came out of his office, looked around, headed for the elevator.

"Why now?" Conklin said.

I didn't have to answer because it was obvious. The Hall was old. Our signal was weak. The building was "seismically unstable." The next earthquake could break it up into chunky granite rubble.

That pretty much summed up my mood.

Richie found Michaels, our most tech-savvy colleague. While they talked about the Wi-Fi, I watched the second hand on the wall clock sweep around the dial, propelling the minutes and hours forward.

At 10:00 a.m. we were no closer to learning the identity of the mysterious Loman or pinpointing his target than we had been when Julian Lambert coughed up the news that a big heist was going down.

I was starting to think that Lambert had made it up.

This morning had begun with another anxious full-house meeting of all available investigators from Robbery, Narcotics, Homicide, and Vice. The law enforcement pros were frustrated, clueless, and resentful that they were working on rumors instead of sitting at home eating sugar cookies and watching a ball game with their families.

I had to admit, I felt that way, too. I had a child and a husband, and the Loman heist was a *potential* robbery. If Lambert was to be believed, he had gotten this breaking news from a street person named Marcus who had overheard a phone call. This tip had resulted in a dead FBI agent and a dead shooter named Dietz who before dying had circled the de Young Museum on a map. For all we knew, the de Young was on the shooter's bucket list of sights to see.

In sum, we were working a crime that hadn't happened. A possible crime, potentially. Maybe. And right now, while I tried to solve a puzzle of random pieces, Mrs. Gloria Rose, our nanny in chief, was standing in for me at home.

I adored Mrs. Rose. Imagine the most loving granny ever living in an apartment across the hall from you. A woman who can cook, who loves dogs and babies, and who is available almost on call. She even had a little OCD, which meant the apartment was tidy when I got home and locked my weapon in the antique gun safe.

I was damned grateful to Mrs. Rose. But right that minute I would have loved to trade places with her, be the one playing reindeer games with Julie. Instead I was at work, as was Joe, and I didn't know when I would be home.

From the cheers around me I gathered that the Wi-Fi had returned. And in the next second Brady's voice startled me.

He said, "Conklin, you get anything on Dietz from the prostitute?"

"TMI," said my partner. "Dietz was twisted, but all he told her about Loman was that he'd hired him to do a job on Christmas."

"Fantastic," Brady said glumly. "Another lucky day. I guess I'll go out and get a lottery ticket. Buncha them."

I said, "Conklin and I are going out to the museum to go over procedures with the head of security. Jacobi is on his way to San Quentin."

"Because?" Brady asked.

"He wants to talk to Ted Swanson."

"Okay. That's smart."

He told me to keep him posted.

I smiled at him and said, "Yes, boss."

He went back into his office.

Conklin and I suited up and headed out to Golden Gate Park. My mood had shifted again. I was getting a paycheck. I was on the Job.

If possible, Conklin and I were going to make sure that that stunning, treasure-filled museum was bulletproof.

CHAPTER **31**

FORMER CHIEF WARREN Jacobi drove the twelve miles north from the Golden Gate to San Quentin, the oldest prison in California. Beautifully situated on 432 acres on San Francisco Bay, it was home to a rotating roster of over thirty-five hundred prisoners.

The Q was also the only men's prison in California with a death row. But Ted Swanson had lucked out—the governor had imposed a moratorium on the death penalty. If he hadn't, Swanson would certainly have been executed by now.

It was a perfect day, but Jacobi hardly noticed. He was inside his head, thinking about Swanson, the dirtiest of dirty cops. He owned that title. Who in the future could match him?

Swanson had done something Jacobi had never seen or heard of before. He had recruited two crews from the Robbery Division he commanded at the SFPD's Southern

Station; one of these crews, wearing SFPD Windbreakers and pig masks, had hit Western Union outlets and payday-loan stores, gunning down moms, pops, and whoever else stood between them and the money, and the second crew had executed the more sophisticated and more dangerous robberies, taking down the distribution point of a drug lord known as Kingfisher. Swanson's cops–turned–armed robbers had stolen millions of dollars in cash and a huge amount of drugs during the fifteen-minute heist, killing four people in the process.

There had been payback for that. Kingfisher had obliterated all of Swanson's forces, although not Swanson himself.

If Ted Swanson's gang hadn't been killed, they might still be robbing drug dealers and check-cashing joints, leaving dead bodies behind and enriching their corrupt and dirty selves to the tune of millions of dollars that they'd tuck away in their fat retirement accounts.

Until the massacre, nobody had guessed that Swanson was behind the robberies. There had been no leaks, no one stepping forward from the ranks. But as chief of police, Jacobi couldn't duck the responsibility and hadn't tried. It had happened on his watch. But while he'd refused to let Swanson's corruption dishonor him, it had tarnished his career.

He couldn't change that. But maybe he could stop what was coming.

In Jacobi's mind, there was one worthwhile thing that had come from the Swanson catastrophe. Swanson knew robbery from both sides. He might have usable information.

And if he did, Jacobi might be able to extract it. But that would depend on who Swanson was now. Would he be cooperative? Unrepentant? Brain-damaged?

Soon Jacobi would know. He parked in the official lot, entered the main building, and walked into the reception area, which was packed with families, young children, and babies. Families making Christmas visits to inmates.

He waited in line, then spoke to one of the guards at the desk. He told her his name and affiliation, why he was there, and whom he was visiting, and he cited prior approval from Warden Jason Blau.

As directed, SFPD's former chief of police emptied his pockets, deposited his wallet, badge, gun, phone, and pen in a tray, and raised his arms for the electronic security pat-down. A guard scribbled a receipt and handed it to Jacobi, saying that he could collect his belongings when he left the prison.

Jacobi was escorted through electronically operated doorways, down corridors loud with shouting of prisoners and clanking of metal gates, and into a cage of an interview room.

The gate closed behind him.

Jacobi pulled out one of two facing chairs and sat down heavily. He hadn't seen Ted Swanson since his conviction a year ago. Now he needed him to open the vault inside his head and give him something on Loman.

He figured Swanson more than owed him.

CHAPTER 32

TED SWANSON SHUFFLED into the interview room, his leg chains rattling and scraping against the floor.

Jacobi hardly recognized him.

Before the massacre, Swanson had looked like a typical guy next door: sandy hair, average build, blue-gray eyes; a very convincing career cop with a future. Then he misjudged a drug lord, was ambushed in a firefight, underwent innumerable surgeries, endured six months of rehab, and suffered through a scorching murder trial. Last time Jacobi saw Swanson, he was being helped into a prison van, looking scrawny, beaten up and beaten down.

But a year at San Quentin in the seclusion of administrative segregation with few visitors, fewer privileges, and no hope of freedom had apparently been good for him. Swanson had bulked up and his face looked sculpted. He appeared fit, healthy, even respectable, for whatever that was worth.

Swanson grinned broadly and said, "My God, Chief Jacobi. So glad to see you, man."

He held out his cuffed wrists so a guard could chain them to a hook in the table.

Jacobi said, "How you doing, Swanson? Accommodations agree with you?"

"Not bad, not bad. First time in my life I've had time to think. Of course, I don't get a lot of visitors, so this meet with you makes my month. What brings you here, Chief?"

"I'm officially retired. Brady hired me to help with a case."

"You're retired? How's that going?"

"As you said—first time in my life I have time to think."

Swanson nodded appreciatively while Jacobi fought back the urge to punch him in the face. Again. And again. And again.

"So how can I help?" Swanson asked.

"It's like this, Swanson. We've got some information about a job going down, but our informant had limited info and our next-best lead is dead."

"You want me to help you?"

Jacobi nodded. "If you're still connected."

"And what do I get in return?" Swanson asked.

The bastard wanted a deal.

"How'd you like a conjugal visit?"

"Ha. Love it," said Swanson. "But you're gonna have to do a little more than twist my ex-wife's arm. Oh, I see. You didn't know Nancy divorced me."

"So what do you want?" Jacobi asked. "A hooker? A generous deposit to your commissary account?"

"Here's what. A 'conjugal visit' with a pen-pal girlfriend of mine. And I'll take that deposit to the commissary. A hundred a month for a year sound okay?"

Jacobi nodded slowly, said, "I can do that."

Swanson reached his hands out the length of his chain as if to shake on it.

Jacobi didn't go for it. "Let's see if you still have your chops. Ever heard of a guy named Loman?"

"He's the one who's doing this?"

"His name came up in the investigation," said Jacobi.

"Look, I don't know him, but I know a little about him. He supposedly knocked off an armored car and a bank, two-for-one heist in LA about five years ago.

"There were about five or six fatalities, if I remember correctly. LAPD got his name from one of his crew who was breathing his last. Then there was a casino job in Vegas a couple of years later that looked like Loman. Close to a nine-million-dollar haul."

Jacobi said, "Black Diamond Casino, right?"

"Yeah, that's it," said Swanson. "Bodies were littering the pit. The robbery crew got out with their mega-score but then fate intervened. They were incinerated in a collision with a gas truck."

Jacobi said, "What about Loman himself? Is that his name or an alias? Where does he live? Known associates?"

"What I heard is that he hires guys for a job or two. They're dispensable. My guess, that's how Loman stays invisible. And I'll tell you something else. A hunch, really."

"Go on."

Swanson grinned. "He doesn't make mistakes. Given the

bodies he's left behind, that's almost impossible. Yet it's apparently true."

"Okay, Swanson. You've given me nothing I didn't know."

Jacobi got up, banged on the door, and called for the guard. Swanson swiveled in his seat and said, "What about our deal, Jacobi?"

Jacobi scoffed. "When you have something I can use, get in touch."

Guards opened the door for Jacobi.

"Have a heart, Chief. Costs you nothing. Come on. Be a person."

Jacobi's mind filled with furious retorts concerning Swanson's legendary crime spree, but he stifled them. He needed to get out of this prison and away from Swanson, the sick son of a bitch.

When he got outside, he called Boxer and then drove to the de Young Museum.

CHAPTER 33

WILLIAM LOMACHENKO WAS washing his car in the driveway when his wife, Imogene, came to the front door and called out to him.

"Willy. Phone."

"Who is it?"

"It's Dick. Should I tell him you'll call him back?"

"I'll be right there."

Lomachenko hosed the soap off the car, moved the bucket out of the way, dried his hands on his pants, and trotted up the steps to his brick two-story house on Avila Street.

Imogene handed him the phone, said, "Give me those."

She took his eyeglasses to the kitchen and cleaned them with Windex. When she returned to her husband, he said, "Dick wants to meet for lunch. I'm going to change."

"Bring back a package of egg noodles. You know the kind. And a cabbage."

Dick Russell was waiting for Loman at a back booth in

Danny G.'s, on Van Ness, not far from his house. He lifted his hand in greeting, and Loman walked through the dark bar and luncheonette to the table. He hung up his jacket and cap on a hook and slid into the seat.

"We've got a problem?" Loman asked his number two.

"None that I can see. We're at T minus forty-eight hours. I want to review."

Loman and Dick Russell had known each other for twenty years. They had done half a dozen major jobs together and had never been caught or even brought in for questioning.

Russell was a gambler with a deep knowledge of mathematics and physics and a PhD in engineering from MIT. He was a numbers nerd, could figure out timing and angles and do scientific calculations that were incomprehensible to Loman.

But Russell was also a player—the markets, the ponies, questionable women. He relied on Loman for the planning, then designed the execution from there.

Loman was nothing like Russell.

He saw the big picture and had leadership skills. His cover was selling a line of gold chains to jewelry stores. He kept his head down and put his earnings in gold bullion that was stored in vaults overseas. This he could convert to any one of eight currencies with a couple of keystrokes. And any or all of it could be put on a debit card. Hell of an escape plan.

The two men gave their orders to the waitress. Loman asked for a heart-healthy salad; Russell went with the fried chicken basket, extra fries. Always the gambler. The waitress stood next to Russell, cocked a hip, played with her hair. When she'd gone, Russell opened his tablet and started at the top.

He listed the first distraction: Lambert's grab-and-dash, leading the cops to Dietz.

The second distraction was Dietz's suicide-by-cop, a good deal all around.

Distraction three was the clue Dietz had left for the cops on his phone, and distraction four was putting out the idea that Mayor Caputo could be hit.

Along with that rumor were the innumerable random tips about a big heist that they had paid bums, snitches, and ex-cons to leak to cops.

Russell said, "The next head fake is set for tonight, Willy. The cops are frustrated and working overtime. This will throw them over the edge."

Loman said, "Oh, no. Let me get out my tiny violin."

Russell laughed and Loman joined him.

Loman pulled his new burner phone out of his pocket and dialed, said into the phone, "Yeah, it's Loman. Go ahead and drop the next bread crumb." He listened, then said, "Right. That's all you have to say. I'll be in touch."

He clicked off, smiled at Russell. He was enjoying his little shell game. "Distraction number five is in play."

Russell smiled back and said, "We are good."

"I'll drink to that."

They clinked water glasses. Lunch arrived and the two men dug into their meals.

Were they friends? Not really. But they enjoyed the benefits of good partnership based on history and results.

Loman had made Russell rich. And Russell allowed him his little slaughters.

Loman stabbed a tomato wedge, thinking how in two days they would be so loaded, neither would have to work again.

Loman had designed the smoke screen of chaos and terror that would settle an old debt and allow him to pull off a job that could net him a billion dollars, easy. It would be the job of his life.

CHAPTER 34

CONKLIN AND I were still at the de Young Museum going over the blueprints and security systems with James Karp, head of security, when news alerts about a possible large-scale armed robbery hit my phone.

The press now had the story.

In minutes 911 and the tip lines would be flooded with unconfirmed reports, adding to the mass confusion surrounding the ID of Loman's robbery target.

Jacobi found us in Karp's office, greeted his old friend with a hug, then filled us in about his meeting with Swanson.

"I didn't punch him," Jacobi said. "I wanted to."

I nodded my understanding. Jacobi went on.

"Swanson theorized that Loman's jobs come with a high number of fatalities intentionally, because dead people don't talk. This is why Loman is a cipher. A ghost. No record, which explains why we don't know who the hell he is."

As Conklin, Jacobi, and I knew, Swanson's own six-month-long robbery spree had left eighteen dead, so his opinion actually had weight. I touched my gun belt reflexively, hoping to hell I could finish my shift without firing a shot.

Jacobi offered to stay with Karp and drill the security team that would be working in the museum overnight. Conklin and I left them to it.

On the way out to the car, I asked Rich what he thought of the museum's security.

"Better than I expected."

"Agreed," I said. "If a gang of robbers come to the door with cop badges and duct tape, they won't get in. But…"

"But what if Loman has a bigger idea?"

"Explosives," I said. "There's so much glass."

"Helicopter," Conklin said. He was exploring that idea out loud, how explosives could be dropped, men coming down ropes, when my phone buzzed.

Brady said, "Boxer, two things. A wallet with Julian Lambert's ID was found on China Beach near the Golden Gate."

"What? Just his wallet? No body?"

"No body. Just the wallet with his driver license, some receipts, and a few business cards. Your card was in there. That's how this piece of news got to us."

I thought about the lightweight thief in the red puffy coat who had led us on a chase that ended with the firefight at the Anthony Hotel.

"Are people searching the area?"

"He could have lost the wallet, Boxer, or it could have

been stolen or thrown there to make us think that Lambert was dead."

"Or he was murdered and his body is out there some-where."

"I sent out a notification request," Brady said. "If a body shows up that matches his photo, we'll hear about it. We don't have anyone to go on a body search right now."

"What's thing two?" I asked.

"An anonymous tip came in that a gallery in Nob Hill is the target," the good lieutenant told me. He gave me the name and address.

It was almost six. I wanted to go home. Into the yawning silence of my hesitation, Brady said, "I'd go, but I'm with the mayor. He wants personal protection. There's no one else I can send."

"No problem," I said. "We'll check it out."

I clicked off and said to Conklin, "A wallet with Lambert's ID was found on China Beach. No body."

Conklin said, "Lambert throwing down a fake clue?"

"Could be," I said. "I can think of a few other possibilities."

It isn't scientific, but detectives solve cases with hunches. My hunch was that Lambert was dead.

CHAPTER 35

THE BANNER IN the long plate-glass window of the Soigne Gallery announced a special Christmas exhibition and sale of an anonymous collector's rare musical instruments.

I didn't get it.

Armored trucks, casinos, banks, and even museums made sense, but if this tip was for real, how would Loman turn musical instruments into big piles of cash?

Conklin and I entered the gallery through the main door and walked into an event in progress. Servers with trays of champagne and canapés skirted around the displays and drifted between the well-dressed prospective customers. The air was perfumed, and the honeyed sounds of a string quartet playing classic carols came from the mezzanine, setting a soothing and spendy mood.

My partner and I, wearing our SFPD Windbreakers over

chinos, stood out like soccer players who'd blundered onto the stage at an opera. We ignored the hard stares of the patrons and took in the scene. The gallery was half a city block long with plate-glass windows fronting the street. I counted six exits, a camera over each, and small motion detectors beaming lasers onto the exhibits, set to chirp if someone got too close.

My attention was drawn to a harpsichord in the window. It was a meticulously crafted piece, with a mosaic of inlaid wood. How much was this doggy, anyway?

I stepped in and read the card on a pedestal beside it. I learned that it had been made by an unknown Italian artist in the mid-fifteenth century; the red dot beside the two-million-dollar price tag told me that it had been sold.

I shifted my eyes to other instruments displayed around the large, open room, each presented like one of the queen's crown jewels. Red dots marked many of the cards, telling me that the money was flowing along with the champagne.

I was beginning to understand. Compared with armored trucks and banks, compared even with the de Young Museum, the Soigne Gallery was vulnerable and as sweet a hit as a chocolate cake with icing roses.

All Loman would need was a half a dozen guys with a couple of vans parked at the rear of the building. And he'd have to have a fence with international connections who could sell this pricey, unusual loot to collectors, a fence with an underground gallery and the ability to keep an illegal haul to him- or herself.

My thoughts were broken by a handsome man in his

midthirties wearing a professional smile and an expensive suit calling out, "May I help you?" He came over to us. "I'm Charles Linden," he said, "operations manager. Has someone left their car lights on?"

If only. I gave him our names and told him our business, after which he reluctantly called over to Soigne's owner, Renata Fabiano.

Ms. Fabiano, standing to my left in the center of the gallery, was a stunning fifty-something woman in black, buffed and polished to a high shine. She'd been showing off her knowledge of fifteenth-century strings to a rapt couple of richies.

She didn't like the interruption. She scowled at her manager and then, even though I was a couple of inches taller than her, managed to look down on me as though I were tracking dog dirt onto her carpet.

I apologized, steered Ms. Fabiano to a dead spot in the gallery, and told her that we'd received a tip that her gallery was a target of an armed robbery.

For a moment I had her complete attention. She didn't even give Conklin a glance. First time I could remember a female failing to take a long look at Inspector Hottie.

But her attention to me was fleeting. "Talk to Charles," Fabiano said. "He knows all about our security systems." Then she returned to her prospects.

The manager took his cue and led Conklin and me to his office just behind the gallery display space. After we all sat down, he said, "How do you know about this impending robbery?"

Conklin said, "Mr. Linden, *how* we know isn't important.

What we know is that the party who may be targeting this gallery is a pro. When he stages a hit, he gets what he came for. And he has a signature. He leaves dead bodies behind."

CHAPTER 36

"WE HAVE *AMAZING* security," Charles Linden told us. "Cameras at the exits, vibration sensors on paintings, and many of the sculptures and alarms are connected to a central station. Our employees have been vetted and their pass cards are registered."

I said, "You're not checking packages and bags at the door. You don't have screening apparatus."

Linden shrugged. "Our patrons wouldn't stand for it. You can see that, can't you?"

Conklin said, "I'd like to look at a list of your employees."

"Why do you need that?"

"Often big-ticket robberies are inside jobs," said Conklin. "I can't force you, but you should let me have that list and the names of anyone who left your employ in the past year."

Linden gave Conklin a cold look, then tapped on his keyboard. The printer on his credenza came to life.

I said, "What other security measures do you have, Mr. Linden? Saturation motion detectors?"

"Yes, in the main gallery, but not in the other wings. I don't see how we could rewire the place every time we have a new exhibit."

Conklin walked over to the printer. "Okay for me to take this?"

Linden said, "Be my guest."

I thought, *What a jerk,* but didn't say it.

Conklin took the list of employee names from the tray and said to me, "I'll be back."

While Conklin was running the list through our car's computer, I told Linden, "Here's what I think. You've got a good system, but it won't withstand a serious professional assault. If I were you, I'd call your security company, have them place three or four guards on premises twenty-four/seven for the next couple of days. And if they have canines, bring them in overnight."

"Uh, I'll talk to Renata."

"Also, since you don't know who is coming in or what they're carrying, I'd close up shop now."

"Our customers, clients, they're making big purchases. We could sell more before Christmas than we will in the next six months."

I wanted to get up, muss his hair, flip his tie, and tell him, *What if someone brings in a smoke bomb? And automatic weapons? What if that person opens the back door for the rest of the crew?*

But I didn't do that.

I said, "Please pass our recommendations on to Ms. Fabiano. I'm putting them in my report."

I got up from my seat feeling almost as tired as I had some months ago. Right before I was given doctor's orders to take time off to rest. I needed to go home.

I returned to the main gallery just as Conklin came back in from the street. He signaled to me.

I said, "Whatcha got?"

He showed me his phone.

"I'll take this," I said.

I walked over to Ms. Fabiano, who was talking to another pair of 1 percenters, all three of them admiring a rare violin. I apologized for interrupting and said, "I need a moment."

Again she looked at me like I'd crawled out of a storm drain, and I gave her a similar look—the homicide-inspector version.

"Are you still in touch with your ex-husband?" I asked.

"Royce? Occasionally. Why?"

"Did you know that three years ago he was arrested for robbing a jewelry store? He flipped on his partner and after six months was released on probation. He lives in San Francisco. Works at the Ritz-Carlton."

I was thinking Renata Fabiano's ex was just the type of bit player Loman considered disposable. If Mr. Fabiano knew the gallery's vulnerabilities, he could be setting it up for Loman's big score.

"Not Royce. I don't believe it. That's a mistake."

But the look in her eyes told me that she was reviewing what she knew about her husband. And I had another thought: Possibly Renata Fabiano was collaborating in the hit. I'd heard weirder things.

I gave her my card and then Conklin and I split. I called Brady from the car.

"Soigne could be the target," I said.

I told him about Mr. Royce Fabiano, about his record, and that he could be a Loman tool. I suggested that cars be stationed in front of the gallery and out by the loading dock.

"Even cruising by could be a deterrent."

Brady said, "I'll do what I can."

"Okay. I'm signing off. Merry Christmas, Brady."

I said it emphatically. I wanted him to hear that I was going home, and no one had better try to stop me.

CHAPTER **37**

CONKLIN AND I had parked our cars on Harriet Street, convenient to the Hall's rear entrance, a half block off Bryant. It was sevenish when I said good night to Richie under the overpass. We hugged, patted each other's backs, and got into our respective cars.

In twenty minutes, tops, I'd be home. Home. A beautiful word, calling up clean clothes, hugs and kisses, shared news of the day over dinner, and then blessed sleep.

As Richie drove off, I realized I hadn't asked what he'd gotten Cindy for Christmas. Our shopping trip to Union Square had careened off the rails when Julian Lambert ran past us shouting, "Merry flippin' Christmas."

Had it been only sixty hours ago? And now he was dead.

I called Joe, told him I was on my way. I kissed at the phone, clicked off, put my key in the ignition, and turned it. The engine coughed. I swore and tried to start her up again.

I'm a fair auto mechanic in a pinch, but not without tools and in a dark alley.

I called Joe back. "Joe," I said into my phone. "My battery's dead. Car battery."

"Oh, crap," he said. "Stove malfunctioned. I don't know. The chicken is raw."

"I'll get a uniform to drive me home. I can pick up some noodles—"

"Just stay in the car," he said. I heard him say, "Jules? Want to go for a ride?"

She screamed, "Noooooooo!" Martha woofed along with her. Joe said, "Lindsay. Stay put. We're on the way."

The entire expedition took an hour, including picking up take-out noodle-shop dinners. Julie cried in the car, and by the time we made it through the front door, she was having a full-fledged, all-about-me meltdown. She didn't like the Christmas tree. She wanted something different. And she didn't like me.

"You're bad, Mommy."

"What do you mean, bad?" I asked her.

She rolled onto her belly, kicked her feet, and cried.

Joe looked at me and mouthed, *I don't know.*

I said, "Julie. This is our tree. I love it. If you don't, I'm sorry you're mad at me, but it's time for bed."

"Noooooooooooo."

Her favorite word.

Joe said, "Yes. Would you like mac and cheese instead of the take-out noodles?"

"Noooooooooo."

Joe said, "That's it, then." He picked her up and headed

with her to her room, saying over his shoulder, "Take a shower, Linds. I'll set the table."

I poured wine for Joe and kibble for Martha. I locked up my gun, kicked off my shoes, and stripped off my clothes.

Standing under the shower felt like being reborn. The whole day dissolved under the hot spray—the staff meeting, the trip out to the de Young Museum and the talk with Karp and Jacobi, the security review of Soigne, and the certain feeling that I'd be hearing tomorrow that the gallery had been hit.

Joe was plating the beef and noodles when I reappeared in the kitchen and heard my phone calling me from the hallway. Joe said. "No. Lindsay, no. Don't do it."

I got to the phone, glanced at the screen. Thank God. It wasn't Brady.

I called out to Joe, "It's okay. It's Mrs. Rose."

Joe said, "I forgot to tell you. Mrs. Rose is stopping over tonight to drop off our gifts. What did we get her?"

"Oh, my God," I said. "Joe, I was doing Christmas shopping when that freaking crime happened in front of me."

"It will be okay. You can tell her that."

The phone buzzed in my hand and I answered, laughing, "Gloria. Our stove malfunctioned…"

CHAPTER 38

THERE WAS A lot of background noise—a siren? A voice I didn't recognize said, "Mrs. Molinari?"

"Yes. Who is this?"

"Doris Dillon. I'm an EMT."

I felt a cold shock of fear as I understood the siren. How did the EMT get Mrs. Rose's phone?

"A woman took a fall at Whole Foods. We're taking her to Metro. She must have been trying to call you. I accidentally hit 'send' when I picked up her phone."

"What's wrong? Can I speak with her?"

Doris said, "She's unconscious. I have to go now."

"Wait. What happened?"

The line went dead.

I shouted, "Hello. Hello?" And I pressed Redial. There was no answer. I pictured Mrs. Rose falling down. Hitting her head. Or having a heart attack and falling. I saw her inside the bus, strapped to a stretcher, lines in her arms, mask over her face. Alone.

She had been there for us whenever we needed her since Julie was born.

Joe was in the kitchen trying to fix the stove. I yelled, "Joe. Gloria fell. She's unconscious and on the way to the hospital. I'd better go."

"Oh, no. But wait, Linds. What can you do for her?" Joe asked.

"Whatever she would do for me. I'll try to reach her daughter. Becky lives in New York. You think she could get a flight out tonight?"

"You stay and I'll go," he said.

Since driving me home from Harriet Street, Joe had had a couple of drinks. I had not. I was in pajamas. He was not. I'd been working for the past twenty hours. He'd been home for a while.

We were batting this all back and forth when Julie woke up and started screaming. I wanted to scream, too.

In the end, there were no good solutions, but we decided on one.

We were all going.

Joe took the noodles out of the microwave and forced me to eat some. Then I got dressed and went into Julie's pale yellow bedroom. She was still fussing in her new big-girl bed.

"Julie, want to go for a ride?"

"Noooooooooooooooo."

"We can watch planes and stuff."

My three-year-old gave me a dubious look, as if she

were in Interview 2 and I had asked her if she wanted to waive her rights. She lifted her arms.

Leaving our senior dog in charge of the apartment, the Molinaris locked up and drove to Metro.

CHAPTER 39

THE WAITING ROOM outside the emergency department at Metropolitan Hospital was packed, standing
room only.

A wrong-way car accident on the Bay Bridge had
resulted in fatalities, many injuries, and all lanes blocked
with burning wreckage. It was some kind of miracle that
ambulances had gotten in and then out to Metro.

I learned from a harried, tight-lipped ER nurse that
some of the injured were still in the emergency room,
others were in surgery, and more were in critical condition
in the ICU.

The stricken faces of the friends and families ripped
from Christmas parties or beds spoke without words of the
devastation.

Joe stood with his back against a wall hung with children's Christmas drawings. I sat a few feet away in a row of
attached chairs, holding Julie in my lap. The woman sitting

beside me was a few years older than me. Her arm was around the shoulders of a young teen, her son, who was cut and bruised and waiting to see a doctor.

The woman turned her stunned face to me.

"My oldest, Jeffrey, went through the windshield. He's...they're operating...it was bad..." She started to cry. Her younger son threw his arms around her and said, sobbing, "He has to be okay. He has to be okay."

Sitting in this waiting room was like being wrapped in sheets of broken glass. I felt for the parents and their children whose lives had been tragically altered. I was also flooded with horrific memories of my own, spanning decades.

I pictured Joe and me sleeping in these chairs, holding hands in this very room when Julie was an infant with a rare disease, not knowing if our tiny baby would survive to see her first birthday.

I flashed back to waiting-room vigils for cops who'd been shot, the death of a partner. And I'd waited in one on that horrifying day, not long ago, when Joe was brought to San Francisco General with a life-threatening head injury after the bombing of the science museum.

How quickly a romantic dinner had changed to what could have been the worst day of my life and the end of his. I felt his presence behind me now and thanked God for his life.

Julie didn't have any memories like these. She was big-eyed, bubbling with questions that I couldn't answer. How could I explain to her why so many people were sobbing, keening, holding on to one another?

I turned to face Joe and we exchanged looks. On a bad-parenting scale of one to ten, bringing Julie here had sent the needle off the dial. And yet how could we leave without knowing what had happened to Mrs. Rose?

Short of an assault on the ER, I had done my best to find out her condition. I had badgered the head nurse, who had explained that since I wasn't a relative, she was forbidden by law to tell me anything about the patient.

I persisted. I produced my badge. I told her that a paramedic had called me from the ambulance, for God's sake, to say Mrs. Rose was being taken to Metro. I told her I was as good as Mrs. Rose's closest relative, that she had no one else in San Francisco.

The nurse shook her head no. But then she relented.

She scribbled on a pad of paper and turned it around so I could see the word *Stroke*. After I read it, she ripped the page from the pad, balled it up, and threw it into the trash.

I told Joe I'd be right back, took my phone out to the street, and looked up emergency treatment for stroke victims. Mrs. Rose was probably having a CT scan right now. Whatever was learned would determine her course of treatment over the next few hours or days.

If she lived.

I had stored her daughter's number, and I punched it in, expecting to get Becky's outgoing message again. But instead I heard her actual voice, a breathless, frantic "Oh, thank God. I tried to reach you so many times. How's my mother?"

I filled her in, telling her I'd hit a bureaucratic wall but that she could get information on her mother's condition. "I have the keys to your mom's apartment," I said. "Let me know your plans. And tell me what I can do to help."

Just after ten, as Joe, Julie, and I were headed back home to Lake Street, my phone buzzed.

It was Conklin.

"I'm outside your door," he said. "Where are you?"

"About ten minutes out. What's wrong?"

"I'll wait," he said. "A hot Loman tip just came in. We're catching."

CHAPTER 40

MEGAN RAFFERTY WAS too smart for this, yet here she was.

Six years ago she'd graduated from high school having been voted most likely to become rich and famous. She'd spent the two years after that in college. Then two years in rehab.

Now she was living in a housing project next door to a Superfund site, sweating in a stinking van, waiting, waiting, waiting for directions from someone she didn't know via the drug-riddled brain of her current boyfriend.

What came from Mr. Loman's call would either set her free or earn her a stretch in a state pen.

She was glad her mother couldn't see her now.

Using. Living with Corey. Not a mother or a school-teacher or a doctor. It would break her heart.

Megan busied herself in the navy-blue transport van neatening the shelves and picking up after Corey, who was a pig.

The van was an aging Chevy with a spunky new motor and amazing pickup. It had rear cargo doors and decals reading TANYA'S CAT AND DOG GROOMING: WE COME TO YOU on the side panels. No phone number. No email. But in Megan's humble opinion, it was perfect camouflage.

They were parked on Donahue Street near the construction dump behind the replacement housing where they lived. The field was four city blocks of radioactive dirt and rubble from the bulldozed former shipyard, polluted with petroleum, pesticides, heavy metals.

What a dump.

Other vehicles were parked at a distance from one another on both sides of Innes Avenue, their occupants steaming up the windows.

Here inside the van, Corey was in the driver's seat, fiddling with his playlist, earbud cord dangling from his ear. He was singing along with some vocalist, killing time.

The two of them, waiting for Mr. Loman. Waiting.

Megan had a high idle. She hated to wait.

She climbed up behind the front seat and pulled the bud out of Corey's ear. He spun around like he was ready to pull his piece.

"What's the latest?" she asked.

"I told you never to sneak up on me," he said.

Corey was good-looking for his age and weight. Thirty-eight. Five foot ten. One ninety. A semiretired drug dealer and not a bad bunk buddy. He was also ambitious. He said he was hooked up with a major-league mobster. That big money was in the future.

His future or theirs? Corey kept secrets. And right now he owned her, one baggie at a time.

Megan said, "You told me that he was calling an hour ago."

"Chill out, will you please. Make coffee. Thassagirl."

"Make it yourself."

Megan pulled back one of the blackout curtains and looked out on Donahue. The apartments across the way were lit up. She could see twinkling lights.

A beat-up '85 Mustang GT parked up the road, and a couple of kids got out. They walked down the middle of the street, smokin', jokin', heading in their direction. One was wearing a Santa cap and a fake beard that was pulled away from his face and hanging over his shirt like a bib.

Santa Claus was coming to town. Ha.

The other one—boy or girl, she couldn't tell—was wearing a flimsy skirt over skinny jeans.

"Corey. Those two look like undercover to you? Corey?"

"What? No. I know the one in the skirt. Calm down, Meggy, will you? You're driving me crazy. Is that what you want? Me on crazy?"

She blew out a long, exasperated sigh, returned to the rear of the van, and threw herself down in the bunk against the wall.

How was she supposed to calm down?

On the one hand, freedom. On the other hand, jail.

She put a T-shirt over her face and was counting backward from a hundred when Corey thundered down the length of the van.

"Get up," he said.

"Get up *please*. Mr. Loman called?"

Corey was standing on the bunk, rummaging in duffel bags in the overhead cabinet.

"Here," he said, handing her a semiauto pistol. He grabbed one for himself, jammed a second into his waistband. He tugged open the blackout curtain.

A line of vehicles came up the road from behind them, some stopping along the sagging chain-link fencing across the street. An SUV with its headlights off sped up and passed their van. She couldn't see where it went. A fire truck stopped, backed up, parked behind them.

"What's happening?" she shouted.

No answer from Corey.

Megan could just make out men in dark clothing clambering out of vehicles. She saw long guns.

Corey's face was next to hers; he was also looking out at the swarm of activity on Donahue. Then, bellowing commando-style, he ran toward the front of the van.

Had he wigged out completely? What was he doing? Were they going to run?

Glass shattered.

No, no, no, no.

Megan Rafferty's life wasn't supposed to go this way. Christ.

Am I about to die?

CHAPTER 41

"SHE WAS CRYING when I left the house," Conklin shouted over the scream of the siren.

"Another night and I'm not home for dinner and cannot say when I *will* be home."

He was driving.

I was bracing myself against the inside of the door and standing on imaginary brakes in the footwell as we followed Octavia Boulevard onto the ramp for 101 South. The skyline winked on our left, and ahead of us cars peeled off into the right lane, getting the hell out of our way.

He said, "She gets that this isn't my choice. She respects what I have to do. But she doesn't like it."

"Do you need a note? I can vouch for you."

Conklin laughed. It was an ironic, tired little laugh, but there was mirth in it.

I made a mental note: If Rich and I survived the

night, the four of us—Joe, Rich, Cindy, and I—should treat ourselves to a first-class outing. Something to look forward to.

My thoughts jumped back to the matter at hand and the "hot Loman tip" that had launched our Code 3 response out to Hunters Point. Information had come from one of Brady's own CIs that Loman was sending a caravan of transport vehicles to an unknown target—tonight. That the targeted hit would be big. According to Brady's informant, two people in a dark-blue 2009 Chevy transport van that was part camper, part arsenal would be spearheading a heavily armed assault team and would join the rest of Loman's crew at an unknown location. We had no clue about what we were about to walk into.

We had some background on Corey Briggs and his partner-girlfriend, Megan Rafferty.

Briggs had done time for a home invasion and petty larceny and for possession with intent. Rafferty had been arrested for possession, sent to court-ordered rehab, then released. The pair had found each other and were now living in a housing project in this predominantly low-rent, high-crime area under redevelopment.

Not the pair I would have pegged for criminal masterminds, but from what we knew about Loman, he needed henchpeople he could manipulate.

As other cops headed out to banks, a museum, and the art gallery, my partner and I were assigned to the takedown of a pair of small-time criminals with big-time aspirations.

SWAT commander Reg Covington and his unit were waiting for us on Donahue, a low-traffic side street near the replacement housing. Covington's unit would approach covertly in unmarked vehicles.

My partner and I were only four miles out, and he was concentrating on his driving. We got off the freeway, followed the signs to Cesar Chavez Street, and slowed as we approached the stoplight at Evans.

Adrenaline had burned off my fatigue and focused my mind. I didn't think about home, bed, Julie, Joe, or Gloria Rose. I thought about my partner. And I hardened my nerves for whatever shit-storm was about to come down. I hoped we could bring these two nobodies in alive.

I hoped we could head off a bloody heist and get our hands on Loman.

Commander Reg Covington's voice came over the radio. He had located the dark-colored van two hundred yards up Donahue Street, right-hand side, registered to Corey Briggs. He told us to kill our lights. His team would isolate and launch an assault against the van, with our car bringing up the rear.

"Boyle will wait for you and hand off the first aid," Covington said.

Conklin hung a squealing right around the bend where Evans becomes Hunters Point Boulevard, and we slowed for local traffic, then crawled for a mile along Innes Avenue, bordering the construction site. I stayed in radio contact with Covington and he guided us in.

Four miscellaneous trucks and SUVs, one small all-terrain fire truck, and Conklin's old Bronco converged on the dog-grooming van up ahead.

Everyone involved was heavily armed.

CHAPTER 42

AT OUR SWAT commander's direction, Conklin eased the Bronco onto Donahue and braked halfway down the stretch of pitted asphalt bordering the bulldozed site.

The last time we'd worked with Reg Covington—two full days ago—he'd led the charge up all those flights of stairs at the Anthony Hotel. Then, like now, the goal had been to take the subject alive. But Chris Dietz had gotten the last word, killing an FBI agent, wounding another, and committing suicide-by-cop, taking everything he knew about Loman's plans with him.

A failed takedown just couldn't happen again.

We needed Corey Briggs and Megan Rafferty to talk while there was still hope of heading off Loman's big, bloody heist. In fact, this pair of small-time dopers might be our only hope.

Covington's plan of attack was classic: Use ordinary-looking vehicles and trucks so that they could get close to the subjects' van without spooking them. Isolate the van so that it couldn't go mobile. Execute disabling tactics so that the subjects couldn't hurt anyone, including themselves.

I saw Briggs's old Chevy van thirty yards up ahead. Covington was on the radio, and I confirmed to him that the vehicle was in sight.

"Do you see Boyle?" he asked me.

A man carrying a duffel bag over his shoulder came down the street singing to himself. I recognized him and said so to Covington.

A moment later Boyle rapped his knuckles on my window. I buzzed it down and he passed the heavy bag to me.

"Here you go, Boxer. Everything you'll need."

I thanked Boyle and watched him get into a vehicle; it crawled up the road and disappeared from sight. It was as if I'd imagined him.

A pickup truck, no lights, turned onto Donahue and pulled smoothly in behind the van. Another vehicle, an SUV, parked a dozen yards in front of the van, backed up.

Tanya's groom-mobile was now locked in bumper to bumper. Men and women in tactical gear exited their repo'd vehicles, stopped between our Bronco and the blue van.

I watched SWAT advance on the van with weapons in hand. One of the team leaned across the hood of a truck and braced a 40mm grenade launcher. He aimed at the blue van.

He fired.

A pepper-gas grenade traveled ten yards, shot through one of the van's side windows, and hit the back wall.

The quality of life inside that van was about to go straight to hell.

CHAPTER 43

I HUNCHED OVER reflexively as the grenade exploded, and when I sat up, everything was in motion.

The masked tactical team swarmed toward the van. The rear cargo doors blew open, and the writhing figure of a young woman tumbled out. She was followed by a screaming man in bulky outerwear.

The two fell to the ground, blinded by the burning gas, their mucous membranes inflamed, making them feel like they were choking. These two had to be Briggs and Rafferty. I watched as they tried to stand, but they didn't have a chance. An all-terrain fire truck rolled up on fat off-road tires, and a SWAT commando aimed the water cannon at the couple and flattened them to the asphalt.

On Covington's "Go," Conklin and I scrambled out of the Bronco, me with the duffel bag, Conklin cutting a path for us through the tac team, which was cuffing our howling, writhing subjects on the ground.

"We need some room," Conklin said as we edged through the SWAT team scrum. This was why we were on the scene: to rescue these two mutts from the punishing takedown, befriend them, and get them to talk.

I crouched beside Rafferty, who was cuffed and rolling from side to side in agony. I set the duffel bag down next to her and told her that she'd be all right soon. I spilled cool water onto a rag, swabbed her face, then poured water directly from the bottle into her eyes.

Only yards away, Conklin was doing the same with Briggs.

I said to Rafferty, "Megan, I'm Sergeant Lindsay Boxer. You have a jacket in the van? I'm going to get you out of here."

I had no idea whether she'd heard me or understood me. Anything inside the van would be permeated with pepper gas, but I wanted her permission to send someone into the van without waiting for a warrant. Maybe Loman's contact number would be written on a wall. Or maybe there'd be a map on a cell phone. It had happened before. Or here's what would be nice: a note with Loman's current location stuck to the fridge door.

She said, "What?"

"Do you need a jacket or your handbag? Can we get you something from the van?"

She groaned. "I didn't do anything wrong."

Pepper gas wafted over me. Tears came.

"I know. I know, Megan. Let's get you back to the station, find you some dry clothes there."

I offered her the rest of the bottle of water. She took it, guzzled it down, and then vomited on my pants and shoes.

"It's okay," I said. "It's okay. I'm going to help you up now." She heaved again.

A uniformed officer assisted Rafferty to her feet and into the back of an SUV.

I shouted to Conklin, "Meet you at the Hall." I settled into the front seat, my suspect crouched in the back. The day wasn't going well for Megan Rafferty.

CHAPTER 44

I USED THE restroom down the hallway from the bull-pen and washed pepper-gas residue from my face, arms, and upper torso. I dried off with paper towels, bagged my shirt and Windbreaker, and changed into the sweatshirt and pants I kept in my locker.

I was damp and still getting whiffs of pepper gas from my hair, but it couldn't be helped right now. I went to my desk and called Joe.

He was pissed, I could tell.

"I got your car back," he said, speaking of my comatose Explorer, which I'd left on Harriet Street when the night was still young. I thanked him sincerely and he talked right over me.

"It cost two hundred twenty-nine dollars for the auto shop to jump the car and drive it to Lake Street."

I sighed into the phone.

"Don't do that, Lindsay," my husband said. "I'm the

injured party here. By the way, Mrs. Rose's daughter called. She's taking the red-eye to SFO. I'm picking her up in the morning. Where are the keys to her mother's apartment?"

"On a hook inside the cabinet next to the microwave. I'm sorry, Joe, but have a little compassion, will you? Do you think I want to be here? Do you?"

He grunted, then said, "Tomorrow is Christmas Eve. What if you just sign out for the night? Get a uniform to drive you home. You think you're going to get canned if you leave? Because that's not going to happen, but it wouldn't be the worst thing if it did."

"I've got to go now," I said. "A suspect is waiting for me in the box."

"We have to talk," he told me.

"Fine," I said. "Just not now."

My eyes were swollen, my skin burned, and beneath my SFPD sweats, my underwear was still wet from the water cannon. And now my husband was mad at me.

His anger was justified.

But still, this hadn't exactly been a day in the park tossing bread to the duckies for me.

Tips and clues were sucking us into black holes of nothingness. And yet Loman was still out there—somewhere.

CHAPTER 45

I POURED COFFEE into paper cups and went back to Interview 2, where Megan Rafferty, also wearing police department sweats, had folded her arms on the table and was sobbing into them.

I checked and saw that the camera in the corner of the ceiling was still rolling. I kicked a chair out from the table and sat down.

I said, "Hey, Megan. Look here."

She lifted her head, saw the container of coffee I put down in front of her, and peeled off the lid. "Thanks," she said. "When can I go home?"

Across the hallway Rich Conklin was talking to the lump of dump known as Corey Briggs, a minor-league drug dealer and likely part of the mysterious Loman's crew.

Conklin had some leverage with Briggs.

Drugs and unregistered guns had been found on his person and inside his van. It was possible that Conklin could get the DA to make a deal in exchange for cooperation and usable information. He could promise to try.

Here in Interview 2, I was trying to get information from a twenty-two-year-old crack addict, a former college girl who no doubt had just about wrecked her parents' dreams and her own future. But there was hope for her yet. The van belonged to her boyfriend. She hadn't been armed and had had no drugs on her when we brought her down. Unless we found something that proved otherwise, she'd committed no crime.

If she helped us catch a dangerous criminal, maybe she'd use her clash with the SFPD to rethink her life, get clean. I knew my reasoning was wishful, but I felt sorry for her.

Megan said, "Corey didn't tell me anything except that he was waiting for a phone call."

"From whom?"

"He didn't say. He didn't tell me anything, Sergeant, I swear to God. Please believe me."

I said, "You're living with him. He had weapons and illegal substances inside the van. Why were you bunking in the van, Megan? You two live only a couple of blocks away. I really, really want to help you, but this makes no sense."

"Corey was protecting me."

"From what, exactly?"

She shrugged. Tears spilled. I patted her back. She said, "I don't know one damned thing. Please let me go home now."

"I'm afraid you have to stay with us for a while."

"What do you mean?"

"We're holding you as a material witness. Look on the

bright side—you're going to be able to take a shower and get some sleep."

"And I can talk to a lawyer?"

I sighed again. A shower and sleep sounded pretty good to me.

"Sure. Just remember to tell him or her that you're not under arrest."

"I'm crashing, Sergeant. Everything hurts."

"Megan, why are you protecting him? He's a known criminal. He's been tagged as a murderer. Could you think of yourself, help the police, and tell us where to find Loman?"

"I don't know who that is."

Be her friend. Be her friend, I counseled myself.

"I'll get you some Advil," I said.

I walked out to the short hallway between the two interview rooms and closed the door behind me to see Rich there with Lieutenant Brady.

My partner's hair was wet. He'd changed his clothes. And he and our good friend were laughing their asses off.

CHAPTER 46

THE WAY I felt right now, watching Brady and Conklin snort and guffaw was like grabbing a downed electric line in the rain. A surge of unexpected fury shot through me.

What the hell was this? I'd been working for three days straight. I could count the number of hours I'd slept on one hand. And the two of them were having a good ol' time.

I glanced at the mirrored observation window with its direct view into Interview 2.

Had they been watching me interrogate Rafferty? Were they laughing at me?

I said, "What's the joke? I haven't had a good laugh since last Thursday."

Conklin pointed at the opposite window, the one with the view into Interview 1, where he'd been grilling Corey Briggs. He sputtered, still laughing, finally getting that I wasn't amused.

"Briggs said that he and Megan were waiting for an

earthquake. Then they were going to drive to Union Square…" More helpless laughing.

Brady added, "They were going to hit the boutiques. The van was their getaway car."

Another jolt of rage just about lit me up.

"You believe them?"

"Nooooo," said Brady and Conklin in unison.

I said, "Brady, I got nothing from Rafferty. Maybe Inspector Charming can get her to squeal. I'm going home. Don't call. Don't write. I'm done."

I jerked the band out of my ponytail, pulled the sweatshirt away from my neck to let out the steam, and marched toward the Homicide bullpen.

Shit. If I didn't find a cop to drive me home, I was going to have to ask Joe to pick me up. I didn't think he'd be talking to me—and he would probably be pissed for days.

As I marched down the hall to the squad room, I heard Brady calling out to me.

"Boxer. Wait up."

I ignored him and stiff-armed the door—and ran right into Jacobi.

"Boxer," he said. "Brady, Conklin—you, too. The shit is about to hit the fan."

"Loman?" Brady asked him.

"Bingo," Jacobi answered. "It's not over yet."

CHAPTER 47

LOMAN LEANED BACK on the sofa and sighed appreciatively.

His wife, Imogene, would love this place. It was a great condo in an upscale neighborhood, high-ceilinged, furnished sparingly with some good modern art, and equipped with high-tech everything—including a great security system that Dick had dismantled in under five seconds.

But Imogene didn't push for luxury.

She loved the husband she believed him to be—a hardworking man who sold gold necklaces to department stores and made just enough for them to get by. He smiled to himself. They'd be getting by in Zurich by the end of the week, living in a great rental under assumed names, wanting for nothing. Just the way he'd planned.

But there was something he had to do first.

Loman listened to the dishwasher chugging through its

cycle in the open-plan kitchen. There was a wine bottle and a half-full wineglass on the dining room table. And here in the living room, the modern, artificial Christmas tree stood near the sliding glass doors that led out to the deck. Beautiful setup.

Loman shifted his eyes to the middle-aged man in pajamas and a blue velveteen robe who was duct-taped to an armchair. He said to his old friend, "Arnie, you're planning to go see your kids over Christmas, am I right?"

Arnold Sloane didn't answer. He appeared to be organizing his thoughts, maybe rehearsing a last-minute pitch. Loman was a reasonable man, but he couldn't imagine Arnie coming up with an explanation that would excuse the betrayal. It had cut deep.

Loman got up and went over to Sloane, pulled the T-shirt they were using as a gag down onto Sloane's neck, and said, "Arnie. Look. I want to understand you better. Why'd you do it? Why'd you even think you would get away with it? A hundred thirty K isn't much to me. Hell, I would have just given it to you. But using a fake email address, picking a drop-off in a parking lot? You shouldn't have blackmailed me to begin with. But then what? You thought I wouldn't know it was you? Answer me. What were you thinking?"

Sloane said, "Why are you putting on this charade, Lomachenko? Just get it over with. I concede. You win."

Dick Russell, Loman's right-hand man, came out of Sloane's home office and entered the living room. He was wearing purple latex gloves, microfiber booties over his shoes, a hairnet. He'd been working on the safe with some whiz-bang electronic tool.

He put four stacks of banded bills down on the coffee table, saying, "That's about two hundred Gs, Willy. Here's a satchel I found on the floor—and here's the combination for the safe at Milano's. He kept it in a box with his coin collection."

Loman said, "Leave the combination on the table, Dick. Give the cops something to think about."

Russell addressed the man duct-taped to his chair. "How ya doing, Mr. Sloane? Going to apologize to Mr. Loman?"

"Go to hell, Dick."

"Very original," Russell said. "But I'll give you this for free. You've got balls."

Loman gagged Sloane again. Patted the top of his head and said, "Don't worry. This will be over soon."

Loman knew Arnold Sloane from when they were both in sales, before Sloane became the manager of Milano's, an upmarket jewelry store. Arnie made only about a hundred fifty thousand a year, but he skimmed. And he'd fenced some things for Loman.

Then he'd gotten greedy.

The wholesale value of the merchandise in the Union Square store averaged about sixteen million on any given day, but even with the combination to the safe in his hand, Loman wasn't about to hit Milano's. Too risky.

Loman was happy enough for Sloane's nest egg. He would distribute the cash to his crew for their work and their silence. And this home invasion would mess with the cops' minds and keep them busy.

In a couple of minutes, after he and Dick had left Arnie Sloane's place, Loman would attach another one of

Dick's gizmos to his spanking-new burner phone. It would disguise both his voice and the pings to the cell tower. He'd call in a tip to the police about hearing shots fired at this address.

By then he and Russell would be on to the *real* deal, the job he'd been planning for the past seven years of his life.

CHAPTER 48

LOMAN LEANED BACK on the sofa and told Russell, "Go ahead, my friend. Enjoy."

Russell smiled. He was better at construction than destruction, but he was open to the experience. He took a folding knife out of his pocket and went to work.

First, he slashed a few abstract paintings and opened up the love-seat upholstery, then he gathered up some art glass vases and dropped them one at a time onto the stone hearth. Made a nice mess of it. Mess wasn't his favorite thing, but this was fun.

Next, he walked down the hallway to the master bedroom, opened all of the drawers, and tossed some things on the floor. Then he shredded Sloane's nice suits and ties, knocked the TV off the dresser. It would look to the police like a home invasion with motive.

Loman had turned up the music and was looking out at the deck garden through the sliders.

"Willy. What next?"

Loman turned to face him. He was holding a .45 in his hand.

His boss was pointing a gun at him.

Russell froze, paralyzed with shock. He imagined the shot going through his head, pictured himself falling to the floor, becoming part of another of Loman's violent tableaux.

This is not fucking happening.

Russell knew that he was useful until he wasn't needed anymore. But Loman still needed him. Didn't he?

He shouted, "What are you doing? No kidding, Willy. Don't be *crazy.*"

He watched Loman's expression. Reversing course was in character for Loman. Loman repositioned the gun and presented it butt-first to Russell.

"How could you think such a thing, Dick? You hurt my feelings. Now take the gun."

Ten feet away, Sloane lunged against the duct tape, rocking the armchair forward and back, whimpering through his gag.

Loman said to Russell again, "Take it."

Russell refocused, moving from seeing himself as a bloody corpse to trying to process what Loman wanted him to do. He had never agreed to shoot anyone—but clearly, this was what Loman had in mind.

He understood that if he didn't finish the job, Loman would shoot him, put Sloane away, and walk out the door. Russell's best chance of surviving the night, of cashing in and disappearing on his own terms, depended on his following this order.

Loman asked nicely, "Got a problem, Dick?"

Russell said, "Our deal, Willy. We have an agreement. I'm Mr. Inside, remember?"

"You're as far inside as you can be without being up Arnie's ass. Dick. Think about it. This is the only way I can trust you."

Russell didn't have to think hard.

He saw himself taking the gun and shooting Loman, but he doused the thought. Loman was his ticket to happily-ever-after. Without Loman, he was a man without a plan.

Fucking Loman. Russell reached out and took the gun, got a two-handed grip on it, and aimed at Sloane's chest. Sloane yelled wordlessly through the gag.

"Ahhhhhhhhhhhh!"

Russell fired.

Sloane bucked, almost knocking over the chair, a forceful reaction in contrast to the soft puff of the suppressed gunshot. Russell fired again and Sloane's body jerked. He was dead when the third round went into his torso. He didn't twitch.

Russell stared, briefly mesmerized by the growing bloodstains around the bullet holes in Sloane's shirt.

He'd done that. He was a murderer.

Loman said, "Good job, Dick. But you got some blood on you. Go put on one of Arnie's shirts and be sure to take yours with us. Make it snappy, eh, buddy? We gotta go."

Loman was satisfied. By killing Sloane, Russell was all in. Loman clapped his hands together sharply, getting his partner's attention.

"Wake up, Dick. The job of the century is waiting."

CHAPTER 49

CONKLIN AND I followed Jacobi to Caselli Avenue and parked behind him in front of number 22.

The curb was already jammed with CSI and medical examiner vans and a herd of black-and-whites. Cherry lights strobed, and the crackle of car radios sounded like a hissing crowd at Candlestick.

I got out of the car and looked up.

At eleven whatever p.m., the clouds had blocked out the moon and stars, leaving a fathomless black sky. Up and down the curving, tree-lined block, reindeer lawn vignettes and roof decor twinkled.

By contrast, every window in number 22 Caselli blazed with halogen lights from our crime scene unit.

The uniformed officer standing outside the door was David Thompsett, a bright kid hoping to get into Homicide one day. He reminded me of Conklin when I first met him.

Thompsett looked at me and did a double take.

"Sergeant. You okay?"

"Why do you ask?"

"Uh, honestly? You look like you've been sleeping in the trunk of your car."

I laughed, sounding slightly hysterical to my own ears.

"I wish," I told him. "Sleep is a distant memory. What have we got here, Officer?"

Thompsett ran the scene for Jacobi, Conklin, and me.

"The vic is a white man in his sixties, duct-taped to a chair. Three shots to the chest. He's still there."

"Who called this in?" Conklin asked him.

"Anonymous tipster called 911, said that he heard gunshots and saw the shooter flee on foot. Said he recognized him as Mr. Loman.

"I knew the name from the APB," Thompsett said. "My partner and I responded and found the front door closed but unlocked. We called for backup and went in. Hogan and I took a quick look around, checked to make sure the victim was dead. CSI got here an hour ago."

Thompsett handed the sign-in log to Jacobi, said, "Nice to see you, Chief. How're you doing?"

"Fired up. Ready to go."

I worked out the timeline while Jacobi signed us in. Dispatch had forwarded the 911 call to Homicide. Jacobi had picked up the call while Conklin and I were interviewing Rafferty and Briggs.

How had the caller recognized Loman?

Who was Loman to the victim?

Thompsett said, "Let me get Lieutenant Hallows for you."

He phoned CSI's night-shift supervisor, Lieutenant Gene Hallows, who came out to the front step to meet us. He cautioned us to follow directly behind him. "It's a bloody mess in there. Watch your feet. Don't sneeze," he said, handing out the shoe-cover booties and latex gloves.

I got it. Don't corrupt his crime scene.

CHAPTER 50

WE THREE COPS stood in the foyer as CSI's Lieutenant Hallows filled us in on the fresh new crime scene.

He said, "My first impression is that this is the work of professionals. The dead man is Arnold Sloane, store manager at Milano's Fine Jewelry. Sloane has finished his dinner for one and refilled his wineglass, and that's when someone rings the doorbell.

"He either looks through the peephole or is expecting company. In any case, he knows this person or, more likely, persons. They come in or they push in, hold a gun on him, duct-tape him to the chair, gag him with a T-shirt. Then they go through the rooms."

I said, "It was a robbery?"

Hallows nodded. "Looks like it. They threaten Mr. Sloane and he gives up the safe combination. The safe in his den was opened without tools or explosives. And there's a little gratuitous vandalism. Either staging a robbery scene for our benefit or working out a grudge. So they break up his stuff, take a knife to the pictures, and slice up his clothes. Some sadism here, I think. He knows what's going on. Maybe praying that after they rob him, they'll leave. Or what? He knows what's going to happen. He can't even bargain with them. So he sits in the chair and then they go ahead and shoot him."

Hallows is a tough old dog, but he was disturbed by what he had seen.

"Damn psychos." He shook his head.

I looked past Hallows and saw the body of an older man duct-taped to an upholstered armchair, a gag made out of a T-shirt tied around his head. Three gunshot wounds bloomed red on his pajamas.

Hallows said, "Shell casings were removed by the shooters. They were careful. Maybe we'll have something for you to go on in a couple of days."

Jacobi said, "Thanks, Lieutenant. Can you give us the tour?"

I realized with a shock that we were the damned primaries on this homicide. This was our case. Mine and Conklin's.

We walked past the techs processing the living room: making sketches of the layout, putting down markers next to blood spatter, shooting photos, and taking prints.

Hallows brought us to the bedroom and showed us the empty safe in the closet and the slashed clothing. We went back to the living room, walking carefully behind Hallows, seeing the horror of a cold, professional murder done at close range.

When the ME's techs came in to remove the body, we got out of the way.

Once Conklin, Jacobi, and I were standing outside in the dark again, I asked Jacobi, "Say the tipster wasn't blowing smoke—what's Sloane's connection to Loman?"

Jacobi said, "Maybe somehow Loman knew that Sloane might have millions in his safe."

Really? Was *this* Loman's big heist?

A man had been murdered and robbed, not in a museum or a bank or an art gallery, but in an eleven-hundred-square-foot condo in the Castro District.

If the killers had left anything of forensic value behind, CSI would find it. The whodunit detective work was going to be first up for SFPD. But Conklin and I were still on the Loman task force. We needed help to secure the crime scene right now.

I conferred with my partner and then took Officer Thompsett aside. As first officer, he and his partner could stand in as primaries until we had forensics.

"Until detectives are assigned, this is your case, Officer," I said. "Draft some uniforms and canvass the neighborhood. Keep records of everything. Call me or Conklin if you get a lead."

"Will do, Sergeant."

I got into the squad car, called Brady, and reported in. I thought of calling Joe, but it was too late. I leaned against the passenger-side window and dropped into a dream about Chris Dietz. I was facing him down that long sixth-floor hallway, and he had TEC-9s pointed at me, one in each hand.

My gun jammed.

Dietz taunted me as he fired, and I knew that this was finally it. Death at the Anthony Hotel.

I was startled awake.

It was still deep night. I was inside the squad car and Conklin was saying my name.

"What's wrong?" I snapped at him.

"Time to go," he said. "Sorry, Linds. We have to go."

CHAPTER 51

BRADY PEERED AT his watch with bleary eyes.

Was that right? He shook his wrist, looked at his watch again. The second hand was still sweeping jerkily around the face.

It was three minutes shy of midnight.

He lifted his eyes and looked out at the squad room through the glass walls of his office. There wasn't another soul in the Homicide bullpen, and that was also true of Robbery, Vice, Narcotics, and Organized Crime.

Mayor Caputo had taken the informant's tip about Loman's threat on his life very seriously. He'd canceled the Toys for Tots Christmas gift giveaway because his presence would be putting citizens in danger. And then he'd gone to his office as Brady had requested and stayed on top of the rumored Christmas heist. He was angry that he could be manipulated, threatened, and he wasn't going to accept anything less than "We locked the bastard up. He's behind bars and under armed guard."

Yes, sir. Brady wanted the same.

Whoever Loman was. Wherever he was. He had to be caught and held.

Every ambulatory cop in San Francisco was working to find Loman, prompting a new phrase for *spinning your wheels*. Now it was *working a Loman*.

Brady had just gotten off the phone with Lindsay when a shadow crossed his desk. He started, then saw that Sergeant Roger Bentley was standing in the doorway.

Brady snapped, "What is it, Bentley?"

Bentley was a solid cop but not a brilliant one. He lumbered into Brady's office and dropped into a chair that hadn't been built for a man of his size and weight.

Bentley said, "My kid is home for the holidays. He's taking computer science at San Jose State."

Brady said, "Uh-huh," thinking, *Oh, man, please. Not his kid's theory of the phantom heist.*

Bentley said, "Declan picked up some information in a…like, a virtual chat room."

"Uh-huh."

Brady's head was spinning almost clear off his neck. He'd never heard of so many tips netting nothing. Meanwhile, three people had been shot in the past couple of hours, he had two possible accessories to a rumored upcoming armed robbery in holding, the mayor was panicking, and every cop in the city who hadn't had the foresight to blow town for the holidays was on the Loman case.

The SFPD was seriously depleted—emotionally,

psychologically, and physically—and they had nothing to show for it.

Brady said, "Bentley, cut to the chase, will you please?"

"Okay, okay. I hardly understand this virtual stuff, but Declan is aces at it. He says the heist has something to do with computer software, a new program or something, manufactured in top secret labs by a company called BlackStar."

"Not exactly a rock-solid lead, Bentley, but thanks."

Bentley said, "You said…never mind. Good night, Lieu."

He took the four steps to the door, then spun around and said, "Lieu, Declan says a guy who is part of this heist is some kind of systems-analyst genius. He kills on the game boards. He calls himself the Low Man's Brain."

"I don't get you, Bentley. I haven't slept in three days."

"The Low Man. Loman. Get it?"

"Okay. Now I get it. Go home, Bentley, and tell Declan I said thanks."

Brady was out of gas. He remembered there was a day-old steak sandwich in the fridge with his name on the wrapper.

He made the trek to the break room, found the sandwich and an unopened bottle of near beer—thank you, Jesus—and brought it all back to his desk.

Maybe it was the protein or the carbs, but when he was halfway through the sandwich, the name BlackStar started ringing a tinny and distant bell. Brady sat upright in his chair, took his mouse in hand, and called up the computer files from the crime scene at the Anthony Hotel.

The photos were numerous, organized chronologically,

starting in the hallway. First shots were of the blood spatter, the markers, the bullet holes, the dead man lying in his blood, and the door to 6F hanging by one hinge. The next photos were of Chris Dietz's body from several angles and then the inside of Dietz's rented crib.

Brady impatiently clicked through the photos of the half-eaten food, the open closet, the electronics lined up on the coffee table.

He didn't know enough about electronics to understand the functions of the assortment of small black boxes, but he could read the logo imprinted on two of them. The corporate name had been unfamiliar to him—until Declan's dad spoke the words five minutes ago.

The gadgets were made by BlackStar VR.

Did that mean something? BlackStar. The Low Man's Brain. He was at a loss. What would Jacobi do?

Well. He'd just have to ask him.

CHAPTER 52

JACOBI HAD HIS key in the ignition of his car and was thinking about home, bed, and blessed sleep when Brady called and asked him to work a new angle on the Loman case.

If Brady was working, how could Jacobi say no?

"Tell me about it," he said to Brady.

Brady filled him in on the BlackStar lead and invited Jacobi to work from his comfortable former office on the fifth floor. Jacobi got out of his car and set the alarm. He said, "I'll use Boxer's desk. She won't mind."

The Homicide bullpen was grim in the daytime, but right now, the flickering fluorescent lights reminded Jacobi of hundreds of late nights working murder cases in this room.

Even after Brady told him all that he knew on this new tip, Jacobi still didn't get it. Sergeant Bentley's kid had turned up a possible lead in a chat room—a video gamer with a screen name sounding like *Loman* hinted that he was part of a crew targeting a computer company. To Jacobi, following up on an anonymous internet tip was like feeling for your glasses under the bed in the dark after a night of drinking.

The odds of finding the glasses were better.

Jacobi adjusted Boxer's chair, typed her password into her cranky old Dell, and brought up BlackStar Virtual Reality's website.

He quickly gathered that BlackStar was privately held, had its corporate headquarters in San Francisco, and employed a couple of thousand employees on a modern campus in the Presidio. The company also had dozens of manufacturing plants and offices worldwide. As Jacobi clicked around the site, he learned that BSVR specialized in sophisticated computer games, corporate intelligence, and cybersecurity and that NASA and the US military were major clients.

That was interesting.

Jacobi pulled the desk phone toward him and dialed Bentley's son at the number Brady had given him. Declan Bentley was a nineteen-year-old college freshman and video gamer. According to his father, he was also conversant in various technical areas Jacobi lumped together under the heading of *computer stuff*.

Jacobi had taught himself to text and program his GPS and play around with some apps on his phone, but he was far from tech-smart. He was a member of the AARP . That's just the way it was.

He figured Declan would be awake, and in fact, the

kid answered his phone on the second ring, said, "Talk to me."

"Declan, it's Warren Jacobi. Maybe your father told you I was going to call."

"Oh, right. I'd be happy to help."

"Excellent. Thanks, Declan. Appreciate it."

Jacobi wrote the kid's name and the time and date on one of the yellow pads Brady left all over the squad room.

"Here's the deal, Declan. Your chat-room conversation with the Low Man's Brain. Tell me everything you remember."

PART FOUR

DECEMBER 24

CHAPTER 53

JACOBI LOOKED AT his watch—early in the morning on December 24. Officially Christmas Eve, and all over the city, cops of all levels and from all departments were staked out at plum targets, watching for a job to begin.

Nothing was off the table.

If the Low Man's Brain was part of Loman's crew, if he had leaked something useful to Declan Bentley, Jacobi had to extract that information PDQ.

He asked the kid, "This guy actually said he was part of a plan to hit BlackStar VR? You believed him?"

Declan said, "Yeah, I did believe him. The Brain says he's a systems analyst. He's online a lot, and he's a killer gamer, so over time he's earned some cred with me."

"What word did he use, Declan? *Hit? Rob? Attack?*"

"He said, 'Put a world of hurt on BlackStar.'"

"Did you save a copy of the chat, Declan?"

"I didn't even think to do that."

Jacobi pressed on. "Did you ask him what he meant by putting 'a world of hurt' on a company?"

"Sure. I said, 'Dude. What the hell?' He just laughed and then said something like, 'You'll read about it,' and then he said he was going to put the hurt on *me* in *Lord of Klandar*—that's a game—and he left the room. If Dad hadn't mentioned that he was working the Loman case, I wouldn't have even put those two names together."

"So help me understand, Declan," Jacobi said. "This Low Man's Brain. That's a screen name, right? He says he's involved in a criminal enterprise, he admits that he's a criminal, and he's confident no one can figure out who he is?"

"No one can," said Declan. "No way, not possible. I don't know if the Brain is a he or a cyborg or a five-year-old girl genius in the Netherlands."

Jacobi said, "Okay, okay. You have any idea why BlackStar would be the target of this hit?"

Declan said, "BSVR is big, man, and profitable. Privately held. They're like the new Intel. Maybe they have a weaponized program that could penetrate any kind of system. That's possible. Their games are all about war. Or maybe the Brain is just full of crap."

"Okay, Declan, I'm drowning in maybes and I need a definite something. BlackStar's founder is a man named David Bavar. Apparently, he's your typical tech genius, very rich, keeps to himself. Do you know anything about him that I don't know?"

"Well, right now he's in Davos. Switzerland."

"How do you know that?" Jacobi asked.

"He's been streaming his ski trip in the Alps. He's pretty good. Want me to show you how you can be, like, sitting on his shoulders going down a black-diamond slope?"

Jacobi said, "Some other time." He thanked the kid and wished him a merry Christmas before he hung up.

Was anything he'd just learned useful?

Loman, whoever he was, did big stickup jobs, or so the story went. As Jacobi understood it, stealing a program wouldn't require a crew with guns and masks. Digital theft would be done over the internet. Wouldn't it?

Jacobi went back to the keyboard with his stiff old fingers and looked up BlackStar's CEO on all available databases. He found him in a court document related to a lawsuit against BSVR for patent infringement. BlackStar had beaten that rap.

Noting that it was around midmorning in Davos, Jacobi made the call. He listened to the phone ring and had just about decided that Bavar must already be out on the slopes when someone answered the phone.

CHAPTER 54

JACOBI PRESSED THE phone to his ear and introduced himself to David Bavar as chief of police, retired, on special assignment.

He gave the tech billionaire Boxer's extension and the phone number of the department so that he could call back on a line that would be answered "SFPD, Homicide." Jacobi drummed his fingers on the desk, got a cup of mud from the break room, and returned to Boxer's desk just as the phone rang.

"Chief Jacobi," he said.

"Ah, this is David Bavar. Now, tell me again what this is about."

Jacobi explained that a criminal with a rumored history of big, bloody robberies on an epic scale was reportedly targeting BlackStar, and possibly this hit would come tonight.

When Bavar laughed, Jacobi felt ridiculous. That pissed him off.

He took a breath and realized that most people would be skeptical if they got a call like this from a stranger. Still. He was trying to help the guy. When Bavar asked him the source of his information, Jacobi took the easy way out.

"I can't discuss this while our investigation is in progress."

Bavar said, "So what is it you think I should do? I'm at the airport in Zurich and will be out of touch for about eight hours. After that, I can be reached at this number. My offices are officially closed until New Year's. We're in the cybersecurity business, Chief, uh, Jacobi, and I guarantee you that no one is hacking into our systems. If we had a vulnerability, I would know about it."

"Say that that's true, Mr. Bavar. Do you have any enemies who might want to do harm to your company?"

"Hundreds. No one likes an overnight success."

"Does the name Loman mean anything to you?"

"I don't think so," said Bavar. "Who or what is Loman?"

Jacobi reluctantly crossed that avenue off his list and moved on.

"Mr. Bavar, do you have any objects of value that a professional criminal with a history of armored-car and casino heists would find worth his time?"

"Like what?"

"You tell me, Mr. Bavar. This isn't my field. Do you have some kind of cutting-edge gizmo or stealth hacking program or top secret government plans, anything like that?"

"Nothing that could be found, recognized, and stolen in

some kind of break-in. It just doesn't work that way, but if you want to drive out to our corporate headquarters in the Presidio—what time is it there, midnight?"

"A little later."

"If you want to take a look around, go ahead."

David Bavar gave Jacobi the name and number of his head of security, then told him he had to board his plane.

CHAPTER 55

JACOBI CALLED THE security guy, Ronald Wilkins, rousing him from bed. Jacobi apologized, then used the magic words "David Bavar asked me to call you."

Wilkins said, "What do you need?"

"A look around your headquarters. A chat with you and your night security guy."

Wilkins said, "I'd better talk to Mr. Bavar. I'll call you back."

"Do it quick. His flight is taking off."

Jacobi leaned back in his chair and drifted off. Soon he was woken up by a ringing phone. He picked up. The voice said, "It's Wilkins. Send me a photo of you."

Jacobi said okay. He took a selfie against the backdrop of the squad room and looked at it. Highly unflattering, but he forwarded it to Wilkins, waited a few seconds, then asked, "Get it?"

"It's out of focus," Wilkins said.

"Jesus," said Jacobi. "I'm white, have gray hair. I weigh two hundred pounds and look like I've been a cop for forty years. I'll have ID to show you. All right?"

"I can meet you at BlackStar, east parking lot. Give me an hour."

Jacobi said, "Make it thirty minutes. Tell your security guy not to let anyone into the building but you. No one but you. You understand me? Call him now. I'll be driving an unmarked car. Gray Chevy sedan."

Wilkins said, "Righto," and Jacobi said, "See you in the parking lot."

Jacobi called Brady, who, despite the late hour, was working in his cubicle at the back of the squad room. Jacobi remembered when he'd hired Jackson Brady a few years back, right out of Miami PD. First time out, Brady took a stance in front of a car with a kidnapped kid inside that was coming straight at him. Brady kept firing until the driver was dead. He was a winner. A great hire. Jacobi had recommended Brady to replace him as police chief. Brady hadn't yet said he would take the job.

Brady picked up his phone, and he and Jacobi looked at each other across the room as they spoke.

Brady said, "Whatcha got?"

Jacobi said, "I want to check out BlackStar's corporate offices. I need a partner with some years in grade and a backup team."

Brady said, "I've got only one live body for you, Chief."

"Ah, don't call Boxer. She's done."

"Not Boxer," Brady said. "I mean me."

CHAPTER 56

CONKLIN STEPPED INTO the apartment he shared with Cindy and switched on the living-room lights.

He hung his gun belt over the back of a chair, sat down, took off his shoes, and massaged his feet. Then he walked quietly down the hallway and into the bedroom, where Cindy was sleeping like an angel, her arms spread out like wings, her blond curls framing her adorable face.

He didn't want to wake her up. But he needed to sleep.

He returned to the living room, took the spare blanket and pillow out of the coat closet, stripped down, and got comfortable on the couch. He blinked in the dark, listened to traffic and a couple of drunk guys singing "Silent Night."

He sighed deeply and counseled himself to turn off his

thoughts. The way he understood it, your brain had to be bored in order for it to go to sleep. His brain couldn't be more agitated.

He pictured himself standing in Sloane's foyer with Jacobi, Lindsay, and Hallows, all of them staring at an older man duct-taped to a chair and shot dead.

The front door behind them had been unlocked by someone with a key, or, more likely, it had been opened from the inside by Sloane himself. He had known his killers. Or he had trusted them. They had asked Sloane to let them in and he had. Why?

Sloane's safe had been open, and according to the handheld print reader, the only prints on the safe were Sloane's. Had he opened the safe for his killers?

Conklin could see a shadow standing behind Sloane, holding a gun to his neck.

The safe had been cleaned out. If Sloane had a phone and a laptop, they'd been stolen. Shell casings had been retrieved by the shooter. CSI picked up a few prints not belonging to the victim and ran them at the scene, but there were no matches in the criminal database.

The killer or killers had worn gloves.

So. A couple of questions: Was this a robbery, and the homicide sprang from that? Or was this a homicide and the robbery staged?

And here were some more questions: Were the robber-killers Loman and an associate? Or was the anonymous tip that Loman had been seen exiting Sloane's place a deliberate misdirection?

If the tip was a misdirection, someone who knew Loman

or worked for Loman, or possibly even Loman himself, had called it in.

Why?

To keep the cops busy while they did their big heist.

Conklin rolled over to face the back of the couch, punched the pillow, and again tried to empty his mind. A minute later he threw off the blanket, got a beer from the fridge, and stood in the bedroom doorway watching Cindy sleep.

She had been working flat-out on her story about Eduardo Varela. Her drop-dead deadline was tomorrow, the day before Christmas. He looked at his watch. It was five after two, so actually, it was due today. He hadn't been able to talk to her about the piece or read a draft of that one or the Christmas-for-immigrants story. He always read her stuff before she sent it in.

He missed the hell out of her, and she was right here.

Rich slugged down his beer, grabbed his phone, and texted Jacobi.

What are you doing?

Chkg out BlkStar w/ Brady.

Find anything? Conklin texted.

Is a dead end anything? Get some sleep. C u in the a.m.

Conklin went back to the couch and turned the case over in his mind again. If the Sloane hit was a ruse, what was the real deal? If Sloane was the real deal, then he'd been killed for what had been in his safe. Would the canvass of Sloane's friends and neighbors turn up a lead or a window into the hit?

What would CSI have to report and how long would he have to wait?

Was there a thread that tied Julian Lambert, the de Young Museum, two druggies in the van in Hunters Point, BlackStarVR, and Arnold Sloane together?

Conklin didn't see it. After a while his brain got tired of cycling through unanswerable questions, and he fell asleep.

CHAPTER 57

YUKI WAS PROPPED up in bed with her laptop. It was just past midnight, which meant Christmas Eve was tonight. She was wearing one of Brady's shirts as a nightgown and was aggravated that he wasn't home.

They'd made no plans for Christmas, not for dinner in or out with friends. Unopened cards and wrapped gifts were on the coffee table, but there was still no tree.

Brady had warned her that his life would belong to the Job if he took over for Jacobi as chief of police and kept doing his other work as well. The situation was meant to be temporary, and she'd encouraged him to see if being the top cop agreed with him. She hadn't realized that he'd be working all the damned time.

Yuki was also mad at herself because she'd fallen for the latest of Cindy's crusades, this one to get Eduardo Varela out of jail. As if that weren't bad enough, she had inveigled her friend Zac Jordan into taking Varela's case. Pressure and more pressure.

When Varela was arrested twelve hours after the murder, the police had administered a gunshot residue—GSR—test. If gunpowder was present, it would prove that he had fired a gun.

Now Yuki knew the results of that test.

No GSR had been found on Eduardo's hands or sleeves. No gun had been found on his person, and the murder weapon had not been recovered at all.

Only the witness statements of three neighborhood boys, gang members with arrest records, tied Eduardo to the murder. Eduardo believed that one of them had actually done the murder. She believed Eduardo.

Why hadn't Peter Bard, Eduardo's attorney, presented the GSR test results to the judge at his arraignment?

Why hadn't Bard discredited the so-called witnesses and pointed the finger at them?

Now they had something to go on. Despite his busy schedule, Zac had gotten Varela a pretrial hearing at nine a.m. But Yuki wanted to talk to Eduardo's original lawyer, Peter Bard.

That was turning out to be impossible. The last place Bard had worked had gone out of business. He didn't answer his phone. Her email to him had bounced back. During the past two years, he could have moved to Fiji. For all she knew, he had died there.

Why didn't he answer his damned phone?

Yuki texted both Zac and Cindy to let them know about what might be exculpatory evidence.

GSR test was negative and never mentioned at arraignment.

She put her phone down on the night table, and when it buzzed, Yuki glanced at the screen. Brady.

He had promised to be home hours ago. She didn't want to break her concentration and get into a long talk with him now on his drive home.

She had her stiff *I'm busy* voice on when she answered the phone.

"Are you sleeping?" Brady asked.

"Working," she said.

"Okay. Me, too. Jacobi and I are patrolling the Presidio. Should be home soon."

"Uh-huh," she said.

She heard the dispatcher's staticky voice coming over Brady's car radio.

"I'll let you go," Yuki said to her husband.

"See you in a bit," he said. "We'll go get that tree in the morning."

"Be safe," she said.

She hung up before any phone kisses could clear the air and got back into the dubious case against Eduardo Varela.

CHAPTER 58

YUKI HAD TURNED out the lights at two, and when she woke up at seven fifteen, she heard and felt Brady sleeping heavily on his side of the bed.

Before she'd conked out last night, she'd uncovered a bombshell that might give Eduardo a get-out-of-jail-free card. But she hadn't had a chance to give this discovery a shakedown cruise. If her reasoning was flawed, it would blow up on Team Eduardo.

Yuki wanted to talk to Brady but didn't have it in her to wake him. As she showered, she reviewed the bombshell, thinking how Zac would present the argument.

Now, only an hour before court convened, she was starting to doubt herself. Judge Lauren Innello was hard-core law-and-order. That could work for or against them. If what she'd found was true, would it be enough to convince the judge to overturn the state's case against Varela?

At twenty to nine Yuki was behind the wheel of her car, navigating the pre-Christmas traffic crush resulting from people doing their last-minute shopping. She was a good driver and managed a faster-than-moderate speed while thinking through the best way to approach the judge.

The prosecuting attorney was Anna Palermo. Yuki knew her only slightly. If Anna was reasonable, if she saw what Yuki saw, maybe she could be persuaded to join with Yuki in taking an official position for the district attorney and withdraw the charges.

If Anna agreed, the judge would go along with them.

The lot across from the Hall of Justice was full, and there were no empty spots on either side of Bryant Street. Yuki circled the Hall, and when she saw nothing, she ranged farther away, eventually finding one-hour metered parking outside a camera shop on Ninth.

She would get a ticket, but it couldn't be helped.

She grabbed her computer case from the seat beside her, fought to release her seat belt, and locked up her car. Then, dodging pedestrians and ignoring red lights, she turned left on Bryant, dashed two and a half blocks northeast, and still had enough wind to sprint up the courthouse steps.

The security guard just inside the courthouse gave her a look—well, Yuki did look frazzled—but after checking her ID and running her bag and laptop through the magnetometer, he let her through.

"You really shouldn't run in heels," he called out. "My wife…"

She was out of range before he finished his sentence.

The elevator door opened on two, and Yuki forced

herself to wait for the frail elderly man standing in front of her to exit the car.

Then she flew down the marble hallway with her ID in hand. The large wooden doors to courtroom 21 were closed, but when the court officer saw the look on Yuki's face, he was persuaded to let her in.

Judge Innello's court was in session.

CHAPTER **59**

CINDY WAS SITTING in the back row of courtroom 21, writing the opening to the Varela story in her head.
  She would first set the scene.

Eduardo Varela, exhausted from his day at the auto shop, has come home for a hot dinner with his wife and kids. He changes into his uniform, his name stitched over the breast pocket of his pressed white shirt. But he's early for his night shift at the convenience store. Getting behind the wheel of his car, parked along Bartlett Street, he reclines the seat and naps until he is startled awake. He's scared. Gunshots have been fired, and by someone close by.

Okay. That would work. But Cindy was sweating it.
  She was an investigative crime reporter. Her work read like fiction, but it was solidly based on journalistic ethics

and principles. Professional. Unbiased. Facts only. Facts checked.

Cindy wanted a good outcome for Eduardo, but if it went badly for him today, Cindy was going to have to write a Christmas tragedy.

Earlier, as the gallery filled, Cindy had made her way down to the front row of the courtroom and met Eduardo for the first time. She'd seen many photos of him as a free man, and she was shocked by how shrunken and pale he was now, how much older he looked than his forty years.

When she told Eduardo who she was, he teared up.

Cindy hugged him, then reached over the seat and hugged his dear wife, Maria, and their three teenage children, sitting behind their father. And she shook Zac Jordan's hand, wishing him the best of luck.

After returning to her seat in the back row, she texted Henry Tyler, the newspaper's editor in chief, to say that she was on the job and would alert him as soon as the case had been dismissed.

Tyler texted back, *Always the optimist.*

She replied with a smiley face.

Tyler was supportive and he trusted her. Good outcome for Eduardo or bad, she must write this story as if her job depended on it.

Today, Judge Lauren Innello would hear dozens of case summaries presented in brief by both the prosecution and the defense counsel. She would weigh mitigating or aggravating circumstances and negotiate sentences or pleas for those defendants who wanted to avoid going to trial.

Would Eduardo get a break? Would he go home or would he go back to jail to keep waiting for trial?

Cindy was jolted out of her thoughts by someone shaking her shoulder.

"Yuki!" Cindy said. "What's wrong?"

Normally, Yuki was immaculately put together, but right now she looked as though she'd taken a few spins inside a clothes dryer. She put her finger to her lips and indicated to Cindy that she needed to speak with her outside the courtroom, then she went to grab Zac.

Cindy left her jacket on her seat and waited for Yuki and Zac outside the courtroom.

What had happened?

Her thoughts went directly to the worst thing she could imagine: that the murder weapon had been recovered, that it was registered to Eduardo, and that his prints were on the gun.

When Cindy, Zac, and Yuki were all gathered in a corner of the teeming corridor outside the courtroom, Yuki said, "I found this."

She pulled a document out of her handbag and showed it to Zac. After he'd read it, Yuki asked, "What do you think?"

"We need to get Palermo in on this," Zac said, referring to the ADA who had brought the homicide charges against Eduardo. "And we have to meet with Judge Innello in chambers."

CHAPTER 60

AT JUST BEFORE six on Christmas Eve, William Lomachenko strolled through the International Terminal at San Francisco International Airport. He wore a loud Christmas sweater—red and green with a big Christmas tree on the chest—jeans, and running shoes, and he had a carry-on bag with the strap slung over his shoulder.

Loman was bareheaded, which felt odd to him. He'd worn a cap almost constantly since he'd started to lose his hair, around age twenty-five. Like many bald men, he sported a full beard and mustache.

There were cameras throughout the terminal, and Loman was counting on that. He glanced at the one inside the entrance as he gazed up at the elongated skylights with structures hanging from the ceiling, then moved on. There was another art installation near the Virgin Atlantic check-in counter, a very grounded sculpture called *Stacking Stones*.

The cameras would show that the man in the garish Christmas sweater took a deep breath of ionized air and continued his self-guided tour. He moved at an unhurried pace, checking out exits, escalators, bathrooms, rental-car booths, the left-luggage section, appearing to be just another traveler killing time.

Eventually he headed toward the shops, most of them with their lights on to capture desperate last-minute shoppers, Christmas music still pouring from the open doors, tinsel and glass ornaments arranged invitingly around merchandise in the plate-glass windows.

Loman checked the time and pulled what appeared to be a boarding pass from a side pouch of his bag. He peered at it, then looked up at the arrival/departure board as if double-checking the time and the gate number.

He still had some time.

Loman scoped out the row of retail stores—the bookstore, the souvenir shop, the candy store, the art gallery, the high-priced toiletries boutique, and Tech4U, an electronic gadgets wonderland.

That was the one.

Tech4U was narrow and deep and lined with shrink-wrapped camera, phone, and computer accessories. The blond, tattooed young woman behind the counter was bored enough to listen as he told her about his nephews and asked her advice on what to get them.

Together they picked out some device chargers and games, and Loman waited as the girl gift-wrapped them. She seemed to enjoy making the square corners, tucking them in, taping them down.

"Will there be anything else?"

"Nope, I'm good," said Loman.

He paid for the gifts in cash, thanked the girl, and headed to the men's room. Inside a stall, Loman opened his overnight bag and removed a pair of gray slacks, a plain navy-blue cotton pullover, a black ball cap, and a pair of glasses with red frames.

He stripped off the fake facial hair, changed his clothes, packed up the ones he'd worn to the airport, and slipped the small gifts inside the bag. Then he left the men's room and exited the terminal, going through the revolving doors and out to the passenger-drop-off lanes.

A Salvation Army Santa was right outside on the sidewalk, ringing his bell. Loman took his wallet out of his bag, peeled off a single, and dropped it into the kettle. Santa thanked him, and Loman touched the brim of his cap, then crossed the road to the median strip.

A seven-year-old gray Prius pulled up and Loman got into the passenger seat.

"Everything okay, Willy?" Russell asked.

"Perfect. I've got it all in here," Loman said, tapping the side of his head. "I think Santa is going to be very good to us. In fact, I know he will."

PART FIVE

DECEMBER 25

CHAPTER 61

THE CHRISTMAS TREE looked beautiful.

It was only seven in the morning, but I'd gotten eight solid hours of sleep in my husband's arms. We were both scrubbed and dressed, tree-side with mugs of hot cocoa in hand, when Julie came out of her room, rubbing her sleepy eyes.

"Was Santa here?"

"Of course he was," Joe said.

I was so relieved that our daughter still believed in the kindly gent from the North Pole. We didn't have to have *that* talk this morning.

Julie climbed onto a chair to check the plate of cookies we'd left for Mr. Claus. She didn't have to know that Joe and I had scarfed them down only minutes ago.

Joe winked at me. I grinned back at him, then I scooped Julie up and brought her back to the tree. Joe had done a pretty good job of last-minute shopping. He'd filled a photo album for Julie with photos of everyone in our circle of family and friends, including Joe's family in New York and my sister, Julie's aunt Cat, and her girls, who lived up the coast in Half Moon Bay.

Martha got a new bowl with her name on it from Julie, and Joe got a cappuccino machine from me. He and I exchanged small treats and new pj's from Santa. Santa had brought toys and outfits for Julie—thank you, internet shopping—and I had a special gift for her.

She opened the small, heavy box, peeled back the tissue, and took out the little globe that my mother had given to me many years ago.

Julie said, "For me?"

"It belonged to Grandma Boxer, then me, and it's yours now, honey. See, this is how it works."

It was a West Coast version of a snow globe and featured a beautiful starfish surrounded by drifts of glittering sand and tiny shells.

I said, "I used to keep this by my bed, and every morning when I woke up, I'd tip it and shake it, and that was the way I started a new day."

Julie looked at her starfish globe with reverence. She tipped it and shook it, and sand fell like snow.

"I love it, Mommy."

She climbed into my lap and hugged me and kissed me, and I did my very best not to cry.

Joe took a picture of us and I took one of him and Julie for her new photo album. The bell rang and we all opened the front door to see our beloved friend, neighbor, and nanny, Gloria Rose. She was on her feet. She was grinning.

I almost shouted, "You can't be out of the hospital. We're coming to see you there."

"It was only a TIA," she said. "I'm cleared, checked out, and good to go." She threw her arms into the air and twirled in the doorway.

I knew about TIAs, transient ischemic attacks. They were like mini-strokes, episodes of oxygen deprivation in parts of the brain. Patients recovered quickly, often within twenty-four hours, and a TIA usually left no permanent damage. But it was a warning. Another stroke, a serious one, could be in her future. I pulled Gloria into the apartment and into my arms.

"So good to see you," I said.

"All I wanted was another year as good as this past one," she said. "And now it seems that I'm getting my wish." She wiped her glistening eyes. "Becky will be here in a minute. She's parking the car."

Becky arrived a moment later, holding a shopping bag. "I bought out the hospital bake sale," she told us.

She had. Suddenly we had enough cake for all twelve days of Christmas.

Joe settled Gloria into his big chair, and I produced hot cocoa, and then Julie couldn't wait any longer. She handed Mrs. Rose our last-minute gift, wrapped with too much wrapping paper and tape. Mrs. Rose pulled the paper apart and gasped with pleasure, then shook out the fluffy blanket and buried her face in the folds. She said, "You're the sweetest, Julie-Bug. Just what I wanted."

"It's from Santa," Julie said, deadpan.

Everyone laughed.

It was a perfect Christmas. Just perfect.

I had no sense of foreboding, no thoughts that I would be jumping into my car and heading toward trouble today.

And then, of course, my phone rang.

CHAPTER 62

YUKI WOKE UP on Christmas morning, cocooned in soft cotton and pillows, grasping for the remains of a dissolving dream—then realized that she was alone.

Brady hadn't come home.

Before she had a chance to get crazy-worried or mad, she heard the shower running in the bathroom. Good.

Yuki threw on a robe and made a dash for the kitchen, and by the time Brady came through the doorway, there was a gift on his plate, eggs by the stove ready for scrambling, and a smile on her face as she sat in her seat at the table. *Still no tree.*

Brady grabbed her up out of her chair and dipped her into a swooping romance-novel kiss.

"Hey," she said breathlessly.

He kissed her again.

This time she took in that he was fully dressed and he was apparently kissing her good-bye.

"Were you working all night?" she asked.

"I slept right next to you, darlin'. You were out cold."

"I don't even remember falling asleep. Hey, how about some hot breakfast?"

"I only have time for coffee. Maybe toast."

"Sit down," Yuki said. "I'll give you coffee, toast, and the thirty-second headline news of what happened in court yesterday. You should feel free to give me thirty seconds of your news, too."

Her big, blond, handsome man grinned and said, "I love you, darlin'. Talk to me. But first…"

He took the little package off his plate and shook it.

Yuki said, "Merry Christmas, sweetie."

She watched him open the box and take out her gift: a gold tie clip, a little grand for work, but she loved it. He turned it around and a beam of sunlight hit it.

"I love this, Yuki. What a major-league tie bob."

He thanked her and fixed it to his tie. She expected him to tell her that he hadn't had time to get her anything but he'd make it up to her. But he said, "I'm taking tonight off, no matter what. I booked us a room on the top floor of the Stanhope. How does that sound?"

Yuki shouted, "Woweeee," and threw herself at Brady, who hugged her, kissed her to pieces, and said, "I'll call you later."

Wearing his gold tie clip but without having had eggs, toast, or coffee or hearing about Eduardo Varela, Lieutenant Jackson Brady was gone.

CHAPTER 63

CINDY HAD KICKED the bedcovers to the floor.

Richie retrieved the blankets and her nightgown from the foot of the bed, tucked himself in, and opened his arms. Cindy, still mostly sleeping, burrowed against him.

He stroked her back, enjoying the little sounds she made as he bundled her up and squeezed her. He said, "Sleep. You don't have to get up yet," then he edged out of bed and headed to the kitchen.

He knew he'd be working the Loman today. He was worn out, angry at the amount of time and manpower that had been dedicated to go-nowhere leads interspersed with bloodshed.

He thought about Arnold Sloane, the man who'd been gagged and terrified and then shot to death.

Who had done that?

He thought again about the anonymous tip they'd gotten that Loman had been seen leaving Sloane's place. Christ.

A blind tip to a possible killer with a fake name. Loman. Whoever, whatever, wherever he was.

He remembered a play he'd read in school called *Death of a Salesman.* The main character was Willy Loman. Sloane had been a salesman before he became the manager of a high-end jewelry store. Was Sloane the dead salesman? Was Sloane's safe Loman's big heist?

The coffeemaker was prefilled with water and coffee, so Rich hit the switch, dropped a couple of frozen waffles into the toaster, and checked his phone.

First on the list was an email from Brady to the whole squad laying out today's assignments. Brady's email was followed by one from Lindsay: *We're on stakeout. C u @ 8.*

And there was an email from Cindy with an attachment. The subject heading was *Cannot wait to tell you.*

Rich opened the attachment. It was Cindy's Christmas-for-immigrants story, now titled "God Was Always with Us."

As his waffles toasted, he read the story, marveling at how close Cindy had gotten to these displaced families. She'd conveyed in a few inches of type their will to overcome hardship, to celebrate their holiday traditions thousands of miles from their homelands in San Francisco.

At the end of the article was a sidebar with the title "After Two Years in Prison, a Miracle Arrives with Bells On."

Cindy had told Rich enough about Eduardo Varela to convince him that the guy had been framed, and Cindy had turned up an innocent man at San Bruno Prison.

Her story laid it all out.

First, Peter Bard, Varela's lawyer, had failed to present

crucial evidence to the DA that might have stopped the whole case against him cold. But there was more. Bard had been a drunk and a no-show for several clients, and after Varela had been locked up, awaiting trial, Bard had been disbarred for malfeasance.

Yesterday, Judge Innello had dismissed the case against Varela for lack of evidence and offered her apologies from the court. ICE had not detained him.

Cindy wrote:

Last night Eduardo and his family led the parade called Las Posadas, a celebration and reenactment of Mary and Joseph's search for shelter that involves stopping at "the inns," neighbors' homes, for food and prayer. Piñatas were smashed. There was much laughter and happy tears.

For the past two years Eduardo sat alone in his cell twenty-three hours a day. On Monday he plans to go to each of his three former employers and ask for his job back. He has much he wants to do to secure a future for the ones he loves.

There was a photo of the Varela family after Eduardo's release. Cindy was at the center of an ecstatic group hug.

Rich had to take a moment.

He wiped his eyes with the backs of his hands and sent Cindy a note: *Great job, Girl Reporter. I'm so proud of you. And I love you. So. Much. Richie.*

He dressed and headed out to his assigned stakeout on Geary Street, where he and Lindsay would be working the Loman. Again.

CHAPTER 64

IMOGENE LOMACHENKO WAS a Christmas baby. Today was her day.

Willy, Imogene, Imogene's brother, Stan, his wife, Gina, and their two kids watched *Goldfinger* on the wide-screen TV over the gas fireplace. Stockings were hung. The tree glinted with lights and was draped with a garland of birthday cards.

The stove's timer pinged. Imogene jumped up from her cozy chair and said, "I sure hope that big Butterball is done. It had better be."

Then the doorbell rang. Ten-year-old Gordo ran to the door and shouted, "It's Dr. Gadgets. Wow, oh, wow!"

Dick Russell, wearing a Santa hat and gripping two large boxes, entered the room with a big "Ho-ho-ho." The kids hustled him over to the tree, where Willy relieved Dick of his gifts and Imogene brought him a hot drink with a candy cane stirrer. After small talk with Willy's in-laws,

Santa told the kids, "On your marks, get set...go. Open your presents."

The boys lunged for the gifts, ripped off the paper, and screamed when they saw the pictures on the boxes.

"Drones! We've got drones!"

After the women dressed the children in coats and scarves and Dick shepherded them outside with their new toys, Willy went upstairs to the spare bedroom he used as his den. While keeping an eye on the football game, he polished the plan for the first day of the rest of his life.

Willy had not yet told Imogene that this would be the Lomachenkos' last Christmas on Avila Street. He was protecting them both, and he certainly didn't want to give her anything to worry about while the job was in progress.

Tomorrow at this time he'd call and say that they were off on a surprise birthday vacation and she should meet him at the airport. She'd say, *We can't afford a vacation, Willy.*

He'd tell her, *Yes, we can, honey. Do not worry. You have to leave now. I've got your passport. Bring a couple pieces of jewelry. Your favorite ones.*

He would tell her how important it was that she pack only an overnight bag and a sweater for the plane. She couldn't say anything to anyone. That meant she couldn't tell Valerie next door, Carmen, who did her hair, or, especially, her sister-in-law, Gina.

Imogene was a good wife and partner. He planned to tell her on the airplane how much he loved her and how grateful he was for her loyalty and trust all these years that he'd been lugging around his sample case, making just enough to get by.

He'd tell her that he'd been making plans for their golden years all along. That she should trust him now. That this was a critical juncture, a turning point in their lives.

She would panic, of course, and maybe get mad when she realized that they were leaving San Francisco for good. There was a chance she'd threaten to get on a return flight as soon as the plane landed, but she wouldn't make a scene in first class. Willy would have about eight hours to paint a picture of upcoming sunny skies forever.

Or maybe he'd tell her the whole truth—that if he didn't leave now, he would get caught, convicted, and sentenced to life without parole. If she saw him again, it would be through a sheet of Plexiglas, and it would be that way until death did them part.

If telling her that didn't work, well, he sincerely hoped he wouldn't have to hurt her.

Willy banished these thoughts and calmed his mind. He'd been smart and careful and thorough. It was all going to be good.

He stood up from the worn brown sofa and looked out the window to the backyard, where Dick was getting the swing and the bird feeders out of the way of the drones. His nephews and his partner in crime were having an unforgettable Christmas.

He took a mental picture.

Then he got ready to go.

CHAPTER 65

WILLY TOOK THEIR wedding picture off the wall and opened the safe.

He removed a short tube of ten Krugerrands and the packet of forged documents they'd need at the airport. He put the papers and the coins inside his bag next to the cash from Sloane's safe. He added a rolled-up pair of trousers and a long-sleeved shirt, some underwear, and his toiletry kit, then zipped up the bag.

He went back to his father's desk and ran his fingers across the top of it, tracing where he'd carved his initials, for which he'd gotten a pretty good beating. The right-hand file drawer held a box of notes and cards and memorabilia. He flipped through it, memorizing the contents, then took out a spare pair of eyeglasses and closed the drawer.

He'd mailed the thumb drive of family photos and passwords to his banker in Zurich. His attorney had his will and Imogene's, dated two years ago, leaving everything to her brother and his family. He'd told his attorney that in some underground circles, he was a wanted man.

That he could be made to disappear without a trace.

You know what I mean, Phil? Take care of my family.

Having buttoned up the past, Willy turned his mind to the next twenty-four hours.

He and Dick had been planning the upcoming job for months. Over the past week they'd flooded the tip lines with a shit-storm of fake clues, exhausted the police department with isolated violent events and rumors of worse to come. They had drilled down on the knowns and unknowns. They had baked flexibility into their calculated terror attack so that they could manage mavericks, the unexpected accidents and incidents, and score as big as their dreams.

Today was their day.

Loman was checking the scoreboard at the start of the third quarter when the program was interrupted by local news. A cop was telling the windblown woman with the microphone that a body had been discovered in a car parked near the bay off Fort Point.

The cop said, "He's a white male in his forties, medium weight and height, medium-length dark-blond hair. This man has been dead for three or four days, approximately. There was no ID on him. He was wearing jeans, a blue plaid shirt, and a red down jacket.

"If any of your viewers have knowledge of a missing person fitting this description, please call our tip line. That's all I can say at this point."

Loman clicked off the TV. It was about time the dead man

made his curtain call. Not a problem. Julian had completed his mission. Loman took another look at the drone airfield in the patch of yard below, watched Dick teaching the kids about the electronic controls and aerodynamics.

Then he went downstairs to help the women and carve the bird.

CHAPTER 66

BRADY SAT INSIDE the surveillance van parked on the verge of JFK Drive northeast of the de Young Museum.

The interior of his command post was lined with video screens, and he had three computer specialists with him monitoring live feeds from dash-cams in patrol cars in and around the target.

While Brady watched over the de Young operation, he was in contact with five other commanders who, like him, had eyes on possible heist targets. SFPD tactical teams and dozens of security companies stood by, braced for a Loman attack, whatever the hell that would look like.

Brady couldn't imagine Loman and his crew getting away with an armed robbery in daylight under the watch of so many cops. Just couldn't happen.

Calls came in from all points, and Brady took them, noting the reports of nothing stirring, not even a mouse.

And then a face appeared on-screen. It was Lindsay Boxer, holding her badge up to the camera, Rich Conklin standing behind her inside the surveillance van on Geary at Stockton.

"Boxer. What's up?" Brady said into the webcam.

"Do you know about the body just pulled out of a car trunk?"

"No, I don't. What's this about?"

She held up a morgue photo on her phone. He recognized Julian Lambert.

"Lambert, huh? What does the ME say?"

"Homicide. Cause of death was two rounds, one to the back of the neck, one to a vertebra. The bullets are the same caliber as the ones taken from Sloane's body."

"Please tell me that the gun is in the system."

"Sorry. No."

"And the car?"

"VIN was traced to a junkyard in Baton Rouge, Louisiana, in '05. That's all I've got, Lieu."

Brady told Boxer he'd call forensics in a little bit, then said grimly, "I'm not surprised that guy turned up dead. While we're chasing our tails, Loman has a game plan. I think he just rubbed out the only known witness against him."

CHAPTER 67

CONKLIN AND I stared out the windshield of our un-marked car, parked near the spot where Julian Lambert had bowled over an old gent holding a bag of belts and ties.

That was the beginning of the Loman affair as we knew it.

Lambert had told us he had overheard a street person named Marcus saying that a guy named Loman—first name, last name, fake name, he didn't know—was planning a big heist on Christmas.

His unconfirmed tip had led us to Dietz, and after two nights in holding, Lambert had been released and then, shortly thereafter, professionally executed.

The morgue photos of Lambert's body showed lividity from lying in a fetal position in the trunk of a car. The shot to the back of his neck, fired at close range, suggested that he'd trusted his killer enough to turn his back to him.

I remembered everything about Julian Lambert, the

way he'd spoken, what he had said, what he'd looked like—vibrantly alive.

Conklin noticed that I'd gone quiet.

"You okay, Linds?"

I shook my head, trying to understand my own mood. I said, "It's weird, but I felt like I knew him. I mean, he was a small-time thief. He was something of a charmer. The lead he gave us to Chris Dietz was the only real lead we've had. Did talking to us put Lambert on Loman's hit list? Is he dead because he talked to us? I think so."

"Lindsay, we didn't kill the guy. Please. Don't torture yourself."

I needed to talk. We kept our eyes on the street, the thickening traffic, the pedestrians with coats and hats going in and out of hotels, going to and from the skating rink in Union Square, near the soaring artificial tree.

I said, "Rich, what are we looking for? We have a bunch of pieces and parts that add up to a big fat pile of nothing."

He agreed, and while watching the scenery, we tried to connect the dots yet again, going from Lambert to Dietz with the circled map to the de Young Museum and Dietz's girlfriend, Dancy, who'd confirmed the name Loman.

Then the mayor was threatened, and informants all over the city gave tips to cops they knew. This bank, that art gallery, the San Francisco Mint—all were named as possible targets.

We took down two nickel-bag drug dealers, dupes or extras who didn't actually know anything about Loman or the job. And then, of course, there was the savage murder of a jewelry-store manager and a reported anonymous tip that Loman had been seen leaving the premises.

That brought us to last night, when a cop's son who had picked up some chat-room braggadocio told Jacobi about a possible plan to hit a big computer company. Rich and I sat in the car overlooking Union Square and chewed on that bit of chatter. We concluded that unless Loman had an army and air cover, hitting BlackStar VR made no sense.

It was Christmas Day. Like almost all businesses, the offices would be closed.

Was the crime teed up and ready to go? Had it already been committed?

Apparently, our mayor didn't think so, and he wasn't going to call off his bodyguards or the SFPD until Loman was in jail.

At the same time, while every cop in the city was chasing the phantom Loman, there'd been a fatal stabbing in the Tenderloin, a shooting at a cash machine in the Marina, a vehicular manslaughter or outright homicide on Jackson, and a domestic dispute in Bayview that had ended with a child dead and a wife in a coma.

I was thinking of phoning Joe just to say hello when dispatch called on our radio channel. I grabbed the mic, and day-shift dispatcher May Hess said, "Sergeant, can you take a call? There's a woman named Cheryl Sandler on the line. She claims to be a close friend of Julian Lambert, deceased."

"Put her through." I couldn't say it fast enough.

CHAPTER 68

A TEARFUL FEMALE voice said, "Sergeant, the medical examiner's office told me to talk to you. What should I do?"

An hour later Conklin and I were in the box with Cheryl Sandler. Tall, thirty, and pretty, she had boy-cut platinum-blond hair and wore a black dress and jacket; her eye makeup was smudged. She had an arrest record for running out on a restaurant check as well as convictions for shoplifting and returning the stolen merchandise for cash.

She and Lambert had petty theft in common.

I asked routine questions about where she lived and worked, and after she'd filled in those blanks, she told me about Julian.

He had a wonderful spirit. She loved him. They'd spent the night together at his place five days ago, before we'd pulled him in for his grab-and-dash on Geary. She told us that Lambert had called her from the jail and they had made plans to get together after his release, but he had stood her up. That wasn't like him. At all. She went to his place and looked around. Nothing had been disturbed since she'd been there last. She was going insane worrying about him but figured maybe the police had moved him. Maybe he couldn't use a phone.

And then, this morning, she'd seen the TV report about the man's body being pulled from a car trunk. She'd called the hotline that was on the screen and was transferred to the ME; she'd ID'd Lambert from his morgue shot.

Cheryl's story seemed logical. She was understandably distraught and jittery. I suspected she was coming down off a drug high.

"I never, ever, ever expected *this*," she told us.

I asked, "When you last saw Julian, how did he seem to you?"

"Excited."

"Excited about what?"

"Christmas was coming and…" She shook her head, wrapped her arms around herself, and cried. "He was the sweetest boy. Ever."

Conklin handed Cheryl a box of tissues and said, "Can I see you for a minute, Sergeant?"

I left the room with Conklin, and we took up a position on the other side of the mirrored observation window. The young woman had put her head on the table and seemed to be sobbing.

"What's your BS meter saying?" he asked.

"Too soon to tell," I said. "What do you think?"

"If it's an act, it's a good one. I'll get her some tea."

"When you come back, why don't you take over?"

Conklin has a way with women. In fact, he's famous for it. I went back into Interview 1 and told the young woman that Inspector Conklin would be right back.

She said, "How can Jules be dead? How did this happen?"

I said, "Let's try to figure it out."

Conklin hip-bumped the door and came in with tea for three in paper containers. He found a clean ashtray for the tea bags, set down a dish of sweeteners, and took his seat across from Cheryl.

He said, "Sorry to have to ask you personal questions, but you may be the only person who can help us."

She nodded. Wiped her eyes. "I want to help."

Conklin asked, "How long have you known Julian?"

"We've been together about three months, but I've known him for a year or so. We hung out at the same bar. Had some bar talk, you know. Flirting."

Conklin said, "Did he seem worried about anything or anybody? Had he been threatened at all?"

"No, that's the crazy thing. Everyone liked Jules. He was friendly. He was funny, too. But can I tell you something off the record?"

She was talking to Richie now. Asking him if she could trust him. The camera in the ceiling was rolling.

Conklin said, "Of course, Cheryl. Go ahead."

"I think there's going to be a big robbery at the airport. Something to do with US Customs."

"Julian told you that? He specified customs?"

"I think he was going to be a lookout. He told me that the crew chief is a big-time robber and that he's cold-blooded.

239

You know what really scares me? If he found out that Jules talked to the police when he was arrested…"

Conklin was still giving Cheryl Sandler his full attention.

He asked her, "You're sure he wasn't making stuff up to impress you?"

"He isn't like that."

"Okay. Anything else?" Conklin asked her. "Do you know the boss's name?"

She shook her head. I wasn't convinced.

"It's okay to tell us," said Conklin. "You won't be connected to this guy. I promise you."

Cheryl leaned across the table and whispered to my partner. Conklin said, "Got it. Thank you. I'll call you if we have further questions. Wait right here, Cheryl. I'll get a police officer to drive you home."

"I shouldn't be seen in a police car," she said.

"Here's my number. If you think of anything we should know," he said, handing her his card, "call, day or night."

She tucked the card into her bag and blew her nose.

Richie said, "Sit tight. I'll call you a cab."

CHAPTER 69

DICK RUSSELL TOOK note of the active police presence as he drove slowly along the arrival lane outside the International Terminal.

Cruisers lingered in the taxi lanes. Uniformed officers talked to each other as they stood near curbside check-ins. No one even glanced at the seven-year-old gray Prius.

Then again, a number of these "cops" were on Willy's payroll.

There was rapid movement up ahead: Willy sprinting across the street to the curb and hailing him. Dick brought the car to a stop but kept the motor running as his partner got into the passenger seat.

Dick quipped, "I guess I should ask you: How was the trip?"

"Short and sweet," said Willy, snorting a laugh.

Dick had dropped Willy off an hour earlier, then parked

in a short-term lot and waited for his partner to inspect the site one last time, making sure it was all a go.

"I had a latte and did some people-watching," Willy said.

Both men were dressed in casual business attire, sports jackets and ties. Willy had on wraparound sunglasses and a billed cap, Dick a toupee and a fake mustache, items that were good enough to thwart facial-recognition software if the security footage was scrutinized.

But the airport was teeming with travelers taking the last possible flights to their family Christmases. No one was watching them. They wouldn't stand out on video.

Dick said to Willy, "Let's take another spin around the terminal. We still have plenty of time."

Willy said, "Sure. Let's go."

He buckled his seat belt, then tapped a number into his burner phone. A sweet young voice said, "Hi there, Mr. Loman."

"Hi, Cheryl. How'd it go?"

"In my humble opinion, I think I was very good. Even I started to believe it. Poor me, losing Julian like that. I felt sorry for myself."

She laughed, and Willy said, "I'm sure he would have liked you. Now tell me everything."

Cheryl described it all, how she'd called the hotline, spoken to Sergeant Boxer, one of the cops who had arrested Julian. She told Mr. Loman about being interviewed in the Homicide interrogation room and how she'd cried over her dead boyfriend.

"I let them drag the airport job out of me," she said. "They totally bought it, Mr. L."

"And why do you think they believed you?"

"Because they didn't grill me. They didn't hold me. They didn't give me a polygraph. They gave me green tea and a cab ride home. Oh, and they'll keep me posted on how the case goes."

"Very good, Cheryl. Proud of you."

He told the girl where to find the key to the box at Mailbox Inc. that held her packet of cash, and he thanked her.

"Be safe, Mr. Loman," she said. "Call if you need anything."

"Will do."

He would never see her or talk to her again. Twenty-four hours from now he and Imogene, using the names he'd bought and paid for, would be flying out of San Rafael Airport. No wait times, runway lit and open twenty-four hours; their private jet would take them to New York, and from there, they'd go to Zurich.

But they weren't in the air yet.

Willy was satisfied that the planning stage was over. Everything on the list was checked off and now they were counting down to the execution phase, which was complicated and risky.

He and Dick still had a lot of work to do.

CHAPTER **70**

I CALLED BRADY and heard police radios squawking in the background as I filled him in on our interview with Cheryl Sandler. He was irritated by this vague new lead about an upcoming hit at the airport, and I understood.

He snapped, "Can you confirm this goddamned tip?"

"No, but we checked Cheryl out, and she is who she says she is," I told him. "She has two priors for petty theft. She is, in fact, a seamstress, and as she said, she does live on Waller Street. With a little prompting, she named Loman. I gotta say, she seemed pretty damned terrified."

Brady didn't speak.

"Brady? You still there?"

He said, "I'll make calls. You'll have contacts by the time you get out to SFO."

"Okay. We're on our way."

Until a few years ago I'd been the Homicide squad's

commanding officer. The job had come with a title of lieutenant, an office the size of a bread box, and a hotline to the mayor, but it had made me feel older and crankier. It took me away from what I wanted to do—catch bad guys and have time at home with my family.

I'd stepped aside and Brady got the job. Good for him. Good for me. He was a first-class boss—honest, admirable, brave. I had no regrets.

Right now he was in a surveillance van handling the current shit-storm, and soon he'd call Mayor Caputo, brief him on the latest unconfirmed Loman tip, and ask him to release funds and send help quick.

The mayor would give Brady what he wanted, of course.

Way before my partner and I reached SFO, the SFPD Airport Bureau, Homeland Security, and International Arrivals and US Customs would be on high alert.

The SFO security command center would have cameras on every individual on-site, and agents manning the operation would relay information on any suspicious persons to undercovers throughout the airport.

All Conklin and I had to do was find and contain Loman, a man we had never seen and wouldn't be able to identify because we had no idea what he looked like. "As they say, they don't pay the big bucks for the easy jobs," I said.

"Still standing by for the big bucks."

We smiled and then left the squad room, trotted down four flights of stairs, and exited onto Bryant Street. We located an unoccupied unmarked car at the curb and signed it out. I felt the day slipping away, and at the same time I was having flashbacks of the shooting gallery on the sixth floor of the Anthony Hotel—the sounds, the smell of my own sweat. I was glad that Conklin wanted to drive.

We strapped on Kevlar vests and buckled our seat belts. Conklin gunned the engine.

CHAPTER 71

WE BURNED RUBBER as our car shot out into stop-and-go traffic. I flipped on the lights and the siren, then called the radio room and asked for a dedicated channel for communications with Brady and airport PD.

"You're blue channel, Sergeant," I was told.

Traffic slowed us down when we hit the intersection of Sixth and the 280 Freeway. Richie swerved, jumped lanes, and sped ahead. I gripped the dash, fighting carsickness, until we pulled off the highway onto the airport access road. We stopped minutes later under the International Terminal's swooping marquee that glowed with the holiday light display.

I buzzed down my window and took a few deep breaths. The airport's curbside looked as crowded as it always did during a holiday.

Travelers arrived and disembarked from cabs and hired cars with their luggage and families. They wheeled and humped their bags to airport check-in, unaware that cameras were on them, that some of the porters were undercover cops, that some of their fellow travelers were likewise plainclothes law enforcement dressed to blend in, all of them connected by wireless coms to the surveillance headquarters below the ground floor of the terminal.

I tried to remember if I had kissed my husband good-bye. Yes, I remembered his whiskery kiss and pat on my rump at the door. But I'd left Julie sleeping under the tree with her arm over Martha. I hadn't said good-bye to Julie.

Conklin turned to me. "Ready?"

An airport cop rounded the front of our car, banged on the roof, and, while blocking my door, shouted, "Move your vehicle. You can't park here."

I tugged on the chain around my neck and showed him my badge, saying, "Sergeant Boxer, Homicide. Step aside."

Brady's voice came over the radio. "Conklin. Boxer. Captain Gerald Herz from airport security is commanding this operation. Good luck."

Conklin crossed himself.

I checked that my vest was lying flat under my jacket.

Together, we got out of the car.

CHAPTER 72

SAN FRANCISCO'S INTERNATIONAL Termi-
nal is an enormous structure, almost two million square
feet enclosed by glass and steel. It's got five floors, two
concourses, and twenty-four gates, and it's built to handle
five thousand passengers an hour.

After entering from the street, Conklin and I stood at
the far end of the Main Hall, staring out at the hundreds of
travelers crossing several football-field lengths of terrazzo
flooring between the airport shops and check-in booths
spanning the hall.

We'd been here before, of course, but this time we were
looking for one particular ant in this mammoth anthill.
Unless that person was holding up a sign reading I AM
LOMAN, I had no idea how we or any of the surveillance
crew in the pit would be able to identify our suspect.

I phoned our contact, Captain Herz of SFPD airport
security. When he answered, I told him our location and

gave him our descriptions. I said, "I'm five ten, blond. My partner is taller. We're wearing SFPD caps and Windbreakers."

Herz answered, "Okay, good, I was told to expect you. Walk to the opposite concourse and you'll see the travel agency."

Chrome letters on the overhead marquee across the terminal from where we stood spelled out AIRPORT TRAVEL AGENCY. A man in a dark-blue police uniform and a billed cap raised his hand. I lifted mine.

We crossed the passageway from the entrance and the wall of ticketing stations and shops to where Herz waited for us in front of the travel agency.

I took note of the twenty-five-foot-wide entrance, the size of an average airport shop. The long counter was at a right angle to the front, and a conveyor belt traveled through an opening in the back wall and out to luggage handling in the rear. I also noted a stack of six black nylon suitcases in front of the counter and two uniformed airport cops going through them.

Herz was wiry and tanned and had a steely handshake. There were laugh lines at the corners of his eyes, but he was deadly serious as he briefed us. He explained that short-term baggage storage, twenty-four hours or less, was available only at this location. All left bags were x-rayed before being accepted for storage.

The captain said, "We found a bag outside the doorway this morning, unlocked, no ID tags. Inside the bag were plastic-wrapped kilos of white powder. It could be anything—drugs, anthrax, talcum powder, I don't know."

I thought how damned easy it was for anyone to bring anything into an airport terminal. Unknown white powder. Semiautomatic weapons. Explosives. Bags weren't x-rayed unless people tried to check them in or take them through security.

Herz went on. "Forensics just picked up the lot of it. We've now gone through all of the bags in storage. Nothing looks hazardous or particularly valuable. Everything is labeled. But..."

I tried to wait him out, but after ten seconds or so, I had to say, "But what?"

He said, "But a tip just came in to airport security, a woman saying that there could be a nerve-gas attack coming over the HVAC system. The operator said, 'Please repeat that,' and the caller said, 'Loman is targeting the cargo area,' then hung up," Herz said. "We couldn't trace the call."

CHAPTER 73

I WAS STARING at Herz, imagining nerve gas billowing through air-conditioning vents, paralyzing airport personnel and travelers—to what end? I pictured rows of body bags.

I could see it in Herz's eyes. He, too, was trying to part the fog surrounding this terror threat, figure out what it was and how to shut it down.

"I've got guys going through HVAC, and the surveillance room is working overtime."

Herz went over the basics, and even though I had a pretty good idea that there were cameras in every niche of this terminal, including the baggage areas and the bathrooms, it was reassuring to hear him describe the pit.

I could see it in my mind's eye: the whiteboards around the room covered with notations, the names of security officers and the number assigned to the unsubs—unidentified subjects— they would follow through the airport.

Until the unsubs were cleared, they were active and would have tails listening to their conversations, looking over their shoulders to see their tickets, following them into restrooms, and staying with them to security check-ins; TSA would take it from there.

Thousands of people an hour had legitimate reasons to be in the airport. It took only one with a weapon to turn the terminal into hell.

Herz said, "Along with the assigned undercover operators, we've got thirty plainclothes on this floor. Homeland Security is working the rest of the terminal, including all points out to the gates. TSA has been notified. Customs has been notified. SWAT is on standby."

I said, "Good, good," as I stared up through the artwork hanging from the high ceiling to the mezzanine levels and then back down to the terminal's vast Main Hall.

"Seeing around corners is one thing," Herz said. "Looking into the minds of psychos is something else. I'd like to shut the whole place down, but I can't. Not based on an unconfirmed tip from an unidentified tipster."

I thought about that as the Ronettes' version of "Sleigh Ride" filled the hall.

Herz continued, "I sent a uniformed detail out to the cargo terminal." He indicated the far end of the hall, where open-sided escalators carried passengers up to the higher floors and the AirTrain station.

"That was fifteen minutes ago," Herz said. "So far my guys have seen nothing suspicious."

I told Herz that although the phoned-in tip sounded typical of false leads we'd gotten over the past four days, sometimes the tips led to killings. I was saying, "We'll head out to the cargo area—" when a woman yelled, *"Gun!"* and three sharp reports rang out across the terminal.

Adrenaline shot through me before the echoes died out. I drew my nine and Conklin did the same. The woman yelled again, this time saying, *"Police. Drop your guns."*

I couldn't see her. I couldn't locate the cop.

People screamed and dived for the floor, threw themselves on top of their children, jumped behind counters, or raced into shops for cover. Others froze, immobilized by fear.

Conklin and I exchanged looks, each knowing what the other was thinking.

Loman's rumored Christmas Day attack had just become real.

CHAPTER 74

MY PARTNER AND I stood shoulder to shoulder, trying to see past obstacles and through a moving scene of terrified and screaming people.

A female cop had shouted, *"Police. Drop your guns."*

Guns had fired. Had she been hit? Where was she?

A thin woman in tights and a long red pullover with a gun in her hand appeared twenty yards down the main passageway from where I stood and took cover in the news shop.

Herz was barking into his phone, and I figured out that the woman was an undercover airport operator, Heather Parsons.

Parsons yelled again, this time at passengers and by-standers, *"Everyone get down on the floor and stay down."*

Three more shots were fired, and I saw a couple of uniformed cops dash out from the souvenir store three shops down from Parsons on the concourse and go out to the ticketing area that bisected the Main Hall.

Parsons took a stance, and, aiming at the cops, shouted, *"Hands up. Stay where you are."*

I saw that she couldn't get a clear shot. She didn't fire.

I said to Herz, "We're going after them."

He nodded an okay.

The uniformed cops who had fired on the undercover were joined by two more cops looking much like them, and all four fast-walked toward the sliding-door exits.

They had a good lead on us, and as we ran up on them, I noticed details of their uniforms that confirmed that they were all wrong. The fabric was slate blue, a color I didn't recognize as a uniform standard. And one of the cops was wearing running shoes, definitely not acceptable in uniform.

These cops were fake, had to be. Were they Loman's crew?

I had tunnel vision now; I was intent on stopping the fake cops from leaving the terminal when I took a sudden blow to my right hip. I fought to keep my balance but failed and slid on the slick terrazzo, my arms windmilling uselessly before I went down.

I was sure I'd been shot, but as I hit the floor, I realized that a man who'd been running with his head down while pulling two heavy wheeled suitcases had T-boned me. Now he cried out apologies and fluttered around me, getting in my way and blocking my view.

By the time I'd brushed him off and gotten to my feet, I'd lost my sight of Conklin.

I started moving, dodging bystanders, yelling out, "Let me through!"

Then more shots rang out, more than I could count.

I took cover behind a shop doorway, and when the gunfire ceased, I peered out into the shrieking, stampeding crowd. I saw Conklin standing behind a column, reloading his gun. I shouted out to him. He waited for me to catch up, and then we sprinted to the next column in the line. Only a minute or two had passed since we'd raced off our mark at the travel agency into a shooting gallery.

But as we reached the end of the Main Hall, we weren't alone.

As airport security and DHS streamed through the terminal, cruisers screamed up to the curb with all sirens and flashers to the max. The fake cops had seen the cars through the glass, and rather than break for the exits, they'd gone for the escalators.

I watched them disappear as the moving staircase took the fake cops to the floors above.

CHAPTER 75

CONKLIN SAID TO me, "They're going to the AirTrain."

It made sense. The AirTrain was a closed-loop shuttle that took passengers around the airport to other terminals, rental-car booths, cargo storage, parking areas, and local transit. An excellent escape route.

Herz had previously sent a detail to the AirTrain, but they had found nothing and were now, no doubt, assisting in the forced evacuation as the terminal was cleared and locked down.

We had the up escalator to ourselves, and we rode it to the AirTrain station on level four. The station was empty when we arrived, but the stubby little shuttle was waiting at the platform with open doors.

I peered through the tinted windows and could just make out a row of passengers huddled in their seats on one side of the train. I counted ten people, men, women, and children, and they looked terrified.

The loudspeaker for this automated train squealed, and the mechanical voice announced, "Please hold on. Next stop Terminal Three."

I conferred with Conklin by hand signal, and with guns drawn, we positioned ourselves on either side of the train's open doorway. I took a breath, let it out, looked at Conklin.

I mouthed, *One, two, three.*

And then we went in.

A horror show was in progress.

A passenger lay on the floor, gripping a bloody hole in his side. At the front of the car, facing us, were the four fake cops. One of them called out, "Drop your guns. Only saying this once."

My heart, already racing, red-lined. My ears rang, my focus narrowed, and the picture fully clarified.

This was a hostage situation.

The primary actor had stringy red hair and was wearing a faded cop uniform that, according to the patch on his shirt, had belonged to a cop in the Las Vegas PD.

Reportedly, Loman had pulled off a nine-million-dollar casino heist in Las Vegas, but the getaway van collided with a gas truck.

Judging from his shooting stance, the red-haired fake cop knew how to use a gun.

Was he Loman?

The other three fakers also wore LVPD uniforms. Two of them had choke holds on two real cops, while

259

the third fake cop pointed his gun at one of the hostages' heads.

I tightened my grip on my nine and spoke in a loud, I-am-not-shitting-you voice. "SFPD. Guns down. Hands up."

A child cried out behind me, "Daddy."

A man's hoarse voice pleaded with the gunman, "In God's name, let us go."

Conklin was on his phone to Herz, saying, "They're on the train."

This was as dangerous as it got. We were outmanned, civilians were in the line of fire, a man was dying on the floor, and we'd just executed our only plan B.

The speaker on the platform screeched. The mechanical voice spoke. "Doors closing. Please hold on."

I had a two-handed grip on my gun, and I knew who I was going to shoot first. In that long second, as the red-haired gunman and I stared each other down, a gloved hand holding an M4 with an EOTech sight came through the open door.

One shot was fired.

The red-haired fake cop's blood and brains and skull fragments splattered on the wall behind him, and he dropped to the floor.

Had we gotten him?

Was Loman dead?

CHAPTER 76

HERZ AND FOUR SWAT commandos in full tac gear came through the open doorway, and the fake cops dropped their weapons. They were thrown to the floor hard, then frisked and cuffed. Their guns were taken into safekeeping.

The automated voice came on: "Doors closing. Please hold on."

Herz opened a compartment near the door and threw a switch. A faint electric hum I hadn't noticed before went quiet. This train would not be going anywhere.

I knelt beside the victim on the floor.

"What's your name?"

"Sandy."

"Take it easy, Sandy. We'll have an ambulance here fast. Who shot you?"

He took one of his bloody hands away from his side and

gestured toward the crumpled body of the headless cop behind him. The injured man groaned and said, "Him."

"Why did he shoot you?"

"I rushed him."

"You're military?"

He nodded. He was going pale, and there was a good chance he could bleed out. Conklin leaned down and told the injured man that he had called for EMTs.

"They're in the terminal now, on their way up to you."

While I took USMC sergeant Sanford Friedman's contact information, Herz ID'd the phony cops, and the sobbing, shell-shocked passengers collapsed against one another.

Herz was holding the fake cops for Homeland Security. They were standing with their faces against the wall, and I noticed that one of them was trembling. He was a big, imposing monster of a guy, but he looked to be the weakest link.

After he'd puked, I told Herz, "I want this one."

Conklin and I took the guy who was definitely not a cop to the far end of the train and I said, "Tell me about Loman."

"I can't."

He didn't say, "I don't know who you're talking about" or "You guys just killed him." The fake cop said, "I can't."

Conklin and I kept him on the train as the flood of law enforcement cleared it. EMTs followed moments later and got the injured man onto a stretcher.

When Conklin and I were alone with the bulked-up dude, I said in a motherly tone, "I want to help you. I'm Sergeant Lindsay Boxer. What's your name?"

CHAPTER **77**

NEWS OF THE dramatic airport closing and cancellation of hundreds of flights out of SFO had flashed across the country.

People were really frightened. They wanted answers.

About ten minutes had passed since we'd begun our witness interview inside an airport interrogation room. The large, trembling fake cop was white, twenty-eight years old, with a thin mustache, a buzzed haircut, and a few messy tats on his neck obscured by the collar of his uniform.

He said his name was Benjamin Wallace.

We had put Wallace under arrest for carrying an unlicensed gun and then read him his rights. I accessed our database with my phone and ran his name through the system. Benjamin R. Wallace was clean, and his DMV photo matched his mug.

He told us that he was currently a security guard for

a clothing shop downtown, the Men's Clubhouse. Conklin called the place, and Wallace checked out.

My partner and I had to work fast to build a rapport with Wallace and make him see that it was in his best interests to give Loman up. Any minute now, the door to this small room was going to swing open and Homeland Security would take Wallace away before we'd heard his story, before he'd told us about Loman.

I'd pegged Wallace as a low-level actor. Chances were this young security guard with no prior record would be open to making a deal. I took a seat across from the shivering hulk and relaxed my face, hoping to look sympathetic.

"Ben," I said nicely, "you understand your situation? If the victim who was shot inside the train dies, even if you didn't shoot him yourself, you're going to be charged with accessory to murder. If you discharged your gun at all, that's assault with a deadly weapon. I see a real chance you're going to be charged with kidnapping."

He nodded, gulped, looked like he was going to puke again. There was a garbage can under the computer stand by the door, and I brought it over to him.

I continued. "Homeland Security is going to charge you with terrorism. That's a federal offense. You're still a kid. You could spend every last day of your life in a maximum-security prison with no chance of parole."

I let that sink in. Tears slipped out of Ben's downcast eyes.

I kept going. "Right now your only two friends in the world are Inspector Conklin and me. We've both been shot at today. Speaking for myself, I'm in a bad mood. But we need help catching Loman. You help us, we'll help you. That's a limited-time offer."

"I don't know Loman," Wallace said. "I know his name. That's all."

Conklin, a.k.a. the good cop, said, "Ben. We know you aren't the key man in this operation. You got swept up in something and now you're in way over your head. You're a small fish. But small fish sometimes end up in the boat if the big fish can't be reeled in."

Ben was nodding.

Conklin said, "Let's start at the beginning. See where we go from there."

CHAPTER 78

I LEFT THE interrogation room, dried the sweat from my face with my sleeve, and reset my ponytail.

Then I wandered the hall until I found the vending machine. After three bottles of water had plunked down the chute, I picked them up and returned to the box.

I pushed a bottle of water across the table to Wallace, handed one to Conklin. Then I sat down next to my partner and just kept quiet while he ran the interview. Wallace appeared to be responding to him.

Wallace told Conklin, "It was my brother, Sam. He's the one who got me into this airport job."

Conklin encouraged Ben Wallace to keep talking. The story he told was this: Ben's brother, Sam, age thirty, had once been arrested for an unarmed liquor-store shoplift, caught with a bottle of ten-dollar hooch under his jacket. He was arrested, pleaded guilty, got bail, and immediately fled. There was a warrant out for Sam Wallace's arrest, but he wasn't one of the top ten, or even one of the top ten thousand, most wanted. So he was free, doing odd jobs, living with whoever would put him up, including Ben, but most often living on the street.

Ben went on to say that last week he'd gotten a call from his brother about a man named Russell—whether that was a first name or a last name, Sam didn't say—who worked with Mr. Loman, apparently as an agent or deal broker. Through Sam, Russell was offering Ben fifteen thousand dollars to be part of a robbery crew. He would be given a uniform and a gun, and all he had to do was put on that uniform and meet up with the three others in the crew at the airport outside the International Terminal. The uniforms would get them through security, and after they were in, they were supposed to take the AirTrain out to the cargo terminal.

He went on to say, "Once we got to cargo, we had to look for a wooden box about one cubic yard in size."

He tried to show us, but the cuffs gave him only about twelve inches of range. "The box was, like, marked with Japanese letters, and some canvas bags of papers were inside. We were told that the papers were none of our business.

"Once we had the bags, we were supposed to leave the cargo area and go outside to the parking lot. Russell was going to pick us up in his van and take us to a drop-off, I don't know where.

"It was supposed to be easy-breezy," Wallace said, sniffling and crying now. "Look like airport cops, act like airport cops. Take the train. Grab the bags. Get the hell out. A half day's work for fifteen K. I'm happy to make fifteen thousand a year."

I believed that Ben Wallace hadn't questioned his third-hand instructions. He hadn't doubted what he'd been told, that the job was a no-brainer.

But I couldn't contain myself. I had to jump in.

"What about the *guns*?" I said. "What did you think about having a loaded *gun* in your possession?"

"It was just for show," he said.

"But you fired it," I said.

He nodded miserably.

Guns for show. *Tell that to the former US Marine with a gut shot that might kill him.*

I'd been keeping my temper in check, but I was tired and I was convinced that Wallace knew where Loman was and how to find him.

I said, "Ben, that's a nice story, and I feel bad for you. You were used. But none of what you've told us gets us to Loman or even to his second in command. I'll bet one of your dumb-ass crewmates might have some information for us. Maybe even be smart enough to throw you to the Feds and take any kind of deal in exchange for revealing Loman's whereabouts."

After pausing to let that sink into his muscle-bound head, I said to Wallace, "Speak now, or I'm going to call, 'Next,' and interview one of the others on your crew. Ralph Burgess looks ripe to spill. And I'm going to launch an APB to grab up your stupid brother. There's a warrant out for Sam. I think we can wring the truth out of him."

Conklin said, "I like that idea, Sergeant. Ben? Anything else you'd like to say?"

Ben Wallace shook his head no.

Conklin and I got up from our chairs. Conklin started to drag Wallace to his feet, but he twisted, bucked, started yelling, "Okay, *okay. Please.* I have a pacemaker. I could die right here."

I believed that. Steroid abuse could do major damage to vital organs.

Conklin and I sat him back down. Gently.

Wallace exhaled, said, "I need a deal."

"No promises," I said, "until we have Loman."

"I'll tell you everything I know," said Wallace.

CHAPTER 79

WALLACE SAID, "BUT first I gotta go."

While Conklin escorted him to the men's room, I sat there in the airless airport interrogation room thinking about our interview a few days ago with Julian Lambert.

Lambert had told us a credible story and we'd believed him. He'd said that he'd heard Loman's name on the street, that he was just a bit player, and that he didn't know Loman at all.

Now he was dead.

Like Lambert, Ben Wallace claimed to be a pickup player. Also like Lambert, Wallace seemed entirely disposable. There was every chance that if he'd gotten out to the parking area, he and his crewmates would have been executed at the drop-off.

In the last hour the airport had been closed. Flights had been canceled. Travelers had been evacuated. News outlets carried the story of a foiled terrorist attack.

Our job was to find Loman, and right now the only living lead to him was Benjamin Wallace. Briggs and Rafferty had been charged with possession of unregistered firearms and drugs—the coke they'd had stashed in their cookie jar. They had a lawyer now and hadn't said a word about Loman.

Wallace was shaky. Was he ready to give it all up?

The door opened, and Conklin settled Wallace back into the plastic chair across from us. Then Conklin started asking questions about Loman's recruiter, Russell. Had Wallace ever met him? Wallace said he had, once. Conklin asked him what Russell looked like, what he sounded like, when he'd said he would pay Wallace his fifteen thousand dollars.

Wallace answered that Russell was above-average height and had dark hair, a pointed nose, and unaccented speech. That he seemed nice. And smart. And that Russell was going to pay everyone off when they got to the van.

I studied everything about Wallace.

I listened to his vocal inflections and observed his body language, eye movements, looking for tells, for lies. I was checking him against all the hundreds of interrogations I'd done, trying to discern if he was telling us the truth.

"This job we were doing," said Wallace, "was supposed to be a whatchamacallit…a head fake."

The little hairs on the back of my neck stood up. A head fake was a ruse. A diversion. A diversion from what?

"How so?" Conklin asked.

"There wasn't supposed to be any trouble. It was supposed to be cut-and-dried, a robbery at the cargo terminal and then out. Loman was doing a different job. I think so, anyway. And it was all going as planned until Leonard went rogue."

What had Wallace said?

Was Loman's big heist still in play?

Wallace took off on a little side road then, talking about how he should have just kept to his lame job, minded his own business, not listened to his dopey brother.

I picked up my water bottle and pounded it once on the table to get his attention. "You said 'head fake,' Ben. That you thought Loman was 'doing a different job.' Dig deep. Tell us about that."

"I don't know," Wallace whined. "I told you five times already, we were just supposed to go to the cargo terminal, open the box, take the bags, and get to the parking lot. Look. Everything that went wrong was Leonard's fault."

"Leonard was the red-haired one," I said. He was the fake cop whose brains were spattered inside the shuttle train.

"Johnny Leonard. I'd just met him, but I knew he was nuts," said Wallace. "He saw cops on routine patrol in the terminal, and he thought he saw someone looking at him wrong, like an undercover, and he snapped.

"Next thing you know, he's shooting and cops are shooting back. And our easy-breezy plan just blew up. It was shoot or be shot. Once Leonard started firing, I knew I was a dead man."

Conklin said, "If you can't tell us about Loman, you've given us nothing."

Said Wallace, "I don't know anything else."

I slapped the table and said, "Okay, then. We're done. Good-bye and good luck."

I meant it.

CHAPTER 80

"DON'T SAY IT like that!" Wallace shouted. "I'm going to be killed. Loman is going to have me killed, understand? Oh God."

Conklin said, "If I'm God, I'm pissed off, buddy. Your crew put a lot of innocent people in danger today, and maybe a US Marine, a passenger on his way to Cincinnati, is going to die. You should pray that he lives."

Wallace nodded and my partner went on.

"You want us to help you? Or do you and your pacemaker want to take your chances with the FBI and DHS?"

Wallace started to sob and shake his head no.

Conklin put his hand on Wallace's shoulder, and I could see something shift inside the young man.

Nowhere to run, nowhere to hide.

He knew that he was done.

Conklin said, "Hey, Ben. We're the good guys. San Francisco police. In about three minutes the Feds are going to come through the door. They outrank us. The federal government trumps local PD. We won't be able to help you, my friend, and that's the truth."

Wallace shook his head some more, choosing between a rock and a hard place. He looked up and said to Conklin, "Loman's going to hit a computer company. That's the real job."

My adrenaline spiked again.

Jacobi had been working on a tip about a hit on a computer company. Had that tip now been confirmed?

I asked, "Where did you get that?"

"Leonard told me."

The dead guy. I said, "What computer company? Give us a name."

Wallace was panting now, sweating profusely, lips trembling. I found him believable. Then again, I'd been wrong before. I cautioned myself not to interrupt Wallace as he went on.

"If I tell you, that's worth something, right? That's worth a cell out of state, where I can get protection?"

Conklin said, "You're going to have to give us the name of the computer company."

"Black Stone," said Wallace. "No. That's not right. Black something. BlackStar."

Conklin put his card in Wallace's breast pocket seconds before two DHS agents came in and took our crying, pleading subject out of the room.

I pulled my phone from my pocket and called Brady.

CHAPTER 81

I RELAYED BRADY'S orders to Conklin as we edged and fought our way through the panicky crowd exiting the terminal en masse.

"Brady says he's rolling out a heavy emergency-response team at BlackStar," I told him. "Jacobi is in command on scene."

The lanes around the airport were packed with patrol cars, taxis, buses, and passenger cars. Travelers on the sidewalk yelled at baggage handlers and anyone in uniform, shouted about flights they absolutely had to be on, about missing connections, about lost luggage, and about having no place to stay. Lawsuits were threatened and shoving fights broke out, fights that could become brawls.

Cops weren't charged with keeping airline customers happy. They had only one order, and it was freaking urgent: to get everyone out of the airport.

The sounds of the stalled traffic, the horns honking and sirens blaring, was the very definition of hell on wheels.

Our unmarked squad car was hemmed in at the curb, and we went Code 3 in place, blasting the sirens and the lights, leaning on the horn, until we were free to move.

Conklin drove, and we had just cleared the airport lanes when Jacobi's voice came over the radio. "I just heard from Brady," he said over our dedicated channel. "You both okay?"

"Yes. What's your location?" I asked.

"I'm in the surveillance van in the Truby Street parking lot. It's right outside the BlackStar VR campus."

"We're on our way out to you," I shouted over the mike to my dear old friend and former partner. "Be careful."

Conklin took us onto the 280 Freeway north and from there past Colma, where the dead outnumbered the living. Colma contains the cemetery where a lot of people I know are buried. My mother is there. When we drove past Woodlawn Memorial Park, I placed my palm against the window. *I miss you, Mom.* And then we were speeding through the Sunset District and Golden Gate Park.

I saw other unmarked cars leaving the park from their stakeout of the museum, some heading out to the airport and some, I hoped, to BlackStar's campus.

Jacobi had sent a map of the BlackStar compound, and as we drove, I told Conklin what we needed to know. He took Veterans Boulevard into the Presidio, then made a series of turns that brought us past the Main Post. Forty-five minutes after we'd left SFO, I could see the BlackStar VR campus on our left.

It looked idyllic, a compound made up of half a dozen brick buildings built in the style of the old army barracks and officers' quarters, located on twenty green acres fronted by a small lake with a waterfall.

I read out the function of each building.

"Buildings one and two are labs," I told my partner. "That's got to be new product development. Could be a Loman target, I'm guessing."

I consulted the map and went on.

"Buildings three and four are executive offices. Building five is the BlackStar museum, and six is a tourist destination devoted to digital displays, like light shows. It also has a bank, a Starbucks, restrooms, a tourist info center."

Conklin pulled the car into the main lot, where we could see the attractive red buildings arranged like two loosely cupped hands, and the roads and footpaths leading to them.

It looked calm, but I knew what Brady meant when he said he'd be rolling out a heavy emergency-response team.

Cars in the lot and streets near the campus would be occupied by cops. SWAT would be manning ordinary-looking vans. A couple of ambulances would be in the vicinity, and Brady would have undercover operatives inside and outside the buildings, whatever he could pull together on Christmas.

I got Jacobi on blue channel. He'd seen our car pull in and was on his way over from his post.

Minutes later I saw his hulking form limping across the parking lot. I buzzed down my window and Jacobi stooped so he could see in.

"Brace yourself," he said.

"I'm braced," I said.

"That mutt you grilled at the airport. Wallace. We picked up his brother, Sam, who gave up a name. Brady sent this."

Jacobi fiddled with his phone. His tech skills were not the greatest. He swore a little, then said, "Okay. Here he is."

He put his phone up to the window so we could see the photo on the screen. It was a candid shot of a balding, middle-aged man carrying a large briefcase, heading into a jewelry store on Post Street.

"Meet William Lomachenko," said Jacobi, "a.k.a. Willy Loman. He has no record. But we now know everything about his public life."

CHAPTER 82

I STARED AT the photo on Jacobi's phone.

The picture was low-res, as if it had been taken from security-cam footage shot at the end of the day. I could see the light from the storefront reflecting off the man's scalp. I noted his double chin, his paunch, his unremarkable clothes. William Lomachenko could be invisible in plain sight.

"*This* is Loman?"

"So I've been told," said Jacobi.

It was a huge breakthrough. We had a name and a photo ID, and with that, we'd learn more.

I passed the phone to Conklin and asked Jacobi, "What do we know about Mr. Lomachenko?"

"He lives on Avila Street. Been in the same house for twenty years. He's self-employed. Buys gold chains from overseas and sells them locally. His wife, Imogene, does the books. We have her in custody as a material witness."

Conklin said, "No kidding."

Jacobi smiled. "Chi and McNeil are questioning her, making sure she doesn't give Willy a heads-up. She says that we've got the wrong man."

Conklin said, "Any chance she mentioned where we could find her husband right now?"

"Imogene told Chi and Cappy that the mister is out doing last-minute errands. He's planning a surprise for her birthday."

I stared through the windshield, hoping to see an ordinary-looking white man in his late forties or early fifties, approximately five foot eight, 180 pounds, balding, with a potbelly, the kind of man who looked nothing like anyone's idea of a criminal mastermind.

Jacobi said, "FBI has people inside the Lomachenko house in case he comes home. If he calls his wife, we'll trace the call."

My old partner looked good for someone who'd been on watch inside a surveillance van for about sixteen hours without sleep. I asked him if there had been any disturbances or if anything on this large campus seemed like a possible target for a heist.

"It's busy," he said. "The CEO told me that BlackStar was officially closed until New Year's. Maybe he meant closed for business, because it looks like Christmas isn't a holiday for BlackStar employees."

We watched people walking between the buildings, most of them millennials in tight jeans and pullovers or satin BlackStar baseball jackets. I also saw several older, professorial types.

I noticed ordinary unmarked cars like ours in the lot, as well as dozens of cars with BlackStar parking stickers. I saw an undercover cop I knew standing by the waterfall, two others smoking cigarettes and strolling as they worked their phones.

"What's the plan, Chief?" Conklin asked Jacobi.

"Special response teams have warrants. Risk warrants to seize weapons, and the Feds will have a search warrant for electronics, computers, and like that," said Jacobi. "Couldn't be more than a few hundred thousand computers in this place. After they lock all of these buildings down, the three of us and everyone else Brady can get will go in looking for Mr. Lomachenko. Just waiting now for the word 'Go.'"

Conklin swept his gaze across the huge campus, the half a dozen buildings and the expansive greens between and surrounding them, some trees scattered around as well. He sighed. "Lot of ground to cover."

I agreed. "I'm getting out," I said, opening the car door. "I need some air. I've got to make a quick call to Joe."

Jacobi held the door for me, and I'd just gotten my feet on the ground when a shot cracked across the campus.

Around us, some people stopped to listen, some dropped to the ground, and others dashed toward doorways.

I saw no gunmen, no sign of the shooter. I got out of my crouch behind the car door and went to help Jacobi to his feet.

That's when I saw that his face was gray and that he was clutching his thigh.

"I'm hit," he said. "Don't worry."

And then his eyes rolled back and he passed out.

CHAPTER 83

AN EMT NAMED Murphy hustled me out of the ambulance.

Doors banged closed, and the bus, with my dear friend Jacobi inside, took off down Lombard Street, turned a corner, and was gone.

I forced myself to come back to the moment.

BlackStar employees who had been crossing the green seconds earlier had hit the ground or were hiding behind trees as SWAT poured out of their vans and took up positions around adjacent buildings.

I stared out over my car-door shield, looking for the shooter—and something stood out to me. Within the scattered BlackStar workers, I saw three men walking away from the executive offices and toward the corner of the grounds leading to O'Reilly Ave.

They weren't taking cover. They walked with purpose, as if unfazed by the shots and the panic. They were dressed differently from the techs I'd seen earlier sauntering through the campus.

They just looked…off.

The tallest of the three was dark-haired and wearing a leather bomber jacket. The shortest of the men wore a khaki-colored Windbreaker and a billed cap. He kept his eyes down.

The third man was bracketed by the other two. His hair was silver. The BlackStar logo was on the back of his jacket, and I had the impression that he was being propelled forward by his companions.

I grabbed my partner's arm.

"Rich. The chunky one with the cap. Tell me. Is that our guy?"

Sunlight slanted through the copse of trees and into our eyes as the three men took the path heading away from us.

Conklin said, "I can't say for sure."

We crossed the lawns, planning to intersect the path the men were traveling. Then they changed course and walked more quickly toward one of the brick buildings.

My heart was banging hard and I was panting even though I was walking at a steady pace. My gut was telling me that the guy with the cap was the man in the picture on Jacobi's phone.

My gut said that it was Loman. William Lomachenko.

CHAPTER 84

THIS WAS JUST brilliant. Had Russell's shot hit a cop?

Loman stood with his hostage and his second in command outside the side entrance to Building 3. He'd seen cops wearing SFPD Windbreakers cluster around a body on the ground, and an ambulance had pulled up to the main parking lot near the lake.

The three of them were hidden from the SWAT team on the green, but Loman still felt exposed. He reached around Bavar and pulled on the door handle. It didn't budge. A tiny red light centered on a metal plate in the brick wall beside the door caught his attention. Below the light was a small lens at eye level.

His screwup associate stated the obvious. "It's an iris reader."

Loman had nothing to say to Russell. His shot, fired in panic when Bavar tried to make a break for it, had hit a cop, launched a law enforcement response, and guttered the smooth execution of their plan.

But he did speak to Bavar. "Look at the lens."

"I don't think so," said Bavar, laughing. "You shoot me, and this becomes the worst day of your life."

Bavar's contempt despite the loaded guns pointed right at him actually made sense to Loman. Bavar was a cocky bastard but he was not stupid. Without him, there would be no payday.

According to the plan, while the airport fandango was going down, Russell's man on the street, Sam Wallace, had been tracking David Bavar, watching and reporting to Russell when Bavar left his home in his candy-apple-red Maserati. So Loman and Russell had been waiting for BlackStar's CEO superstar when he arrived at his private parking space behind Building 4.

It had worked just like it was supposed to. Until now.

Russell was sputtering, spinning excuses for why he hadn't known that BlackStar would be overrun with staffers today, unable to explain the police presence.

Loman burned as he looked at Russell, standing there with his gun in Bavar's gut.

"I can't know everything, Willy," Russell said. "I had excellent information. It's well known that Bavar always comes in alone on Christmas—"

Bavar said, "Oh. I guess you didn't get my memo to staff last night. BlackStar has a rush order. Santa says all those who work on December twenty-fifth get a bonus."

It was like a lit match had been dropped into a gas can. Loman's anger at Russell exploded.

He moved his gun out of his retirement plan's back and pointed it at Russell's chest. Russell's eyes widened and he started backing up.

"Willy, no, no, no."

"I thought I could count on you, Dick."

Loman fired twice.

Russell dropped, then rolled on the ground, moaning. When he opened his eyes, he saw that Loman still had the gun on him. Russell held up his hand, palm facing Loman, a plea not to shoot.

Loman shot him again, through his palm and into his heart, and Russell, the big gambler, the deep thinker with a scientific mind, exhaled his last breath. Loman wished he could kill him again. Russell had blown their carefully choreographed hit-and-escape strategy.

Loman had planned to milk Bavar for information for a while before killing him, but a reboot was possible. His flight was paid for and the jet was still waiting. He had seed money in Zurich. He'd figure out how to finance his new life once he was out of the country.

He said to Bavar, "Look into the scanner."

Bavar had gone pale. He wasn't joking and smirking now that he'd seen how easy it was for Loman to kill. He put his eye up to the iris reader. The lock thunked open, and Loman pulled on the door, held it open with his foot, and poked Bavar with the gun.

Loman said, "Move."

Bavar did it.

Loman's pulse was pounding loudly in his ears. Shooting Russell hadn't alleviated his anger at all. He flashed on his wife, imagining Imogene sitting in her rose-colored chair in the living room, having packed for an overnight trip like he had told her to. He thought she'd be wearing her engagement ring and the diamond pin he'd gotten her for her birthday. Sweet woman born on Christmas Day.

He had planned a wonderful life for them. Now he thought that he might never see her again.

CHAPTER 85

CONKLIN AND I lost sight of maybe-Loman when the three men suddenly ducked into the space between Buildings 3 and 4. Speeding up, our guns holstered, we continued along the footpath in their direction.

Two shots rang out, then a third.

Conklin and I now ran toward the gap in the staggered line of brick buildings, and there, in front of a side door, was a body that matched Ben Wallace's description of Loman's number-two man. Bullet holes had punched through the tall man's flight jacket, and blood was pooling around him.

Conklin stooped, felt for his pulse, then shook his head no.

I went for the door, pulled on the handle, shook it a couple of times, and looked at my partner.

"Go ahead," he told me. "If this circumstance isn't exigent, I don't know what is."

I fired shots into the door around the lock, hammered in the glass with my gun butt, reached inside, and opened the door.

The lights were on. The hardwood floors gleamed. The white walls were hung with large, framed graphics, and a Christmas tree twinkled in a corner of the sparsely furnished reception area.

Ahead of us, against the far wall, was an unoccupied reception desk festooned with pin lights. Beside the desk, a short staircase and a wheelchair ramp led to an elevator bank.

To our left was a wooden interior door. I tried the handle but the door was locked. Across the room on our right was an identical door—ajar, as if it had been opened in a hurry and not pulled shut.

I phoned Brady and got him. I said, "There's a gunshot fatality outside the south side entrance to Building Three."

"Noted. What else have you got?" I told him I thought that the shooter was inside the building, that he wasn't alone, that the building had to be evacuated and a perimeter set up around the murder scene.

"Conklin and I are inside the building, going after the shooter. We need backup."

I clicked off, and moments later a bullhorn cleared its throat with an electronic squeal and a voice announced, "This is SFPD. We need everyone to evacuate the building right now. Use the front entrance only. Repeat, evacuate through the front entrance only and go to the main parking lot, where you will receive instructions. Thank you."

Conklin and I blocked the shattered side entrance to protect the murder scene. At the same time, we had a clear view of the large, open lobby. Workers appeared, young people in ones and twos, speaking excitedly into their phones, pouring down the stairs from the elevator bank, threading around coworkers, heading toward the main exit.

I searched the faces of every person coming into the reception area.

If my gut was right and Loman was here, he was wearing a khaki Windbreaker and trousers and maybe a billed cap. He'd been herding a silver-haired guy in a black baseball jacket with the BlackStar logo on the back.

Richie said, "Old guy in blue boiler suit at two o'clock."

The man crossing the lobby was wearing dark-blue workman's coveralls. He was balding and paunchy, and he avoided looking at me as he headed for the front doors.

That was *him*, the man in the photo on Jacobi's phone.

Rich yelled out, "You! In the coveralls. Stop. We need to talk to you."

Coveralls said, "Me? Sure. No problem."

Conklin shouted, "Keep your hands where we can see them!"

The subject said, "I work here. I've got ID."

His hand darted into his coveralls.

Rich and I yelled in unison, *"Hands in the air!"*

But the man in blue pulled a gun and, gripping it with both hands, aimed it at us.

"Talk to *this*," he yelled.

We were fifteen feet away from him, but the lobby was swarming with panicked human obstacles who were running between us and the man and his gun as they streamed toward the exit.

We didn't have a clear shot, and neither did Loman.

A young man racing for the doors slammed into Loman's back and shoulder. Loman spun, staggered, then caught himself. He whipped around toward the young man who'd run into him and who was now sputtering apologies as he backed away.

Loman had shifted his eyes away from us. We were closing in on him when the front doors exploded inward and the reception area filled with a dozen SWAT team commandos, fully armed. Terrified BlackStar employees tried to break around the men in black, but the exit was now blocked.

Conklin and I reached Loman in two strides, and I saw his expression change as his mood went from defiance to defeat. There was no way out alive. He was done.

His gun clattered to the floor. He raised his hands high over his head and shouted at us, "Don't shoot. Don't shoot!"

We threw him to the floor, and not too gently.

I cuffed him behind his back, and my partner patted him down. Loman was packing a roll of duct tape in a hip pocket and had no wallet or ID, no other weapons.

Conklin and I dragged Loman to his feet, and still high on adrenaline overload, I arrested him on suspicion of murder and read him his rights. Conklin bagged his gun and handed him off to the SWAT commander, Lieutenant

Reg Covington, who grinned at us, then marched our prisoner out to the van.

Conklin's hands were shaking.

I, too, was shaken. And I still had a question.

"Rich, that *is* Loman, right?"

"Yeah," he said. "We got him."

CHAPTER **86**

ONCE THE FEISTY man in the blue coveralls was inside a squad car heading to the Hall of Justice, Conklin and I, along with a dozen other cops, searched the four-story building for two men: the silver-haired man wearing a BlackStar jacket and the janitor whose uniform Loman was wearing.

We found a brown-haired man inside a supply closet, tied up with strips of undershirt and gagged with his boxers.

When he was unbound and ungagged, he thanked us and told us his name was Steven Kelly. He was in his mid-forties and had been working at BlackStar in janitorial services for five years. When he was partially dressed in the baggy trousers his captor had left behind, he said, "The guy who made me strip held a gun on Mr. Bavar. He made Mr. Bavar tie me up."

I said, "Mr. *David Bavar*? Head of BlackStar?"

"That's him," Kelly said. "The boss of bosses. This is his company."

Kelly walked us to a nearby conference room and pointed out the portrait of David Bavar, founder and CEO of BlackStar VR. That was him, the silver-haired man I'd seen walking between Loman and the tall man wearing the satin baseball jacket.

I called Brady, and this time I got his outgoing message. I left him one of my own, saying that David Bavar, BlackStar's CEO, may have been kidnapped and that we had a suspect in custody.

"Could be Loman," I said. "Brady, we need the security footage, especially from the south side entrance to Building Three and everything you can get from inside."

Conklin drove us to the Hall, and by the time we were back in the squad room, Loman had been booked and the dead man had been identified as Richard Ross Russell of San Francisco.

Russell's prints were on file because he was in the education system, an adjunct professor at San Francisco State University with advanced degrees in science and math. He was unmarried and had no known criminal associates or a record of any kind.

But we had forensics.

A gun had been found in the shrubbery near Russell's body. Russell's prints were on the gun, and GSR was on his right hand. Ballistics had put a rush on the bullet taken from Jacobi's thigh, and the lab matched that bullet to those fired from Russell's gun.

I leaned back in my desk chair and stared up at the TV

hanging high on the front wall. The airport shooting was still top of the news. There were first-person reports of bystanders and porters, and interviews with Gerald Herz and with airline executives.

A mention of the shooting at BlackStar was just a chyron, type crawling along the bottom of the screen, and there was no mention of David Bavar.

I still couldn't make sense of what had gone down at BlackStar. What was the point of it all?

Who had shot Russell—and why? What was the connection between Russell, Lomachenko, and David Bavar? Was this, in fact, a kidnapping?

And, most urgent, where was David Bavar now?

If we were very lucky, security footage might have the answers.

CHAPTER 87

AT JUST AFTER 6:00 p.m., William Lomachenko was wearing an orange jumpsuit and chilling in a holding cell.

Conklin and I were at our desks, eating ham sandwiches for Christmas dinner, drinking coffee, and talking over our upcoming interview with Loman.

We had done our research.

Loman didn't have a police record, and outwardly, everything about him spelled Mr. Average Guy. His house was of the cookie-cutter variety in a working-class neighborhood. He and his wife had an import business, and Loman sold gold chains to local stores. He had an old car. Wore big-box-store clothes.

We had a search warrant for his house, but so far nothing incriminating had turned up. And we were able to get a warrant to look into Lomachenko's finances. The banks were closed today, but we did have a few facts to work with.

One, we had a positive ID on Lomachenko from the DMV photo on file.

Two, we had caught him red-handed at BlackStar, and he was in our seventh-floor lockup now.

I should have felt frickin' elated, but we had to make a case against him or turn him loose. Right now, the man we called Loman hadn't left his fingerprints on anything but the gun he'd been holding when we took him down. I would bet anything that Loman had used that gun on Russell, but even though we had a skeleton crew at our lab over Christmas, it might be days before forensics would process it and get back to us.

Conklin and I talked about how we were going to approach Loman: make him comfortable, befriend him, show him the way out and work from the outside in—or go straight at him hard. If we went at him wrong, he could stop talking. It was his right.

Rich and I were in agreement.

Finding David Bavar was critical and urgent. Getting Lomachenko's confession to killing Richard Russell would hold him as we put the pieces of assorted murder and mayhem—Julian Lambert, deceased; Arnold Sloane, deceased; and the Keystone Cops caper at SFO this morning—into a believable whole.

We didn't yet have proof that Loman had murdered anyone or kidnapped Bavar, but we were prepared to work on him until the sun came up—or until he said, "Get me my lawyer."

Which wouldn't be a good thing. With a good lawyer and a sympathetic judge, he might get bail. And then he might jump.

I balled up my brown bag of sandwich crusts and dunked it into the trash can.

Conklin said, "Ready?"

"After I brush my teeth."

Minutes later we were in our chairs at the scarred gray metal table in Interview 1. With Loman facing the glass and the camera rolling, I took the lead.

I asked our suspect nicely, "Mr. Lomachenko, we don't get it. Why were you at BlackStar VR this afternoon?"

"Tell ya the truth, I'm not entirely sure," he said. "Dick Russell, friend of mine, asked me to come with him. I thought he just wanted company. Someone to talk to or hold his coat."

"Why did you disguise yourself?"

Loman stared at me without answering for a long moment, then he said, "There were cops everywhere. I knew Russell was dead and you guys would try to pin it on me. I wanted to disappear. Saddest thing. That man has been my friend for twenty years. He was almost family."

I said, "Okay. But why did you have a gun? What was that all about?"

"Ah. Well. Russell told me that the head of the company, Mr. Bavar, had stolen an invention of his, some kind of software hack. He said it could be worth millions. Dick wanted to scare Bavar into paying him for this intellectual theft. So he tracked down the information that Bavar would be alone in his office on Christmas. Apparently, it was a habit of his to go to his office and write seven-figure bonus checks for his inner circle."

I listened, teeing up my next question.

I asked, "So how did this go wrong, Mr. Lomachenko? Why did you shoot Russell?"

"*Me?* No. You've got it all wrong, Sergeant Boxer. *Bavar* shot Dick. Not me. But it was understandable. Russell was out of control," Lomachenko said. "He was getting madder and madder, threatening to shoot Bavar if he didn't get a million bucks. Like I said. Dick was shaking him down. I was just standing there, watching, and then Bavar snatched Dick's gun away from him and *bang.* Just like that, he shot him. *Bang, bang, bang.* I didn't stick around to see what happened after that."

"Yes, I see," I said, thinking Loman didn't seem or act nervous. No blinking, no tears. Lying came easily to him. I would even say he enjoyed the attention.

I went on. "So, do I have this right? You say you were just tagging along, and next thing you know, a fight breaks out. Bavar gets the gun away from Russell and shoots him."

"Exactly right. I had nothing to do with this, except that I saw Bavar shoot Dick. Honest to God, I was just window dressing."

No. He was just full of shit.

For the next hour Conklin and I took turns asking Loman about BlackStar. When he'd gotten to the point where he was repeating himself, we asked about other elements of the Loman-related crime spree we'd been chasing for the past five days—the false leads, the dead bodies, and the airport terror attack this morning.

We had a lot. We wanted to let him know how much we had and how closely we'd been keeping track of him, hoping he would slip up or try to make a deal.

But he denied every piece and part of it with a smile.

"Whatever you think you've got on me, you're just wrong. I have nothing to do with any of that." That's what he said.

And we had no proof that he was lying.

CHAPTER 88

LOMACHENKO ACCEPTED THE offer of a cup of water, and Conklin and I had the same.

When the lying sack of crap was hydrated, he said, "I want to call my wife. It's her birthday. She's got to be worried about me."

I said, "You can call her in a little while, Mr. Lomachenko, but we're just getting started here."

"Look, let me say this one more time. You've got me wrong. I'm just a jewelry salesman. Small potatoes. Hey, I've *got* to call my wife. That's my one phone call, all right?"

I said, "You want to speak to Imogene?"

"How'd you know her name?"

I said, "We're holding her, Mr. Lomachenko. In a jail cell."

"What? No. What for? She's a *housewife.*" Finally we'd rattled him.

"And she's also your business partner, actually, because she keeps your books. In fact, we've charged her as an accessory to everything you've done. Including the murder of Richard Russell."

Loman blew up.

"She's a *housewife*. She cooks, does laundry. I'll sue you for harassing her. I mean it. I want to talk to her!"

"We can discuss that later," Conklin said, "after you tell us what you've done with David Bavar."

"I already told you. I don't know him. I don't know where he ran off to when the shit hit the fan," said Lomachenko. "All of this is bullshit. And I'm tired of talking to you. I'm done."

He was done, but we weren't.

Conklin, a.k.a. Inspector Good Cop, said, "Mr. Lomachenko, we have pull with the DA. We've both known him for years. We might be able to help you with the shooting if you tell us where to find Mr. Bavar."

"Fuck if I know where he is. I told you."

We still had no clue as to Bavar's whereabouts. His wife hadn't heard from him, and she insisted that Bavar *would* call home if he could. His car was still in its private underground slot at BlackStar, but a sweep through Building 3 hadn't turned him up. He could be dying or dead. We had to find him.

I jumped back in.

"You know your hands were tested for gunpowder at booking."

"Yeah? No, I didn't know."

He still didn't blink.

"The test was positive."

"Bullshit."

"You fired a gun and we have that gun," I said. "Ballistics is working overtime. About now, they're test-firing bullets from your gun and will compare them with the bullets the ME takes out of Mr. Russell's body.

"Mr. Lomachenko. Your friend is on the ME's table now. Do you want to wait for us to have conclusive proof that you shot him? We don't mind. Because once we have you sewn up for Richard Russell's murder, we're done with you. No bargaining. No deals for cooperation."

Loman stared at me for a long time and I stared back.

He blinked now.

"I shot him."

"You shot who?"

"I shot Russell. It was self-defense. He was paranoid and going nuts. He said that I was on Bavar's side, was waving his gun at *me*. Are you getting this down?"

I pointed to the camera.

"Good. Because this is the truth. He was waving the gun like this, fanning it back and forth between Bavar and me. I didn't recognize him anymore. When he told me that he was going to kill me, I had to shoot him. Bavar opened the door and I ran inside. I wasn't thinking about Bavar. I was thinking about hiding until the coast was clear." He scanned our faces to see if we were buying it. "You can understand that, can't you?" he said. "There's a good chance I was going to come forward and tell the police, but first I had to get my head straight. I never shot a gun before. I never shot a person."

"I hear you," said Conklin. "A gun pointed at you is a life-changing experience. I'm sure you're very upset. But I just want to remind you that right now you've got some leverage. The DA may make some allowances when he charges you for shooting Russell. You know what I mean?"

Lomachenko was silent.

Conklin said, "Tell you the truth, Mr. Lomachenko, the best thing you can do for yourself is to tell us where to find Bavar."

Lomachenko looked my partner straight in the eye and said, "No offense, but I think the best thing I can do for myself is not say another word until I speak with my lawyer."

CHAPTER 89

OUR SQUAD ROOM was empty, and not because the guys on the night shift had stayed home with their families.

Every cop in the Hall of Justice, including the sheriff's department and the motorcycle division, was at either SFO or BlackStar, mopping up after Loman.

I called Brady and gave him the shorthand version of our four-hour interrogation.

"He copped to shooting Russell in self-defense," I said. I asked him again about obtaining security footage from Building 3. "Brady, the footage shot from the doorway could show us what happened to Bavar."

"Boxer, I'm dancin' as fast as I can. We had to locate someone who could access the system. We've pulled the tapes, and we're finding people to look at them. It's late. We'll have pictures from the side doorway as soon as humanly possible. *If* the camera was running. Go home. Now. That's an order."

"I'm defying you," I said. "I'm not done with Loman, not yet. I just had an idea."

Brady told me that he was going to crash his car if he didn't get some sleep.

I said, "Go home now. That's an order."

He croaked out a laugh. "Yes, ma'am."

I texted Joe, told him I was alive but didn't know when I would be home. I sent a long string of *X*s and *O*s, and he texted back: *I'm up. And awake. Julie's asleep. Be safe.*

I went looking for Conklin. I found him in the break room.

"Wut up, Linds."

He looked like he'd been run over by a garbage truck, and I was pretty sure he looked better than me.

I had stashed a chocolate bar in the back of the silver-ware drawer. I sat down, offered to share my snack with Conklin.

He said, "Thanks. But no." I could feel it coming. In another minute he was going to tell me what time it was and put on his jacket.

I said, "Just reviewing what we know."

He nodded.

"We saw Bavar walking with Loman and Russell before they hooked a fast left to the side door of Building Three."

"Right," said Richie.

"So Loman shoots Russell. Maybe Bavar takes off?"

"Possible. And as soon as he can get a phone or find a squad car in the parking lot, he tells the police."

"Or Loman points the gun at Bavar and orders him into the building."

"Let's assume that," said Conklin.

"If that's true, dead or alive, he's in Building Three."

Conklin and I had gone all through that building, look-ing for the janitor and for Bavar. The ground floor had the reception area and a half a dozen conference rooms, all open spaces. The top three floors were filled with small offices. "Is David Bavar's body lying behind a desk in one of the offices?" I wondered out loud.

Conklin said, "Tac teams also went through those offices."

"Yep. But it was fast, a security sweep, looking for a shooter, a body, a person in distress. It will take days before they get maintenance and security people to take them through the building with blueprints. Dismantle it brick by brick."

Conklin nodded his agreement.

I said, "We know one person who can tell us where to find Bavar."

"I'll go up to the jail and tuck Loman in," Conklin said. I washed the chocolate bar down with coffee, went back to my desk, then called Metro Hospital and said that I was Warren Jacobi's sister and I wanted to talk to him.

The nurse on duty wasn't forthcoming. "Says here his phone is off."

"What's his condition?"

"I don't have that information," she said.

"Can you take a message?"

"Sure."

"Please tell him that Lindsay called."

I hung up to see that Conklin was in his seat across from me.

He said, "Loman says his lawyer isn't around. He left an outgoing message: 'Mr. Doheny is away from the office until January second and cannot be reached. He'll get back to you when he returns.' Words to that effect."

Good. This bought us some time.

Conklin said, "He's insisting on talking to his wife. Not that he has any right to."

I said, "You know what? We should go talk to her first."

CHAPTER 90

LOMAN WAS LYING across the narrow bench in his brightly lit holding cell at an unpopulated end of the line.

He jumped to his feet when we brought his wife, Imogene, into the jail. We set her up on a chair outside his cage.

Loman grabbed the bars and greeted her sorrowfully. "Bunny, are you okay? Are you okay?"

She, too, was wearing an orange jumpsuit. I'd woken Brady from REM sleep and filled him in in less than thirty seconds. What we were doing wasn't illegal, but it was unorthodox. We needed our lieutenant/chief to help us make it happen. He had put in the call, and Mrs. Lomachenko had been transported pronto from the women's jail a few blocks away.

She looked her husband directly in the eye. She didn't bother with pleasantries, just got right to it.

"Willy, they said you killed Dick Russell. That's a lie. That's *got* to be a lie. You love him."

Loman's eyes watered up. He looked past his wife and directed angry looks at me and Conklin.

"Can we have some privacy?"

My partner and I stepped ten feet away and turned our backs. Cameras monitored by techs lined the cell block and one was pointing at the Lomachenkos.

Loman said, "I had to do it, Imogene. It was self-defense. He was going to shoot me."

She responded in a strong, unmodulated voice, "William. The police are charging me as your coconspirator. Your accomplice to a *murder*. I must be dreaming. I must be having a very bad dream."

"I'm sorry, Bunny," he said. "Very sorry."

"Sorry for what, exactly, Willy? I don't understand any of this. What did you do?"

He told her a version of the story he'd told us, but this time it was a confession of involvement—and there was motive. It took all the restraint I had to keep my hands still and my eyes on the far end of the hallway.

"I wanted us to have a better life," Lomachenko told his wife. "There was going to be a huge payday and no one was going to get hurt. No one. Believe me, Imogene. Please. I did this for *us*. I had a private jet waiting. You and I were going to fly to Switzerland. I bought a place there for us and filled it with modern art. A beautiful high-rise condo, three bedrooms, overlooking Lake Geneva."

A mirror was angled at the juncture of two walls, giving a view of the block. I saw Mrs. Lomachenko shaking her head vigorously, displaying disbelief and anger.

Her husband went on. "This was your birthday surprise.

We were going to be rich and have nothing but the best for the rest of our lives. You can thank Dick for screwing it up."

"I don't know you," Imogene Lomachenko said. "Twenty years of marriage. A nice life. And you wanted to what? Take all of that away from me? You wanted me to live as a fugitive in a foreign country? Are you crazy?"

Imogene Lomachenko's fury and indignation reverberated throughout the cellblock. Other prisoners laughed. They jeered.

Lomachenko's head was down.

Imogene went on.

"And now what's going to happen to me? I'm going to die in a high-rise cell in San Francisco with a view of a wall?"

"It was an accident," he said. "A terrible accident. If Dick had done his research, we'd have—"

That was my cue.

I said, "Mr. Lomachenko, this just came in."

I looked down at my phone and called up the video our computer specialist had just sent to me.

I said, "There was a camera above the doorway to Building Three."

"What…and so what? I don't believe you. I didn't see a camera."

I said, "It saw *you*."

CHAPTER 91

I'D PREVIEWED THE video with Conklin a moment before, and now I held up the phone so that both Imogene and her husband could see the screen.

The visual quality was exceptional. And now that I could hear the audio, it, too, was clear. What you'd expect from a cutting-edge technology company.

Russell: "Willy, no, no, no."

Willy: "I thought I could count on you, Dick."

Lomachenko was on his feet, shaking the bars. He yelled at me and Conklin, "*Stop that.* For God's sake, stop the film."

The video continued running, and I made sure that Imogene could see every bit of it: Loman pointing the gun at Russell and firing once, then again. The same overhead view showed David Bavar cowering beside the side door and Lomachenko standing over the body of Russell.

Imogene's expression was of wide-eyed horror. She gasped loudly, then covered her mouth with her hands.

We all heard Russell's dying moans and the third shot, the coup de grâce, followed by Lomachenko's voice saying to Bavar, "Look into the scanner."

We watched Lomachenko open the door, tell Bavar to get inside, then follow him in.

I stopped the recording and addressed the man doubled over on his bench, his hands clasped across the top of his head. "Mr. Lomachenko, this is what we call irrefutable proof. Rock solid. We've got you."

When I was sure he'd absorbed that bombshell, I went on.

"Here's your Christmas gift from my partner and me. You tell us right now where we can find David Bavar. You confess in writing to all of it—Richard Russell, Julian Lambert, Arnold Sloane, the airport scam, and the kidnapping.

"Do that, and when we have Mr. Bavar, I'll call the DA and ask him to withdraw the charges against your wife. No promises, but I'll call in favors, and he's a friend."

Lomachenko didn't move, just stayed in his crouch. What was he thinking?

I said, "If you love your wife, Mr. Lomachenko, do the right thing. Let her go home."

PART SIX

DECEMBER 31

CHAPTER **92**

THE HORNS, KAZOOS, and steel drums playing a jazzy version of "Yellow Bird" could be heard halfway down the street from Susie's Café.

It was New Year's Eve.

Cindy, Yuki, and I, along with our spouses and significant others, had commandeered the Women's Murder Club's favorite booth in the back room. Another table had been pushed up for Claire and Edmund Washburn, who were on their way.

Cindy leaned across the table and asked me to pass the bread, her new emerald pendant sparkling.

I asked, "What bread?"

Cindy cracked up. "I said, 'You look good in *red*.'"

I fell apart laughing and Joe joined in, saying, "I keep telling her that a blonde in red is what used to be called a hot tomato."

Now we were all laughing, Yuki spitting tequila, and

I didn't think it was because of my sweater or because I looked like a vegetable or because the joke was so funny.

It was just fantastic relief. Tonight the beer pitcher was bottomless, the spicy food had never been better, and everyone at the table had much to celebrate.

We were all finally off duty. Mayor Caputo had commended Conklin, Brady, and me for going above and beyond the call with Lomachenko and for locating Bavar, whom Lomachenko had bound with duct tape and then stashed in an air-conditioning closet on the main floor.

Bavar had been unharmed and had since made a sizable gift to the San Francisco Police Officers Association, turning a horrible week into *Yahoo*s going into the next year.

Only one thing nagged at me on this happiest of evenings.

I hadn't spoken to Jacobi since he was shot in the thigh almost a week ago. We'd exchanged texts, and he'd sent me a cheery message saying, *Boxer, I'm fine. I'm comfortable in my own bed. Have a drink for me*, but I still hadn't heard his voice.

Joe squeezed my shoulder and said, "Check it out."

I looked up and saw Claire and Edmund cha-cha-ing down the narrow hallway from the bar to the back room. She was wearing a sparkly, low-cut black dress, and they were both glowing from their week in San Diego.

Once they were seated, my closest friend and I got caught up. I told her what she had missed—the hairy, scary tightrope-walking Lomachenko interviews and his complete and somewhat unexpected capitulation.

"We have him on suicide watch," I told her.

"That depressed, huh?"

"Yes. And in Miller's play *Death of a Salesman*, Willy Loman kills himself."

"But the one in the play does it by crashing his car, right?"

I laughed. "Loman is pretty creative. He might go tried-and-true with strips of bedsheet. We don't want that."

I poured a beer for Claire, and she told me about the go-get-'em students in her extra-credit Christmas-break class.

"Some of those kids moved me to tears," she said. "I know at least three of them are going to make stellar pathologists. Two of them are going to be better than me, if you can believe it."

I looked up from her grin to see another friend headed our way—the lovely Miranda Spencer, a daytime-TV-show actor who was both glamorous and down-to-earth. She was also Jacobi's girlfriend.

I was out of my chair, already beginning to shout greetings and a lot of questions, when she smiled broadly and said, "Lindsay. He's right outside. And he's got a surprise."

CHAPTER 93

IT WAS AFTER eleven. I had fully expected to kiss my husband at midnight right here at Susie's.

But Miranda was getting us up and hustling us out, saying, "Hurry, hurry."

We paid up and pushed our way through the raucous bar crowd and out to Jackson Street, where a limo was parked at the curb.

Brady opened the rear door—and there was my dear friend in the back seat, holding a crutch and wearing a huge smile.

"The mayor has had some seats cordoned off for us," he said. "Let's go, let's go."

We all piled in and took off on a fifteen-minute drive through our city, still lit up for the holidays. When we disembarked at Rincon Park, Brady and Conklin helped Jacobi out of the car and blocked for him. Joe put his arm around Jacobi's back and said, "Lean on me, Chief. Put all your weight on me."

We found our reserved-for-SFPD block on the seating walls. We had a primo view of the bay, the ferry terminal, and the bridge decked out in swags of lights.

This was San Francisco in her party dress.

Thousands of people had collected on the Embarcadero to watch flowers blooming in the sky. We had just gotten settled into our seats when the first fireworks were launched from barges off Pier 14. Music was synced to the display, and the crowd cheered with each new explosion.

When the ten-second countdown to midnight came over the sound system, my husband grabbed me. Nearly squeezing the breath out of me, he showed me without words how afraid he'd been for me and how he couldn't bear to lose me.

For the next twenty minutes the sky crackled with rockets and pyrotechnics, all reflected in the water below and capped off with a brilliant grand finale.

My husband and I kissed in the New Year.

I told him, "I love you, Joe. I love you so much."

"I'm so lucky, Blondie. Do I say it enough? I love you, too."

"You say it a lot."

He kissed me again.

And then I cried. The feeling had been building, and it came out in full waterworks with heaving sobs. Joe held on to me until I was laughing again.

My best and dearest friends were all around us, hugging one another, kissing their partners, and I noticed that

I wasn't the only one with wet cheeks. I'd never seen Brady cry.

At Jacobi's urging, we huddled, rugby-style, to wish one another the best of everything. We girlfriends pressed cheeks and ruffled one another's hair before settling back into the arms of our men.

This was it. The best New Year's Eve of my life.

I felt ready for whatever the New Year would bring.

EPILOGUE

JANUARY 2

CHAPTER 94

THE NEW YEAR'S holiday had ended, and for Joe, January 2 began as a workday like any other.

He had kissed Lindsay good-bye as she left for the station, walked Julie to the pre-K school bus, and settled her into her seat next to her favorite aide. Then he went back home, made a roast beef snack for Martha in exchange for a handshake, and sat down at his desk. At ten-something that morning, as he was paying bills in his home office, his desk phone rang.

The caller ID said *Drisco,* a landmark hotel in Pacific Heights.

He picked up the phone and said, "Joe Molinari."

All he heard was soft breathing, so he said, "Hello?" and was about to hang up when a young woman's voice said, "Papa? Papa, it's Francesca."

Joe felt the floor drop away beneath him. The receiver nearly slipped from his hand. He got a grip and said, "Franny? Is that you?"

There was nervous laughter and then she said, "It's me. All grown up and right here in San Francisco."

It felt crazy but he believed her.

The last time he'd seen Franny, she was Julie's age. Just about four. Talking. Asking questions. *Why, why, why?* He hadn't been able to answer the important ones.

He filled the lengthening silence by asking, "Okay to call you Franny?"

"Of course. Okay to call you Papa?"

"Of course."

They both laughed and then Joe asked, "How long will you be here? Who or what brings you?"

The daughter he hadn't spoken to in more than twenty years said, "You, Papa. I came to see you. I have to fly home in two days. To Rome."

Joe loved the sound of her voice, Standard American with a hint of Italian. He said, "Two days? When can I see you? What's your schedule?"

"I'm free until my flight on Friday."

The last time he'd seen Franny, she'd been wearing footie pajamas and sleeping under a mobile of the cow jumping over the moon in the small bedroom with baby-farm-animal wallpaper in the Washington, DC, apartment. The time before that, she was also asleep. And before that, also sleeping, ad infinitum.

He tried to picture her as an adult. "Would you like to have lunch?"

"Today?"

"Yes. I can pick you up at your hotel at say—noon?"

"Perfect," said his daughter—his elder daughter.

They ended the call and Joe spun his chair around and stared out the window at the blue sky. He remembered saying good-bye to her as she slept and then leaving their apartment, not knowing that Isabel was packed and ready to grab Franny and fly away.

What was her last memory of him?

Fighting with her mother, Isabel?

He shook his head, remembering his fractious marriage to his college girlfriend that had shown cracks and fissures right away and had only gotten worse after Franny's birth. His work, the lengthy assignments away from home—it wasn't what Isabel had wanted or expected in marriage.

One day in June he'd come home to find a note stating that she had taken their baby girl to Rome, where her parents lived. Next to that was her lawyer's business card. After that, she'd cut off all contact.

Neither one of them had pushed for divorce, she for religious reasons, he because he thought she would change her mind. Fifteen years later, when Isabel finally filed, he had signed the papers and had to accept that his ex-wife's parents were kind and that Isabel would take good care of Franny.

But had she?

What kind of woman had Franny become?

He swiveled back to face his desk and touched the phone, thinking now of other things he should have asked his all-grown-up daughter. One of them was "How will I know you?"

He just would.

Joe picked up the phone again and called Lindsay.

"Linds? I have something to tell you."

CHAPTER 95

JOE DRESSED IN a blue shirt, blue pants, and a blue-striped tie.

He brushed his teeth again, combed his hair again, ran a soft rag across his shoes. He wanted to look good for Francesca. He had never even said a proper good-bye to her. What if she hated him for some abandonment story Isabel had told her?

He shook his head. Would Isabel have done that? Yes.

Joe looked at the stiff staring back at him in the full-length mirror. He untucked his shirt, stripped off his tie, and pulled on his blue jacket. In the kitchen, Joe poured kibble into Martha's bowl, locked up the apartment, and pressed the elevator call button.

He thought about Lindsay. She had known about Isabel and Franny since their first date, but they rarely talked about his first marriage—or hers. He was imagining the first meeting between Lindsay and Francesca when Mrs. Rose came out of her apartment across the hall.

"Wow, Joe, you look nice."

"Thanks, Gloria. My daughter Francesca. She just called me. I haven't seen her in a long time, not since she was this big." He held out his hand to show someone about three feet tall.

"Oh. I didn't know…how exciting," she said, looking completely dumbfounded. "Have fun. Take pictures."

Joe patted his phone in his jacket pocket, waved, and, telling himself to calm the hell down, got into the elevator. Out on the street, he unlocked his car, got behind the wheel, and drove toward the tony section of town called Pacific Heights. Even with heavy traffic, he arrived at the Drisco at a quarter to twelve.

To steady his nerves, Joe drove around the block twice, slowly, and finally parked in front of the hotel. He sat for a few minutes, awash with feelings—guilt, concern, excitement, more guilt. Should he have fought harder? Gone after Isabel with legal remedies? But he remembered how he'd felt at the time, that they'd put each other through enough stress and that being part of that had to be bad for Franny.

Joe got out of his car, took the short flight of steps to the hotel entrance, went to the front desk, and waited for a woman with four bags and several special requests to get checked in. When the clerk was finally free, Joe said, "I'm here to see Ms. Molinari."

The clerk picked up the desk phone and listened, then said to Joe, "No answer. She must be on her way down."

Joe walked over to the small seating area, two chairs with a round marble coffee table in between and a newspaper lying open on top of it. Joe sat down and began his habitual pattern of close observation, looking around the lobby at the flower arrangements, the gilt mirrors, the pattern of the carpet, the couple speaking to the clerk, and a man on his phone just coming in.

Five long minutes passed. Joe couldn't relax while waiting for Francesca, so he stood up, went outside into the noontime glare, and stood next to his car, where he had a view of the lobby through the doors.

Only a minute later, a tall young woman approached the front desk. Her long hair was dark, wavy. She wore a slim-cut leather coat, a white turtleneck, a pencil skirt.

That was her. That was his daughter.

The clerk spoke with her and then pointed though the glass door.

She walked through the doorway, paused at the top of the steps, saw him, and offered a sweet two-part smile—first tentative, then a grin. She waved and came down the steps.

Joe waved back as images of Franny as a little girl flashed in front of his eyes. The slim young woman stopped an arm's length in front of him and said, "Papa?"

"Franny."

Joe opened his arms to her, and she went to him. He felt her shaking as he enveloped her in a hug.

He wanted to blurt out to her that he was sorry for everything, that what he regretted the most in his life, his biggest heartbreak, was that he couldn't be close to her.

He wanted to spill it all right then, explain that he had no choice but to go along with her mother's unilateral decision, her refusal to let him be part of Franny's life.

Instead, he put his hands on her shoulders and held her away from him. Her eyes were blue eyes, like his. She had Isabel's nose and mouth, his hair.

"You're beautiful, Franny. I'd know you anywhere."

She leaned over and kissed him on the cheek and he kissed hers, but he wasn't expecting her to kiss his other cheek in the European manner.

"I'm a mess," he sputtered. "I can't quite believe this is happening. That you're here."

"Let's go to lunch," she said, smiling and taking his arm. "We have a lot of catching up to do."

CHAPTER 96

FRANNY SAT ACROSS the table from Joe in Spruce, a neighborhood restaurant that catered to business clientele.

The main room was soothing, softly lit, the walls lined with mohair the color of café au lait, hung with black-and-white drawings of Paris street scenes. It had seemed to Joe to be the right place to bring her—low-key, near her hotel, great food—but Franny looked uncomfortable.

He asked, "Everything okay?"

She said, "I've never been to a place like this." She waved her hand around, indicating the whole of the up-scale space.

He understood. She was all grown up, but she was still a kid. He said, "I should have thought more of what you'd want, Franny. I have client lunches here. It's close to home."

"The room is beautiful," she said. "I love it."

They ordered drinks, wine for Joe, a glass of tea for Franny, and as they waited for their entrées, Franny told Joe more about what had brought her to San Francisco.

"When Mama found out that she had cancer, it was too late to do anything about it. Ovarian cancer. It's fast and deadly."

"Franny, that must have been terrible."

"We went over everything during her…last weeks. The loads of photos she'd taken since she graduated from Fordham. Letters from my grandparents. Baby pictures. Some pictures of you."

Joe said, "I have so few things like that to show you, Franny. Why didn't you let me know you were coming?"

"How could I know what you were going to say?"

"I would have said, 'I'll pick you up at the airport.'"

"I know that now, Papa, but a week ago, I wasn't sure if I would come here or even if I would call you. Mama gave me a key to a safe-deposit box in a bank in DC and said she'd left some things there for me. I went to the bank and then, while I was at the airport, I decided to postpone my flight to Rome and come to San Francisco. Spur of the moment."

"I'm so glad you did it. Over-the-moon glad."

"I'm jumping all around. I'm sorry, Papa. Listen, I'm my mother's messenger. She was very sorry, too. About keeping you away. She told me that several times over the last years. She said, 'I screwed up. I was so young. I didn't understand about marriage.' She said if she could do it over again, she would have behaved differently, but it took her about ten years to figure it out. By then, it was too late. This is what she told me. I was a teenager. I had friends. I was growing up Italian. I hope this doesn't hurt, Papa, but she got married again."

"I didn't know. But it's okay. Was he good to you?"

"Giovanni. Yes. He is temperamental, I think you'd say. But a good man. He's a tailor. He made my coat," she said, smiling.

"Giovanni. That's Joe," he said.

She nodded.

He said, "I want you to know that I missed you like crazy. I thought about you every single day. I asked myself a million times what I had done to you by giving in to your mother. Wondering if I'd done the right thing. Your mother was...I don't know the word."

He knew lots of words for her—*spoiled, selfish, uncompromising, willful*—but none of them were appropriate at the moment.

The waiter brought their salads, unfurled their napkins, and placed them on their laps. He asked if they wanted anything else. They said, in unison, "No, thanks."

Franny said, "She told me everything. That she'd left you a note, taken me away, and made sure you couldn't find us."

"I was with the CIA. Of course I found you."

Franny laughed. "Well, there's that."

Joe said, "I wrote. I called. I couldn't even get her to talk to me. In the end, all I could do was trust her. I couldn't offer you much without Isabel."

Franny poked at her salad.

"Since you're an intelligence man, I think I'd better tell you the truth, Papa."

334

"Yes, you should. We intelligence men have our methods of extracting it."

She laughed. And then she said, "Here's what was in the safe-deposit box."

She reached into her purse, pulled out a little black satin bag, and removed two items from it. One of them was a small velvet box. Franny opened the box, and Joe recognized the small but good diamond engagement ring he'd given to Isabel.

Franny showed Joe the other item, a leather-bound book with a lock and key. She said, "This is her diary.

"She tells her diary all about falling in love with you."

"I'm…I'm glad you showed me. I don't know what to say, except that I'm proud of you."

"She said it. She loved you."

Joe felt his throat closing. He nodded. "I loved her, too. Love isn't always enough."

Franny's face was flushed.

"Thank you for showing me your mother's things," Joe said.

"I had an ulterior motive, Papa, for my spur-of-the-moment decision to show up unannounced."

"You have my full attention."

"I grew up as an only child. I was afraid to ask you this in case you said no."

Joe put down his fork.

"I want to meet my sister," Franny said. "I want to meet Julie."

CHAPTER 97

JOE CALLED ME from the car.

He told me that he was taking Francesca for a ride around San Francisco, showing her the landmarks—the Golden Gate Bridge, Union Square.

My husband sounded elated. I could hardly hear him. Not because of the traffic sounds, although there was a lot of that, but because I was trying to take in this earthquake that had come without warning.

Joe asked me questions. When would I be home from work? Would it be okay to bring Franny home for dinner? What would be the easiest for me? We could go out, but he thought it would be best to have a home visit. Because Franny wanted to meet her sister.

I thought about Julie getting this sudden news. She was a well-balanced and secure little girl, but still, she was three and a half. And very attached to her dad. Daddy's baby girl.

I could see her stamping her foot and saying, "No, no, no."

I said, "Can you do the cooking, Joe? Stuff always happens just when I'm leaving work. You know."

"Can I do the cooking? You couldn't stop me. I have a few authentic Italian recipes I'd like to try out."

"I'll pick up dessert."

"Great," he said. "Love you, Linds."

"Okay. Me love you too. Wait, Joe—what is she like? Do you like her?"

"She's great."

"Good. Good. What kind of work does she do?"

He laughed.

"What, Joe? Doctor? Lawyer? Schoolteacher? Nun?"

"Believe it or not, Blondie, Francesca is a cop."

I tried to leave work early, but Brady called an impromptu squad meeting to start off the New Year. Naturally enough, I was required to attend. And make a report on staffing.

"Homicide is bracing for a busy year ahead," I said, and I left it at that.

As soon as escape was possible, I bolted from the Hall and drove to our neighborhood pastry shop, where I picked up a box of cannoli and an assortment of cookies. Then, at just under the speed limit, I drove home.

Joe's car was parked in front of our apartment building. The engine was cold. I checked.

I took the elevator, opened our front door, and called out, "Helloooo. I'm home."

But no one answered. No one was there, not even Martha. I looked around for any kind of clue—Joe's shoes under the coatrack, a woman's jacket on the hook—but there was nothing.

I took the white string-tied boxes to the kitchen counter and smelled marinara sauce, saw covered pots on the stove. Then I saw a folded sheet of notepaper addressed to me.

What now?

I read, *Linds, we've gone for a walk. Be back in a few.*

Joe had noted the time. I checked. It was ten minutes ago.

I took the opportunity to jump into the shower, rinse off, and cool down. Then I thought about what to wear to meet my husband's daughter. I was under the spray, reviewing my scant clothing options, when I heard the sound of footsteps on hardwood and voices in the living room.

I turned off the water and heard Joe and a woman talking, and Julie was piping up, too. I wrapped myself in a towel and was reaching for the doorknob when the door opened. I hadn't locked it. I suppose I gasped.

"Mommy."

Julie was there on the threshold, looking up at me. Still hearing people talking, I looked over her head, but only Julie could see into the bathroom. I stooped down and said, "Honey, I'll be out in a minute—"

"Mommy, guess what?"

"Let me get dressed before I guess, okay?"

I shooed Julie out of the bathroom doorway and darted into the bedroom with my little sweetie calling behind me, "Hurry up."

I reached into the closet for pants, a top, flat shoes. My hair was damp, but I finger-combed it and put it up in a ponytail, and then, ready or not, I joined the party in the living room.

Joe stood up from his chair and so did the lithe young

woman who'd been sitting on the sofa. Martha, wagging her tail, ran to me and pushed at my hand.

My husband said, "Lindsay, this is Franny."

"Hi, Franny," I said, walking toward her. She said, "So good to meet you," but my arms were already outstretched as if they had a mind of their own.

I wrapped her in a hug.

Julie ran over and hugged my legs and Joe stood behind Franny, where I could see him beaming.

My little girl tugged at my shirttails and I looked down at Julie-Bug's precious face. She was grinning.

"Guess what?" she said.

"What?" I said, releasing my stepdaughter.

"Mom. Mom. This is Franny."

"Yes, darling, I know."

"Franny is my *sister*, Mom. I have a *sister*."

There were smiles all around, and then Joe said, "Who's hungry?"

"I'm starved," said my stepdaughter.

"Me, too," said Julie.

"I can always eat," I said.

Franny helped in the kitchen as Joe set the table and then lifted the pan of his amazing lasagna from the oven. I tossed the salad, and very soon, we were all gathered around the dining table. I sat across from Joe; Julie sat between Franny and me.

The awkwardness, the tension, the fear of God only knew what—that was gone.

All of the Molinaris were home, together.

ACKNOWLEDGMENTS

The authors wish to thank the many people who have been essential advisers to our fictitious characters: Capt. Richard Conklin, BCI Commander, Stamford, Connecticut, PD; attorneys Phil Hoffman and Steve Rabinowitz, partners at the law firm of Pryor Cashman, NYC; Hugo Rojas, who advised us in immigration law for this book; Chuck Hanni, arson investigator in Youngstown, Ohio; and the late Humphey Germaniuk, medical examiner and coroner of Trumbull County, Ohio, who sadly passed away in 2018.

We are also grateful to Ingrid Taylar, our on-location researcher in San Francisco, to Mary Jordan, who successfully keeps the many moving parts and pieces in order and on time, to our supportive spouses, Sue and John, and to Team Patterson.

Merry Christmas and happy holidays to all.

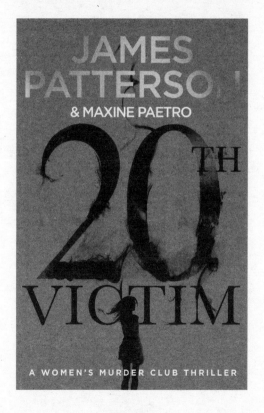

CHAPTER 1

CINDY THOMAS WAS tuned in to her police scanner as she drove through the Friday-morning rush to her job at the *San Francisco Chronicle*.

For the last fifteen minutes there'd been nothing but routine calls back and forth between dispatch and patrol cars. Then something happened.

The Whistler TRX-1 scanner went crazy with static and cross talk. It was as though a main switch had been thrown wide open. Codes in the four hundreds jammed the channel. She knew them all: 406, officer needs emergency help; 408, send ambulance; 410, requested assistance responding.

Cindy was an investigative journalist, top dog on the crime beat. Her assistance was definitely not requested, but she was responding anyway. Tips didn't get hotter than ones that came right off the scanner.

The location of the reported shooting was a Taco King

3

on Duboce Avenue. Cindy took a right off Otis Street and headed toward the Duboce Triangle, near the center of San Francisco between the Mission, the Castro, and the Lower Haight.

With the sirens from the patrol cars ahead and the ambulance wailing and honking from behind, she sure didn't need the street number. She pulled over to the side of the road, and once the emergency medical bus had passed her, she drafted behind it, pedal to the floor and never mind the speed limit.

The ambulance braked at the entrance to the Taco King at the intersection of Duboce Avenue and Guerrero Street. Cruisers had blocked off three lanes of the four-lane street, and uniformed officers were already detouring traffic. People were running away from the scene, screaming, terrified.

Cindy left her Honda at the curb and jogged a half block, reaching the Taco King in time to see two paramedics loading a stretcher into the back of the bus. She tried to get the attention of one of them, but he elbowed her out of his way.

"Step aside, miss."

Cindy watched through the open rear doors. The paramedic ripped open the victim's shirt, yelled, "Clear," and applied the paddles. The body jumped and then doors slammed and the ambulance tore off south on Guerrero, toward Metro Hospital.

Police tape had been stretched across three of the four lanes, keeping bystanders from entering the parking lot and the restaurant. At the tape stood a uniformed cop—Al Sawyer—a friend of Cindy's live-in love, homicide inspector Rich Conklin.

She walked up to Sawyer with her notebook in hand, greeted him, and said, "Al, what the hell happened here?"

"Oh, hey, Cindy. If you hang on, someone will come out and make an announcement to the press."

She growled at him.

He laughed.

"I heard you were a pit bull, but you don't look the part." She wore blond curls, with a rhinestone-studded clip to discipline them, and had determination in her big blue eyes. That was how she looked, no manipulation intended. Still.

"Al. Look. I'm only asking for what everyone inside and outside the Taco King saw and heard. Gotta be forty witnesses, right? Just confirm that and give me a detail or two, okay? I'll write, 'Anonymous police source told this reporter.' Like that."

"I'll tell you this much," Sawyer said. "A guy was shot through the windshield of that SUV over there."

Sawyer pointed to a silver late-model Porsche Cayenne.

"His wife was sitting next to him. I heard she's pregnant. She wasn't hit and didn't see the shooter. That's unverified, Cindy. Wife's inside the squad car that's moving out of the lot over there. And now you owe me. Big time. Give me a minute to think so I don't blow my three wishes."

Cindy didn't give him the minute, instead asking, "The victim's name? Did *anyone* see the shooter?"

"You're pushing it, Cindy."

"Well. My pit-bull reputation is at stake."

He grinned at her, then said, "Can you see the SUV?"

5

"I see it."

"Take a picture of the SUV's back window."

"All right, Al, I sure will."

Sawyer said, "Here's your scoop: the victim is almost famous. If he dies, it's going to be big news."

CHAPTER 2

SAWYER SHOOK HIS finger at Cindy, a friendly warning.

Cindy mouthed, "Thank you," and before she could get chased away, she ducked the tape, got within fifty feet of the SUV's rear window, and snapped the picture. She was back over the line, blowing up the shot, when Jeb McGowan appeared out of the crowd and sidled up to her. McGowan looked like a young genius with his slicked-back hair and cool glasses with two-tone frames. He played the part of journo elite, having worked crime in his last job at the *LA Sun Times*. He had a daily column—as she had—and had done some interviews on cable news after he reported on the Marina Slasher two years ago.

Back then McGowan had implied that San Francisco was small-time and provincial.

"Why are you here?" she'd asked.

"My lady friend has family in Frisco. She needs to see them more. So whaddaya gonna do?"

Cindy had thought, *For starters, don't call it Frisco.*

Now McGowan was in her face.

"Cindy. Hey."

That was another thing. McGowan was pushy. Okay, the same had been said of her. But in Cindy's opinion, McSmarty was no team player and would love to shove her under a speeding bus and snatch the top spot. Or maybe he'd just stick around, like gum under her shoe, and simply annoy her to death.

"Hiya, Jeb."

She turned away, as if shielding her phone's screen from the morning sun, but he kept talking.

"I had a few words with a customer before she fled. I have her name and good quotes about the mayhem after the shooting. Here's an idea, Cindy. We should write this story together."

"You've got the name of the victim?"

"I will have it."

"I've already got my angle," she said. "See you, Jeb."

Cindy walked away from McGowan, and when she'd left him behind, she enlarged the image of the Porsche's back window. A word had been finger-painted in the dust.

Was it *Rehearsal*?

She sucked in her breath and punched up the shot until *Rehearsal* was clear. It was a good image for the front page, and for a change, no friend of hers at the SFPD was saying, "That's off the record."

As she walked to her car, Cindy wondered, *Rehearsal for what?* Was it a teaser? Whatever the shooter's motive for

8

shooting the victim, he was signaling that there would be another shooting to come.

Cindy phoned Henry Tyler, the *Chronicle*'s publisher and editor in chief, and left him a message detailing that her anonymous source was a cop and she was still digging into the victim's identity.

Back in her car, she listened to the police scanner, hoping to catch the name of the victim. And she called Rich to tell him what she'd just seen.

He might already know the victim's name.

CHAPTER 3

YUKI CASTELLANO LOCKED her bag in her desk drawer, left her office, and headed to the elevator.

A San Francisco assistant district attorney, Yuki was prosecuting an eighteen-year-old high school dropout who'd had the bad luck to sign on as wheelman for an unidentified drug dealer.

Two months ago there'd been a routine traffic stop.

The vehicle in question had a busted turn-signal light and stolen plates. The cop who'd pulled over the vehicle was approaching on foot when the passenger got out of the offending vehicle and shot him.

The cop's partner returned fire, missed, and fired on the vehicle as it took off on Highway 1 South. The cop called for assistance and stayed with the dying man.

A few miles and a few minutes later the squad cars in pursuit forced the getaway car off the far-right lane and road-blocked it. The police found that the passenger had ditched, leaving the teenage driver, Clay Warren, and a sizable package of fentanyl inside the car.

The patrolman who'd been shot died at the scene.

Clay Warren was held on a number of charges. The drugs were valued at a million, as is, and impounded. Warren and the car were identified by the dead cop's partner, and Forensics had found hundreds of old and new prints in the vehicle, but none that matched to a known felon.

Bastard had worn gloves or never touched the dash, or this was his first job and he wasn't in the system.

Yuki doubted that.

So in lieu of the killer dealer, the wheelman was left holding the bag.

The DA was prosecuting Clay Warren for running drugs in a stolen car and acting as accomplice to murder of a police officer, but largely for being the patsy. Yuki had hoped that Warren would give up the missing dealer, but he hadn't done so and gave no sign that he would.

Using the inside of the stainless-steel elevator door as a mirror, she applied her lipstick and arranged her hair, then exited on the seventh floor and approached Sergeant Bubbleen Waters at the desk.

"Hi, B. I have a meeting with prisoner Clay Warren and his attorney."

"They're waiting for you, Yuki. Hang on a sec."

She picked up the desk phone, punched a button, and said, "Randall. Gate, please."

A guard appeared, metal doors clanked open, and locks shut behind them. The guard escorted Yuki to a small cinder-block room with a table and chairs, two of the chairs already occupied. Clay Warren wore a classic orange prison jumpsuit and silver cuffs. His attorney, Zac Jordan, had long hair and was wearing a pink polo shirt, a khaki blazer, jeans, and a gold stud in his left ear.

Zac gave Yuki a warm smile and stood to shake her hand with both of his.

"Good to see you, Yuki. Sorry to say, I'm not getting anywhere fast. Maybe Clay will listen to you."

ZAC JORDAN WAS a defense lawyer who worked pro bono for the Defense League, a group that represented the poor and hopeless.

During a brief break from her job with the DA, Yuki had worked for Zac Jordan and could say that he was one of the good guys and that his client was lucky to have him.

In this case, his client was facing major prison time for being in the wrong car at the wrong time.

Yuki sat down and asked, "How's it going, Clay?"

He said, "Just wonderful."

Clay Warren looked younger than his age. He was small and blond haired, with a button nose, but when he glanced up, his gray eyes were hard. After his quick appraisal of Yuki, he lowered his gaze to his hands, the cuffs linked to a metal loop in the middle of the table. He looked resigned.

"Clay," she said, "as we discussed before, a police officer is dead. You know who shot him. I'm asking you again to help us by telling us who did that. Otherwise, I can't help you, and you'll be charged as an accomplice to murder and for possession of narcotics with intent, and tried as an adult. You're looking at life in prison."

"For driving the car," he said.

"Do you understand me?" Yuki asked. "You're an accomplice to the murder of a *cop*. If you help us get the shooter, the DA might help you out. The charges could be lowered significantly, Clay."

"I don't know anything. I was driving. I heard the siren. I pull over and get charged with all of this bullshit. It's wrong. All wrong. I was speeding. Period."

"And the drugs inside the car? Where'd you get a million dollars' worth of fentanyl?"

Yuki knew that there was a tentative ID on the dealer. The cop who'd watched his partner die on the street had reviewed photos of likely suspects, big-time drug dealers, and thought the shooter might be Antoine Castro, but he wasn't entirely sure.

Yuki said, "Why are you taking the weight for scum like Antoine Castro?"

The kid shook his head no.

Castro was on the FBI's Most Wanted list. By now, Yuki was willing to bet, he'd left the country and assumed a new identity.

Zac said, "Lying isn't helping you, son. I know ADA Castellano. I'll negotiate for you."

"For God's sake," Warren shouted. *"Leave me alone."*

Yuki imagined that if the killer dealer was Castro, he'd gotten word to the kid. Warned him.

You talk. You die.

14

Clay Warren wasn't going to talk. Yuki stood up.

"I'm sorry, Zac."

"You tried," he said.

She went to the door and the guard opened it for her. She left Zac Jordan alone with his client, a scared kid who was going to die in prison, just a matter of when.

CHAPTER 5

FRIDAY MORNING AT 9 a.m., give or take a few minutes, homicide lieutenant and acting police chief Jackson Brady strode down the center aisle of the bullpen.

The night shift was punching out, day shift straggling in, calling out, "Hey, boss," "Yo, Brady." He nodded to Chi, Lemke, Samuels, Wang, kept going.

At the front of the room there were two desks pushed together face-to-face. Boxer and Conklin's real estate. Brady had partnered with both of them when he first came to the SFPD as a switch-hitter. Stood with them with bullets flying more than once. He counted on them. Would do anything for them.

Brady slid into Boxer's desk chair. He looked at Conklin over Lindsay's small junkyard of personal space, swung the head of the gooseneck lamp aside, moved a stack of files and a mug to make space for his elbows.

Conklin looked up, said, "You okay, Lieu?"

Brady knew that he looked like shit. Too many hours

here. Too much junk food. Too little sleep. Worried eighteen hours a day. His collar was tight. He loosened his tie. Undid the top shirt button.

"So the way I understand it," Brady said, "Boxer had a doctor's appointment yesterday afternoon. A checkup. She calls to say, 'I'm fine, boss. Doctor said I need to start taking me time.'"

Conklin said, "She told me the same."

Brady thought about when Boxer had been very sick. Took off a couple of months and came back. Said she felt perfect. So now what was she saying?

"You think she's all right?" said Brady.

Conklin said, "She's fine. Doctor told her she shouldn't run herself into the ground like she does. So her sister has the wild child, and Lindsay and Joe took off to parts unknown for the weekend, maybe another day or two. You know, Brady. Most people take weekends off."

"Oh, really? I don't know many."

Brady gathered up loose pens and pencils and put them into a ceramic mug.

Conklin said, "What worries me is how *you* look."

"Don't rub it in."

Brady had been working two jobs since Chief Warren Jacobi had been retired out. Filling Jacobi's old chair on the fifth floor as well as running the Homicide squad room felt like having his head slammed in a car door.

The mayor was pressuring him; choose one job or the other, but decide.

Brady had talked it over with Yuki, who'd offered measured wifely advice, not pushing or pulling, just laying it out as a lawyer would.

"I can make a case for taking on more responsibility while working fewer hours per day. I can also give you reasons why Homicide is where your strengths lie. And you love it. But you have to make a decision PDQ, or the mayor is going to make it for you."

Conklin was saying, "I can work with Chi and McNeil until Boxer is back."

"Yeah. Do that."

Brady left Conklin and the bullpen, took the fire stairs one flight up to five. When he got to his office, his assistant said, "Lieu, I was just about to look for you. Check this out."

He took a seat behind the desk. Katie leaned over his shoulder and brought up the *Chronicle* online, paused on the front page, and read the headline, "'Roger Jennings Shot at Taco King,'" then added the takeaway, "He's in critical condition."

Jennings was a baseball player, a catcher nearing the end of his professional career.

Why would anyone want to kill him?

CHAPTER 6

I'D CALLED JOE as soon as I left my doctor's office and told him what Doc Arpino had said: "Lindsay. Live a little. Get out of town for a few days. Go to a spa."

My dear husband had said, "Leave this to me."

I'd left word with Brady and Conklin: "I'm off duty."

Words to that effect.

Now, with our phones locked inside the trunk, Joe and I were heading north, breezing across the Golden Gate Bridge, sailboats flying below us across the sparkling bay.

Joe was at the wheel and I was sitting beside him, saying, "I did not."

"You did, too. You came to the airport. You said, 'I want you. And I want the jet.'"

I laughed out loud. "You're crazy."

"You remember the company plane?"

"Oh. Yes."

"Louder, dear."

"Oh, YES."

We both laughed.

Joe and I had met on the job, heads of a cop and DHS joint task force charged with shutting down a terrorist who was armed with a deadly poison and a plan to take down members of the G8 meeting in San Francisco. He killed a lot of people, including one very close to me, before we nailed the bastard and took him down.

I blocked thoughts about all of that and said, "You remember when we broke away from the G8 case for the investigation in Portland?"

"Do I ever," said Joe. "Inside that conference room with a dozen people working a national-security murder and you saying, 'If you keep looking at me like that, Deputy Director Molinari, I can't work.'"

I laughed and said, "I told you that afterward. I didn't say that out loud."

I was sure I was right, but it was also true that working with Joe under so much adrenalized fear and pressure had unleashed some pretty amazing magic between us. And before we'd left Portland for San Francisco, we'd fallen in love. Hard.

Was it perfect from then on?

Hell no. We lived on opposite sides of the country, and so we rode the long-distance relationship roller coaster for a while, cured loneliness and longing with adventures for a few days a month until Joe gave up his job and moved to the City by the Bay.

About a year after our wedding, I gave birth to Julie Anne Molinari while home alone on a dark and stormy night with electric lines down across the city. While I panted and pushed and screamed, surrounded by firemen, Joe was thirty-five thousand feet overhead, unaware.

He'd made it up to me and our baby girl when he finally reached home. Joe Molinari, intelligence agency consultant and Mr. Mom.

He asked now, "Where are you, Lindsay?"

"I'm right here."

I leaned over, gave him a kiss, and said, "I was remembering. Where are *you,* Joe?"

He put his hand on my thigh.

"I'm here, Blondie, thinking about what a good mom you are, and how much I love you."

I told him, "I sure do love you, too."

This weekend Julie was staying at the beach with her aunt Cat, two cousins, and Martha, our best doggy in the world, while Joe and I got to be two fortysomething kids in love.

Joe turned on the radio and found the perfect station.

We were cruising. The weather was sunny with a side of sailboats, and we were singing along with the oldies: "Free to do what I want any old time."

When we reached our first destination, Joe and I were in a honeymoon state of mind.

CHAPTER 7

JOE SLOWED THE car and parked us in front of a modest-looking two-story building made of river stones and timbers, surrounded by greenery.

I recognized it from photos of where to go in Napa Valley. This was reportedly one of the best restaurants in the world, as it had been for the last twenty years.

Yes, best in the *world*.

I shouted, "The French Laundry? Seriously?"

I'd read about how hard it was to get into this place, revered by foodies all over and winner of Michelin's top ranking, three stars. A two-month waiting period for a lunch reservation was *typical*.

"You didn't pull this off overnight."

"I have a connection," Joe said, giving me a twinkly grin.

Wow. After the burger-and-coffee diet that went with being on the Job, I wondered if I could even appreciate fine dining. But now I knew why Joe had said to wear a dress—and surprise, surprise, I had one on. It was a navy-blue-and-white print, and I'd matched it with a blue cash-mere cardigan. I pulled the band from my sandy-blond ponytail, flipped down the visor, and looked at myself in the mirror.

I fluffed up my hair a little and pinched my cheeks.

I looked nice.

The restaurant's farm garden was across the street, and it was open to visitors, a lovely place for a Friday stroll. I told Joe I was going to need my phone after all so I could take pictures. He got out of the car, and the trunk lid went up.

That's when a panel van pulled up to the rear of the car and buzzed down its passenger-side window. I couldn't see the driver, but I heard him yell, "Joeeey."

Joe called back, "Dave, you crazy SOB."

I watched him go over to the van, open the door, lean in, and hug the driver. Then he came back to me and said, "You're finally going to meet Dave."

When Joe spoke of David Channing, it was always with love and sadness. Dave had been Joe's college roommate at Fordham back east in the Bronx. I'd seen pictures of them on the field. Dave was a quarterback and Joe played flanker. He'd shown me pictures of the team, whooping, high on victory, both Joe and Dave tall, brawny, handsome, and so young.

Joe had told me that after a day like that, a win against Holy Cross, there'd been a sudden cold snap and a snow-storm had blown in from the west. Dave had been driving his girlfriend, Rebecca, home to Croton-on-Hudson, about forty-five minutes up the Taconic, a lovely twisting road with a parklike median strip and beautiful views.

23

But, as Joe had told me, on that late afternoon the snow had melted into a coating of black ice on the road. Dave had taken a turn where a rocky outcropping blocked his view of a vehicle that had spun out of control and stopped across both lanes. Dave had braked, skidding into the disabled car, while another, fast-moving car had rear-ended him.

Before it was over, thirty-two cars had crashed in a horrific pileup. Rebecca had been killed. Dave's spine had been crushed, and the young man who was being scouted by NFL teams had been paralyzed from the waist down.

His parents, Ray and Nancy, had brought Dave home to their little winery just outside Napa, and there'd been years of painful rehab. During those years, Joe had said, Dave had walled himself off from his friends and pretty much the whole world. Lately, he kept the company books, ran a support group for paraplegics, and mourned his mother's death from lymphoma. That was all Joe knew.

Joe opened my door, offered me his hand, and helped me out, saying, "I've been waiting a long time for this, Linds. Come and meet Dave."

Why everyone loves James Patterson and the Women's Murder Club

'It's no mystery why James Patterson is the world's most popular thriller writer. Simply put: **nobody does it better**.'
Jeffery Deaver

'**Smart characters, shocking twists . . .** you count down to the very last page to discover what will happen next.'
Lisa Gardner

'No one gets this big without **amazing natural storytelling** talent – which is what Jim has, in spades.'
Lee Child

'**Boxer steals the show** as the tough cop with a good heart.'
Mirror

'**Great plot, fantastic storytelling** and characters that spring off the page.'
Heidi Perks

'Patterson boils a scene down to the single, telling detail, the element that **defines a character** or moves a plot along. It's what fires off the movie projector in the reader's mind.'
Michael Connelly

'James Patterson is **The Boss**. End of.'
Ian Rankin

Have You Read Them All?

1ST TO DIE

Four friends come together to form the Women's Murder Club. Their job? To find a killer who is brutally slaughtering newly-wed couples on their wedding night.

2ND CHANCE
(with Andrew Gross)

The Women's Murder Club tracks a mystifying serial killer, but things get dangerous when he turns his pursuers into prey.

3RD DEGREE
(with Andrew Gross)

A wave of violence sweeps the city, and whoever is behind it is intent on killing someone every three days. Now he has targeted one of the Women's Murder Club . . .

4TH OF JULY
(with Maxine Paetro)

In a deadly shoot-out, Detective Lindsay Boxer makes a split-second decision that threatens everything she's ever worked for.

THE 5TH HORSEMAN
(with Maxine Paetro)

Recovering patients are dying inexplicably in hospital. Nobody is claiming responsibility. Could these deaths be tragic coincidences, or something more sinister?

THE 6TH TARGET
(with Maxine Paetro)

Children from rich families are being abducted off the streets – but the kidnappers aren't demanding a ransom. Can Lindsay Boxer find the children before it's too late?

7TH HEAVEN
(with Maxine Paetro)

The hunt for a deranged murderer with a taste for fire and the disappearance of the governor's son have pushed Lindsay to the limit. The trails have gone cold. But a raging fire is getting ever closer, and somebody will get burned.

8TH CONFESSION
(with Maxine Paetro)

Four celebrities are found killed and there are no clues: the perfect crime. Few people are as interested when a lowly preacher is murdered. But could he have been hiding a dark secret?

9TH JUDGEMENT
(with Maxine Paetro)

A psychopathic killer targets San Francisco's most innocent and vulnerable, while a burglary gone horribly wrong leads to a high-profile murder.

10TH ANNIVERSARY
(with Maxine Paetro)

A badly injured teenage girl is left for dead, and her newborn baby is nowhere to be found. But is the victim keeping secrets?

11TH HOUR
(with Maxine Paetro)

Is one of Detective Lindsay Boxer's colleagues a vicious killer? She won't know until the 11th hour.

12TH OF NEVER
(with Maxine Paetro)

A convicted serial killer wakes from a two-year coma. He says he's ready to tell where the bodies are buried, but what does he want in return?

UNLUCKY 13
(with Maxine Paetro)

Someone returns to San Francisco to pay a visit to some old friends. But a cheerful reunion is not on the cards.

14TH DEADLY SIN
(with Maxine Paetro)

A new terror is sweeping the streets of San Francisco, and the killers are dressed in police uniform. Lindsay treads a dangerous line as she investigates whether the criminals are brilliant imposters or police officers gone rogue.

15TH AFFAIR
(with Maxine Paetro)

Four bodies are found in a luxury hotel. Lindsay is sent in to investigate and hunt down an elusive and dangerous suspect. But when her husband Joe goes missing, she begins to fear that the suspect she is searching for could be him.

Also by James Patterson

ALEX CROSS NOVELS

Along Came a Spider • Kiss the Girls • Jack and Jill • Cat and Mouse • Pop Goes the Weasel • Roses are Red • Violets are Blue • Four Blind Mice • The Big Bad Wolf • London Bridges • Mary, Mary • Cross • Double Cross • Cross Country • Alex Cross's Trial (*with Richard DiLallo*) • I, Alex Cross • Cross Fire • Kill Alex Cross • Merry Christmas, Alex Cross • Alex Cross, Run • Cross My Heart • Hope to Die • Cross Justice • Cross the Line • The People vs. Alex Cross • Target: Alex Cross • Criss Cross

DETECTIVE MICHAEL BENNETT SERIES

Step on a Crack (*with Michael Ledwidge*) • Run for Your Life (*with Michael Ledwidge*) • Worst Case (*with Michael Ledwidge*) • Tick Tock (*with Michael Ledwidge*) • I, Michael Bennett (*with Michael Ledwidge*) • Gone (*with Michael Ledwidge*) • Burn (*with Michael Ledwidge*) • Alert (*with Michael Ledwidge*) • Bullseye (*with Michael Ledwidge*) • Haunted (*with James O. Born*) • Ambush (*with James O. Born*) • Blindside (*with James O. Born*)

PRIVATE NOVELS

Private (*with Maxine Paetro*) • Private London (*with Mark Pearson*) • Private Games (*with Mark Sullivan*) • Private: No. 1 Suspect (*with Maxine Paetro*) • Private Berlin (*with Mark Sullivan*) • Private Down Under (*with Michael White*) • Private L.A. (*with Mark Sullivan*) • Private India (*with Ashwin Sanghi*) • Private Vegas (*with Maxine Paetro*) • Private Sydney (*with Kathryn Fox*) • Private Paris (*with Mark Sullivan*) • The Games (*with Mark Sullivan*) • Private Delhi (*with Ashwin Sanghi*) • Private Princess (*with Rees Jones*) • Private Moscow (*with Adam Hamdy*)

NYPD RED SERIES

NYPD Red (*with Marshall Karp*) • NYPD Red 2 (*with Marshall Karp*) • NYPD Red 3 (*with Marshall Karp*) • NYPD Red 4 (*with Marshall Karp*) • NYPD Red 5 (*with Marshall Karp*)

For more information about James Patterson's novels, visit www.penguin.co.uk